Chick & Other Stories by Edgar Wallace

Richard Horatio Edgar Wallace was born on the 1st April 1875 in Greenwich, London. Leaving school at 12 because of truancy, by the age of fifteen he had experience; selling newspapers, as a worker in a rubber factory, as a shoe shop assistant, as a milk delivery boy and as a ship's cook.

By 1894 he was engaged but broke it off to join the Infantry being posted to South Africa. He also changed his name to Edgar Wallace which he took from Lew Wallace, the author of *Ben-Hur*.

In Cape Town in 1898 he met Rudyard Kipling and was inspired to begin writing. His first collection of ballads, *The Mission that Failed!* was enough of a success that in 1899 he paid his way out of the armed forces in order to turn to writing full time.

By 1904 he had completed his first thriller, *The Four Just Men*. Since nobody would publish it he resorted to setting up his own publishing company which he called Tallis Press.

In 1911 his Congolese stories were published in a collection called *Sanders of the River*, which became a bestseller. He also started his own racing papers, *Bibury's* and *R. E. Walton's Weekly*, eventually buying his own racehorses and losing thousands gambling. A life of exceptionally high income was also mirrored with exceptionally large spending and debts.

Wallace now began to take his career as a fiction writer more seriously, signing with Hodder and Stoughton in 1921. He was marketed as the 'King of Thrillers' and they gave him the trademark image of a trilby, a cigarette holder and a yellow Rolls Royce. He was truly prolific, capable not only of producing a 70,000 word novel in three days but of doing three novels in a row in such a manner. It was estimated that by 1928 one in four books being read was written by Wallace, for alongside his famous thrillers he wrote variously in other genres, including science fiction, non-fiction accounts of WWI which amounted to ten volumes and screen plays. Eventually he would reach the remarkable total of 170 novels, 18 stage plays and 957 short stories.

Wallace became chairman of the Press Club which to this day holds an annual Edgar Wallace Award, rewarding 'excellence in writing'.

Diagnosed with diabetes his health deteriorated and he soon entered a coma and died of his condition and double pneumonia on the 7th of February 1932 in North Maple Drive, Beverly Hills. He was buried near his home in England at Chalklands, Bourne End, in Buckinghamshire.

Index of Contents

I

CHICK

Mr. Jonas Stollingham was station-master, head porter, local switchman, ticket-collector, and dispatch clerk at Pelborough Halt. He was also Chief of the Information Bureau. He was an aged man, who chewed tobacco and regarded all innovation as a direct challenge to Providence. For this reason he spoke of aeroplanes, incubators, mechanical creamers, motor-cars, and vaccination with a deep growling "Ah!" Such intangible mysteries as wireless telegraphy he dismissed as the invention of the newspapers.

Jonas knew most of the happenings which had occurred within twenty-five miles of Pelborough Halt during the past forty-seven years. He could tell you the hour and the day that Tom Rollins was run over by a hay-cart, and the number of eggs laid at Poolford Farm on a record day. He knew the Vicar's family skeleton, and would rattle the same on the slightest encouragement. He had had time in his life to form very definite ideas about most subjects, since only four trains stopped at Pelborough Halt on weekdays and half that number on Sundays.

It was a cold, moist Sunday in January that the 10.57 "up" discharged a solitary passenger, and Jonas moved toward him with a gathering frown.

"Where's your ticket?" he demanded.

The passenger, who carried no baggage, dived into the pockets of his worn overcoat, and, increasing the pace of his search till Jonas could hardly follow his movements, he patted and prodded successively his trousers, waistcoat, and jacket pockets.

"If you ain't got a ticket, you've got to pay," said the hopeful Jonas. "You ain't supposed to keep me waiting here all day. I'm only doing the company a favour by being here at all on Sunday."

He was disappointed when the young man produced a piece of pasteboard, and scrutinized it suspiciously as the train moved out.

"Date's all right," he confessed.

"Mr. Stollingham—er—is my—er—uncle well?"

Mr. Stollingham fixed his steel-rimmed spectacles nearer his eyes.

"Hullo!" he greeted. "Mr. What's-your-name?"

"Beane," murmured the youth apologetically. "Charles Beane. You remember I was here for a month."

"I know ye." Jonas chewed accusatively, his rheumy eyes on the passenger.

"The old doctor ain't well." He emphasized the negative with some satisfaction. "Lots of people round here don't think he's all there." He tapped his forehead. "He thinks he's a dook. I've known fellows to be took off to the lunytic asylum for less. Went down to Parliament last month, didn't he?"

"I believe he did," said "Chick" Beane. "I didn't see him."

"Asked to be made a lord! If that ain't madness, what is it?"

"It may be measles," said Chick gravely. "The doctor had an attack last year."

"Measles!" The contempt of Jonas was always made visible as well as audible. "We don't like your uncle's goings-on; it's bringin' the village down If a man's a lord, he's born so. If he ain't, he ain't. It's the same with these air'planes. Was we intended to fly? Was we born with wings? Suppose them crows over there started to chew terbaccer like a human bein', wouldn't the law stop it?"

"But chewing tobacco isn't human, Mr. Stollingham—it's nasty! Good morning!"

He left the station-master gazing after him with a baneful stare.

Charles Beane had never had any other name than "Chick." It had been given to him as a child by one of his father's "helps." For Chick was born at Grafton, in the State of Massachusetts, whither his male parent had gone as a young man to seek the fortune which rural England had denied to a gentleman-farmer. There he had married and died two years after his wife, and Chick, at the age of seven, had been brought to England by an aunt, who, on passing from this world to a better, had left him to the care of another aunt.

Chick saw life as a panorama of decaying aunts and uncles. Until he was fifteen he thought that mourning was the clothing that little boys were, by the English law, compelled to wear. Hence, too, he took a cheerful view of dissolution which often sounded callous. He had the kindest of hearts, but he who had seen the passing of mother and father, three aunts, one uncle, and a cousin, without human progress being perceptibly affected, could hardly take quite so serious a view of such matters as those to whom such phenomena are rare.

Chick appeared a little more than medium height and weight. Both impressions were deceptive. His trick of bending forward when he spoke gave him the slightest stoop, and his loose carriage favoured the illusion. Nor was he deaf; that strained look and bent head was his apology for troubling people with his presence and conversation. This also was innocent and unconscious deception. Many people mistook his politeness for humility, his fear of hurting people's feelings for sheer awe and shyness.

He was not shy, though few believed this. His characteristic was a certain bald frankness which could be disconcerting. The art which is comprehended in the word "diplomacy" was an esoteric mystery to him. He was painfully boyish, and the contours of the face, the rather high cheek-bones, the straight small nose, the big forehead and the baby-blue eyes, no less than his untidy yellow hair, belonged to the sixth form, though the average boy of the sixth is better acquainted with a razor and lather brush than was Chick.

The way to Pelborough Abbey lay through the village of that name. The bell of the parish church was tolling mournfully, and in consequence the straggling street was as crowded as could be. He walked quickly past the curious worshippers and turned into the dilapidated gate of the Abbey, a large and ugly cottage which at some time had been painted white. Once a veritable abbey had stood on the very spot where Josephus Beane had laid the foundations of his house. A few blocks of masonry, weed-covered and weathered, until the very outlines of the dressing had vanished, remained to testify to the labours of the forgotten monks.

An untidy servant opened the door and smirked at the visitor.

"He's in bed," she said cheerfully. "Some say that he'll never get out again. But, lor, he's always makin' people liars. Why, last winter he was took so bad that we nearly got a doctor to him!"

"Will you tell him I'm here, please?" said Chick gently.

The room into which he was ushered was on the ground floor, and normally was Dr. Beane's library. The walls were hidden behind book-shelves; a large and aged table was literally piled with papers, pamphlets, and deed-boxes, books and scattered manuscript. Over the mantelpiece was a brilliant coat-of-arms which always reminded Chick of a public-house sign.

Into this literary workshop had been insinuated a narrow high bed with four polished posts and a canopy. Supported by large pillows, the slips of which had not been changed for a week, lay a man of sixty-five—a grim, square-jawed, unshaven man, who, with a stiff cardboard pad on his doubled-up knees, was writing as Chick appeared.

The invalid's face took a turn for the worse at the sight of the figure in the doorway.

"Oh, it's you, is it?" he growled.

Chick came cautiously into the room and put his hat down on a chair. "Yes, sir, it's me. I hope you're better."

The old doctor snorted and shifted in his bed. "I suppose you know I'm not long for this world, eh?" he scowled up under his tremendous eyebrows. "Eh?" he repeated.

"No, sir, I don't think you are," said Chick agreeably, "but I'm sure a gentleman of your experience won't mind that?"

Dr. Beane swallowed and blinked.

"I am very glad you are alive today, sir," Chick hastened to add, feeling that perhaps he had better say all the nice things he could think of whilst he had the opportunity.

"You are, are you?" breathed the doctor.

"Oh, yes, sir," Chick was eager to help. "I don't, of course, like coming to Pelborough, because you are usually so very disagreeable, owing, I often think, to your age and your—er—infirmity." He looked down at the speechless invalid with solemn eyes. "Were you ever crossed in love, sir?"

Dr. Beane could only stare.

"One reads in books that such things happen, though, of course, it may be sheer invention on the part of the novelists, who aren't always quite correct in their facts—unintentionally, I am sure—"

"Will you shut up?" bellowed the sick man. "You're annoying me, sir! You're exasperating me, sir! Confound you, I'll outlive you, sir, by twenty years!"

The old man almost hissed the words, and Chick shook his head.

"I am sure it is possible," he agreed, "but of course it is against the law of average—we know a great deal about that in the insurance business. Are you insured, sir?"

Dr. Beane was sitting bolt upright in bed now, and he was terribly calm.

"Boy," he said awfully, "I am not insured." And Chick looked grave.

"One ought to insure," he said; "it is the most unselfish thing one can do. One ought to think of one's relations."

"Confound you, sir! You're my only relation!" wailed the doctor.

Chick was silent. That idea had never struck him.

"Isn't there anybody who is fond of you?" he asked, and added regretfully: "No, I suppose there isn't."

Dr. Beane swung his legs out of bed.

"Get out, sir—I'm going to dress, sir—into the garden—go to the devil!"

Chick did not go into the garden. It was cold out of doors. He went instead to the big vaulted kitchen, where Anna, cook and housekeeper to the doctor for twenty-five years, was preparing the invalid's midday meal.

"How did you find him, sir?" asked Anna. She was a stout, heavy woman, who breathed with difficulty.

"I found him in bed," said Chick. "Could you make me some coffee, please?"

Anna filled the kettle and put it on the fire, shaking her head.

"It's my opinion, Mr. Charles, that this here lord nonsense is killing the old gentleman."

There was a furious ring of the bell, and Anna waddled from the kitchen, to return with a face expressive of amazement.

"He's up," she gasped, "and he wants you, Mr. Charles." Here the bell rang again, and Chick bolted back to the library.

The doctor was sitting up in an arm-chair before the fire. Placed within reach were those familiar scrap-books, the contents of which had poisoned one summer holiday for him.

"Come in! What did you run away for? I suppose that's the infernal American blood in your system—never still! Never in repose! Hustle, hustle, hustle!"

Chick opened his mouth to protest against a desire for rapid movement of any kind, and shut it again.

"Sit down!" The doctor pointed fiercely at a chair. "You know that I've been fighting these brainless Law Lords over the peerage? Of course you know it—the newspapers have been full of it! We shall have the Lords' decision in a week. The scoundrels!"

Dr. Beane had spent thirty years of his life in a vain endeavour to establish his claim to the extinct Marquisate of Pelborough. He had dissipated a handsome competence in lawyers' fees, genealogical researches, and had not hesitated at demanding from the Home Secretary an exhumation order to test a theory. The Secretary of State had shown less hesitation in refusing. It was Dr. Beane's hobby, his obsession, his one life passion. Chick groaned within himself. The one hope he had cherished was that the precarious condition of his uncle's health would have precluded all possibility of argument on the doctor's fatal illusion.

Dr. Beane lifted up and opened one of the large scrap-books. "The basis of the claim is the relationship of Sir Harry Beane to Martha, the Countess of Morthborough. Is that clear to you?"

"No, sir," said Chick patiently, but truthfully.

"Then you're a fool, sir!" thundered the invalid. "You're a dolt and a dunderhead! It's that infernal American blood in you, sir—nothing more or less! Do you understand that the Countess of Morthborough was a sister of Sir Harry Beane, who died in 1534?"

"I'm sure you're right, sir," said Chick handsomely.

"That is the crux of the whole problem." Dr. Beane tapped the scrap-book violently. "Martha, Countess of Morthborough, had two daughters. Do you know what she did with 'em?"

"Sent them to school, sir?" suggested Chick. At first he had it on the tip of his tongue to say, "Poisoned them," because that was the sort of thing that unnatural parents did to their children in the Dark Ages.

"Sent them to school!" sneered the doctor, "No, you jackass! She married 'em off to the two sons of the Marquis of Pelborough. Jane, the eldest daughter, died without issue; Elizabeth, the younger, had a son, who eventually became Marquis of Pelborough."

The room was warm, and Chick experienced a pleasant sensation of ease and restfulness. He closed his eyes.

"...upon that fact I argued my claim to the House of Lords..."

"Certainly," murmured Chick.

It was summer, and the doctor's garden was a patchwork of gorgeous colours. And Gwenda was walking with him...

"My father often said—Confound you, sir, you're asleep!"

It was by the most amazing effort of will that Chick opened his eyes.

"I heard you, sir," he said a little huskily. "One was called Jane, and one was called Elizabeth. They both married the Marquis of Beane."

Ten minutes later he was on his way to Pelborough Halt, ejected with a fury and originality of expletive that had jerked him wide-awake. A providential ejection as it proved, for the railway times had been altered, and Chick had to sprint, or he would have lost the only down train of the day.

Jonas thrust him into a third-class carriage with unnecessary violence.

"You ain't stayed long?" he said inquiringly. "Ain't your uncle bright enough to see you?"

"Oh, yes, Mr. Stollingham," said Chick, as the train began to move; "he's very bright—very!"

He sank back into the seat of the carriage with a long sigh of relief, and gave himself up to the real problem of life—a problem which centred about the future of Mrs. Gwenda Maynard. The more urgent was this problem since the last time he had seen her—which was on the previous night—it was as she was coming out of Mrs. Shipmet's room with a queer drawn look in her face.

Mrs. Shipmet called her own drawing-sitting-room her "senctum," and for quite a long time Chick thought that "senctum" was French for "counting-house." It was in the "senctum" that the boarders paid their just debts, a ceremony which was enveloped in an atmosphere of mystery, largely due to the child-like credulity of Mrs. Shipmet's paying guests, all of whom cherished the illusion that they had been received on terms which, in comparison with their fellow-boarders, were ruinously favourable.

Since they had pledged themselves to secrecy, at Mrs. Shipmet's serious request, and also, presumably, because they feared that the disclosure of the lady's philanthropy was liable to cause a riot, if it were revealed, the weekly ritual of settlement was carried out behind closed doors.

"May I see you a moment, Mrs. S.?" a boarder would ask in low tones.

"Certainly, Miss G. Will you step into the senctum?"

And the door would close behind them, and Mrs. Shipmet would stand smiling inquiringly, one hand, waist-high, resting upon the palm of the other.

And when the boarder produced his purse, Mrs. Shipmet would start in surprise, as though sordid money was the last thing in the world she was expecting to hear about. Nevertheless, she would take the cash, though she invariably said:

"Oh, but you shouldn't have troubled; to-morrow would have done. H'm!"

She always said "H'm!" at the end of things.

The ritual which was observed in the senctum was one of two varieties, either that which has been described, or else...

Picture Mrs. Shipmet with an expressionless face, save that her eyebrows were unusually arched; imagine a slow inclination of the head, such as a judge will sometimes give when a murderer says "Not guilty!" and at the end...

"I'm awfully sorry, Mr.— er." She always forgot their names in these circumstances, "but my expenses are very heavy, and I have a big bill to meet on Monday, and I'm afraid I must ask you to vacate your room."

From such an interview had Gwenda Maynard come on the Saturday night.

Chick did not see her on his return from Pelborough until the afternoon, when Acacia Lodge was nearly empty. The young ladies and gentlemen who were guests of Mrs. Shipmet invariably had engagements on Sunday afternoons, and those who were too old for the thrill and glories of love either went to church or to bed.

"Mrs. Maynard"—Chick came eagerly from the sitting-room and intercepted the girl in the hall—"I'm sorry I missed you; I didn't get back until after lunch."

She smiled a greeting, but the smile was a little strained. "Hello, Chick!" she said, squeezing his arm. "I looked for you before I went out. How is your uncle?"

"He's very—robust," Chick could think of no better words. "You're not going up to your room, are you?" he asked anxiously.

She shook her head. "I don't know where I'm going. Chick," she said, and laughed. "Do you want to go out?"

He nodded. "If you're not busy," he said, and she hesitated. "It isn't raining," he urged.

"All right." She turned on her heel and walked through the door into the street, and Chick followed.

Mrs. Shipmet's boarding establishment was situated in the residential district of Brockley, and all properly constituted persons who "went out" gravitated instinctively to the Hilly Fields, which are to Brockley what Hampstead Heath is to London and Central Park to New York.

They strode out together toward the magnetic fields, and the girl did not speak for some time.

She was pretty and slight, and Acacia Lodge had voted her "vivacious" in the days when the sensational advent of a real actress had set all the boarders the agreeable task of analysing her charm. Her popularity had not been maintained at the high level it reached during the first week following her arrival. The men she had subsequently snubbed—and with good cause—decided that she suffered from swelled head. The girls she had momentarily eclipsed set their lips tightly together and looked at one another significantly when her name cropped up in conversation. For Gwenda wore a wedding ring; she was immensely pretty, and she made no reference to her husband.

"Chick," said the girl suddenly, as they turned on to the tar path leading to the hill, "I'm going!"

Chick stood stock still and turned pale.

"Going, Mrs.—I mean Gwenda?" He pronounced her name a little fearfully. "Where?"

Gwenda shrugged her shoulders. "I don't know, Chick, but Mrs. Shipmet told me that she would want my room. I owe three weeks' rent."

Chick looked at her in amazement. "Do you really?" he asked in a hushed voice.

"Yes, I do really," she said savagely. "I had to buy a lot of clothes for this new piece at the Strand-Broadway. Solburg makes you buy your own things, and, Chick, now I've got 'em"—she gulped back a sob—"Solburg talks of not putting mo into the show! There is another girl whose father knows a lord, and this Lord Chenney has asked Solburg to give her the part."

"Let us sit down," said Chick, a little overcome. "But isn't he obliged to let you act Gwenda?"

She sat down on an empty bench, and he took his place by her side.

"No, Chick," she said. "I have a contract, but what is the use of my fighting him? I can only smile and hang on for something else. He is too powerful a man to sue. I should be barred by almost every management."

Chick was stunned. He had guessed the tragedy in the air when he had seen her face on the Saturday night. And this news was a tremendous blow to him. She was the first woman he had ever met on terms of equality—the first girl who had not giggled at him or been rude to him-his first and his greatest comrade, and she was going out of his life.

Suddenly a brilliant thought struck him.

"Mrs.—Gwenda," he said excitedly, "three weeks is only seven pounds ten! I've got over thirty pounds in the bank! Good gracious, fancy my forgetting that!"

She looked at him for a long time, till the tears came up and overflowed, to Chick's horror.

"You queer, dear boy," she said softly, and shook her head. "No, Chick, my dear, I can't take your money. I'm very, very grateful, you dear old Chick!"—and she swallowed hard.

"Why do you call me a boy, Gwenda?" he asked. "I'm a year older than you. Of course I know that you're a married lady, but that doesn't make you older."

She smiled as she dabbed her eyes.

"I feel a million years older than you, Chick. Now tell me about your uncle."

"When are you going?" asked the young man doggedly.

"Next Saturday. I must say Mrs. Shipmet is fairly reasonable. I have paid next week's board in advance. I can't expect her to keep me for nothing. If I had got the part in this new play—" She shook her head. "What is the use of blubbing?" she said impatiently. "I'm getting silly. And here is that awful creature Terrance. I don't want him to see that my eyes are red."

Mr. Fred Terrance described himself as a man of the world. This proud title carried with it the right to wear highly decorative linen and neckwear which nearly harmonized in colour with his socks. He was invariably referred to as "Mr. Fred," and, in addition to his worldliness, he sustained the difficult role of born humorist. He was one of those—indeed, the first—who discovered in Gwenda Maynard a person too big for her boots.

Now he sauntered across the grass, being superior to urgent notices warning him off, swinging his malacca cane and puffing at a large cigar.

"Hello, Chick! Did you enjoy yourself?"

Chick looked up slowly.

"No," he said.

Terrance was looking at the girl with curious eyes.

"What on earth is the matter, eh?" he asked. "Crying! Come, come, this will never do! What is it all about? As a man of the world—"

"I don't think you had better stay," said Chick in that grave tone of his, as the man of the world prepared to seat himself.

"Eh? Why not?"

"Because we don't want to talk to you," said Chick simply.

Though they had lived together in the same house for eight months, Mr. Terrance had never come to grips with Chick, and the very simplicity of the reply took his breath away.

"Another thing, Mr. Terrance, I should like to say is this," Chick went on. "I am not called 'Chick' except by my very near friends."

"Oh, indeed!" said Mr. Terrance, breathing heavily and growing redder and redder of face. "And whilst we are on the subject of what you like and what you don't like, you young puppy—"

It is no exaggeration to say that Chick was terrified.

"I'm very sorry you're annoyed, Mr. Terrance..." he began, but the man of the world overwhelmed him with words.

"You keep a civil tongue in your head, my friend," he said, his voice growing louder and louder, to Chick's embarrassment, "I've got a few things I could say about you! Where do you go every Tuesday and Friday, hey? Perhaps Missis Maynard would like to know that." He emphasized Gwenda's title.

And this being a good line on which to make his exit, he stalked into the gathering gloom, only to return as a much better peroration occurred to him.

"You're the kind of sneaking, snivelling humbug that breaks women's hearts," he said, "and if Missis Maynard had any sense, she'd keep away from you."

The youth glared after him speechless.

"Shucks!" said Chick at last. It was the one word which he had carried with him from the State of Massachusetts.

The girl was laughing softly. "Oh, you heart-breaker!" she mocked.

"But—but I'm not," said the indignant Chick. "I've never broken anybody's heart in my life!"

She was laughing aloud now and rose suddenly.

"It is cold, Chick," she said. "Let us go back to the menagerie."

They did not go back to Acacia Lodge immediately, and when they did return they met Mrs. Shipmet in the hall, and she favoured them with a smile, the cordiality of which was so adjusted that Chick should not feel reproved or the girl encouraged.

Before he went to bed that night Chick was invited into the "senctum."

Mrs. Shipmet closed the door carefully behind him.

"I'm sure you won't mind my saying, Mr. Beane, that looking upon you as I do, as my own son, I think you're very unwise being seen so much about with an actress."

"With Mrs. Maynard?" asked Chick in surprise.

Mrs. Shipmet nodded.

"You're young," she explained, "and sus—er—sus—er—easily influenced. An actress is naturally used to admiration, and doesn't mean all she says. I can't stand by and see your heart broken, Mr. Beane."

"Oh, my heart?" said Chick, relieved. "My heart isn't broken, Mrs. Shipmet. Thank you very much. Good night!"

"I only speak to you for your good," said Mrs. Shipmet, one hand on the handle. "I speak as a mother."

Chick looked at her oddly. "As my mother or her mother, Mrs. Shipmet?" he asked.

"As yours!"

Mrs. Shipmet made haste to disclaim any maternal sympathies with her unprofitable boarder.

Chick nodded.

"I think she wants a mother more than I," he said simply. "I'm awfully sorry she owes you money. I think you would feel nicer to her if she was out of debt."

He left Mrs. Shipmet feeling—as she afterwards said—"very hurt."

Chick received from the executors of his father a sum equivalent to two pounds ten shillings a week, which, added to the two pounds fifteen shillings he received from Leither and Barns, enabled him to live, if not riotously, at least without anxiety.

His work hours were from 9.30 in the morning to 5.30 in the afternoon, except on Saturdays, when the office closed at 12, to allow Mr. Leither—there was no Barns—to get away for his golf, and the work was not exhausting. Mainly Chick's task was to bombard incautious people who had answered Mr. Leither's advertisements with literature and form-letters. It was work which, as Mr. Leither had often pointed out, a child could do, or a very small and ragged boy. He always insisted upon the sartorial deficiencies of his mythical boy.

On the Monday morning he was carpeted before his chief for a grievous error of the week before. In sending a "follow up" letter to a gentleman who had inquired about a workman's compensation policy, he had sent a "Though-you-have-not-answered-our-earlier-communication" when he should have dispatched a "We-are-delighted-to-hear-from-you" epistle. For the client in question had written.

Mr. Leither, who was a stout, careless man generally covered with cigarette ash, shook his ponderous head in despair as Chick came in.

"This work a child could do," he said tragically, after he explained the crime, "or a little ragged boy off the streets! And yet you! I'm surprised at you, Beane! Now, don't let it occur again."

"I didn't let it last time, sir," said Chick. "It just occurred."

"That will do," said Mr. Leither, flicking the ash of his cigarette on to his waistcoat.

But Chick lingered.

"Mr. Leither, you know Solburg, the theatrical person?" he asked.

Mr. Leither frowned.

"Yes, I know him," he said, "but he's not a good life, Beane. He has heart trouble."

"I'm not thinking about him from an insurance point of view," said Chick. "The fact is, Mr. Leither, I'm interested in a young lady who is an actress."

His employer looked at him with wonder and respect. At the same time he shook his head.

"I'm old enough to be your father, Beane," he said soberly, "and whilst I do not wish to put myself in a false position by acting in loco parentis—which is a Latin phrase meaning in the place of your parents—I say to you: Don't do it!—Actresses are all very well on the stage, but a young man like you ought to see 'em there. It's better for your peace of mind, Beane."

Chick had already made his desperate resolution, and was not to be turned aside by his chief's pardonable misconception.

"This young lady was in Solburg's company," he went on. "She has been rehearsing six weeks, and now she is going to be put out because Lord Chenney's daughter knows a girl who wants the part."

He recited this a little breathlessly.

"Lord Chenney is insured with the Commercial and Legal Company," murmured Mr. Leither. "I tried to get him to take a policy with the Peninsular Company. He's a first-class life, if ever there was one."

"Do you think it would be any use my seeing Mr. Solburg? In fact, Mr. Leither," said Chick a little hoarsely, "could you give me an introduction?"

Mr. Leither shook his head.

"Give it up, Beane, give it up," he said, with unusual kindness. "It will be a wrench at first, but you're young."

Chick arrested his protest, and Mr. Leither went on:

"If you want to meet him, I'll give you a letter of introduction. You might give him particulars of the Short Policy system—we might get him in under Schedule D."

Chick did not tell the girl of this interview with the "theatrical person." It had been a surprisingly pleasant experience. Mr. Solburg was a man of the world, too, a smiling Hebrew gentleman with a heart which he admitted was as big as his body, and a sense of humour. He had been frankness itself. Mrs. Maynard was a fine actress, but the influence which Lord Chenney had exercised was oblique. Mr. Solburg had apparently three 'angels'—he spoke of them as such—and Chick's first impression, that Mr.

Solburg was an intensely religious man, was dissipated when the manager explained that an 'angel' was a "backer," and that a "backer" was one who affords financial assistance to the producers of a play. It was to please his "backers," who were flattered by the lordly interest, that he had given Miss Moran the part he had planned for Mrs. Maynard.

"No, my dear boy, I don't mind your coming. You're Mrs. Maynard's brother, are you—or her son, perhaps?"

Mr. Solburg had lived so many years in an environment where nothing was as it appeared, and men and women successfully defied the appearance of age, that he was not greatly impressed by Chick's indignant denial.

"They all look young, my boy," said Mr. Solburg. "Why, I've had chorus girls in my touring companies who had grandchildren!"

It was not a happy week for Chick. All his spare time was employed in the scrutiny of theatrical journals and in cutting out likely advertisements. These he put into an envelope and left in the rack for Gwenda, a proceeding which afforded Mr. Terrance much amusement, and made the meal hour a very trying one for Chick, for Mr. Fred had his reputation of humorist to maintain, and into his wit had crept a note of malice. Chick did not worry about these passages when the girl was not present.

On the Saturday evening, when, as he knew, Gwenda's boxes were packed ready for carriage to the room she had taken in Bloomsbury, and when she herself sat at his side through the "high tea," the badinage became unbearable.

"I suppose we shall see less of Chick now that Mrs. Maynard is going," said Mr. Fred to the table at large. "He'll be hanging round the stage door of the Broadway every night—except Tuesday and Friday!"

He winked, and then, with an exaggerated start of surprise:

"Oh no, he won't! You're not playing at the Broadway in the next piece, are you, Mrs. Maynard?"

"I'm not," said the girl calmly, buttering her bread.

"Ah, that explains many things!" said Mr. Fred, with a significant nod. "Well, Mrs. Maynard, you'll soon be in another play, and be able to pay everybody."

Gwenda flushed and made a movement as if to rise, but it was Chick who got up.

"Mr. Fred," he said gently, "could you give me a minute of your time?"

Mr. Fred smiled.

"Say it here, Chick," he said.

But Chick shook his head and walked to the door, and Mr. Fred, with a smile, followed.

The passage was empty, and the street-door was open, Chick was standing outside.

"If you've got anything to say, say it here. I'm not going to catch a cold."

"Come outside!"

Chick's voice was peremptory.

"What the dickens do you mean?" demanded Mr. Fred wrathfully, as he joined the other.

Smack! The back of Chick's hand struck him across the face. Terrance stood dumbfounded for a moment, and then lunged out with all his strength.

The only light was that which came from the hall, but it was enough. Chick sidestepped and took the blow over his shoulder. Once, twice he drove to the body, and each time his fist got home. It was a favourite opening of his.

Mr. Fred gasped and staggered, and like lightning Chick brought up his left. Mr. Fred did not see it—he did not even feel it.

His first conscious impression was of being pulled to his feet and shaken.

"You wanted to know where I spend my Tuesdays and Fridays," said Chick; "now I'll tell you. At the Polytechnic, training for a lightweight competition."

Mr. Fred said nothing. He went up to his room a little groggily, and Chick returned to the table. He was neither agitated nor angry. He even glanced at the letter rack as he passed, and, seeing an envelope addressed to himself, took it with him into the dining-room.

Gwenda looked up anxiously as he came in. Chick could order nerve and muscle, but the flow of his blood was beyond his control, and he was pale.

"Mr. Fred is not coming back to tea," he smiled at Mrs. Shipmet, and opened his letter.

The girl looked. His knuckles were raw and bleeding.

"Chick," she said under her breath, "what has happened?" But Chick was staring at the letter in his hand. It was from the Vicar of Pelborough:

"...He died quite peacefully. I think the shock of the news must have been responsible. The letter enclosed from the Clerk of the Committee, announcing that Dr. Beane's claim to the extinct peerage of Pelborough had been recognized, was, I know, totally unexpected by your uncle. May I offer at once my condolences for your loss and congratulate you upon the honour to which your lordship has succeeded..."

Chick got unsteadily to his feet, still gripping the letter, and went out into the hall, where the telephone was. He turned the pages of the directory with a shaking hand, and presently gave a number.

The girl had followed him from the room, and was a silent audience,

"Is that Mr. Solburg?" asked Chick, and Gwenda gasped. "I want you to put Mrs. Maynard in that part—yes, give her the part you took away from her."

"Who is that speaking?" asked Solburg's voice, and Chick tried to keep his own voice steady.

"It is the Marquis of Pelborough speaking," he said.

II

FOR ONE NIGHT ONLY

"Good morning," said Chick cheerfully, as he hung up his hat and walked to his writing-table.

His three fellow-clerks and the lady typist were already at their desks, and their eyes had scarcely left the door.

"Good morning," they all said in gruff unison.

There had been a long and serious discussion that morning in the office. Bennett, the head clerk, was admittedly a Socialist, a Communist, and a believer in the theory of violence, yet it was Bennett who had insisted that Chick should be addressed as "my lord."

"Personally," he said, "I regard titles as a ridiculous survival of class privilege, but Chick Beane has always been respectful to me, and I regard him as a comrade and an ornament to the proletariat."

"Bit formal, isn't it?" demurred the ledger-clerk. "I mean to say, we can't very well treat him as an equal if we 'my lord' him."

"What about saying 'sir' to him?" suggested Miss Commers, the typist.

But "sir" was vetoed as impinging upon the privileges of their employer. So that it was agreed that they should studiously avoid calling him anything.

Chick noted the flowers on the desk—they were snowdrops—and stopped to sniff their faint fragrance.

Mr. Leither was also an early arrival, for he had read the tremendous news in the evening newspaper.

"City Clerk Succeeds to Marquisate of Pelborough.

"Successful claimant to an extinct peerage dies, and title goes to a young insurance agent."

He had given (by telegram, the reply to which was prepaid) a somewhat grudging permission for Chick to be present at his uncle's funeral. He had never dreamt that such an amazing romance lay behind the ceremony.

He, too, waited in his office, the door of which was left ajar so that he should know when his lordly subordinate arrived.

Chick sat at his desk, unlocked the drawers, and took out his form-letters. The funeral of his eccentric uncle had not saddened him; it was a far greater tragedy that he should be obliged to dispose of Dr. Beane's domestic staff and place the contents of the house in the hands of a local auctioneer. There had been an unpleasant day of sorting the doctor's personal papers, and Chick began to understand faintly how absorbing an interest this peerage had been to his uncle. He came back to work with a sense of relief. Fortune he had none. The doctor was living on an annuity, and had left something under five hundred pounds.

The cottage, and the land on which it stood—and which Chick refused to sell—might be worth another five hundred pounds, and that was all.

He had hardly taken up his pen before the untidy Mr. Leither walked from his bureau, a cigarette drooping from his lips, his waistcoat speckled grey with ash.

"Morning, Pelborough," he said, almost defiantly.

Chick stared and grinned. He had not grown accustomed to his noble title, and Mr. Leither was the first man who had addressed him as though he were a railway station.

"Good morning, sir," said Chick.

Mr, Leither coughed.

"The sad event was duly carried out?" he asked. "In fact, the late Marquis is—er—interred?"

"The doctor—oh, yes, the Marquis, of course," said Chick hastily. "Yes, sir, that is all over,"

Mr. Leither coughed again.

"Can I see you a moment—er—Pelborough?"

Chick's heart sank.

"Have I made another mistake, sir?" he said. "I was very careful about the work on Saturday."

Mr. Leither regarded him with pain.

"Mistake, my—er—dear Pelborough?" he reproached him. "Of course not! How absurd! Come in."

The insurance agent closed the door behind him.

"Sit down—er—Pelborough. What wage-fees are you getting, my boy?"

"Fees—oh, you mean wages? Two pounds fifteen a week."

"Ridiculous!" murmured Mr. Leither. "Preposterous! Tut, tut. Of course that is absurd for a man of your position, my—er—dear Pelborough."

He paced the room with determined strides.

"I've been giving your position here a great deal of thought lately. Your work is highly specialized, Pelborough, never forget that!"

Chick gasped. Was this the man who, only four days ago, had reminded him that the work he performed could be done, and better done, by a child, and a ragged child at that?

"I've been thinking things over," said Mr. Leither, lighting another cigarette, "and I've come to" this conclusion—this business is growing, but it isn't growing fast enough. We are losing 'lives' that we ought to get. There are scores of members of the aristocracy who can't be got at, Pelborough. Good lives— first-class lives. Now, I'll tell you what, Pelborough. A partnership!"

"A partnership?" said Chick. "Are you taking a partner, Mr. Leither?"

Mr. Leither inclined his head.

"What about my obliterating myself, turning this little business into a company—the Marquis of Pelborough's Insurance Agency, eh?"

Chick scratched his nose thoughtfully.

"I don't see exactly how you could do that, Mr. Leither," he said. "I have no money."

"Money!" said the scornful agent. "Money! I've got the money, my boy. You have the influence. Now, what do you say?"

Chick shook his head.

"I'm not clever enough, Mr. Leither, and I certainly have no influence. It's very kind of you, but I can't see how I could help you."

"Think it over, Pelborough." Mr. Leither screwed himself up to clapping the noble back of the new Marquis. "Think it over, my dear boy, and come and lunch with me at one o'clock."

But Chick had a luncheon engagement which he would not have missed for the world.

"Not your—er—actress friend?" asked Mr. Leither; and when Chick admitted that it was his actress friend, Mr, Leither smiled with meaning.

Gwenda Maynard was an actress and an employed actress, to her joy and relief. If she was no longer a fellow-boarder of Chick's, that was no fault of his obliging landlady, Mrs. Shipmet, who had literally begged her to forget that so sordid a matter as an arrear of rent should come between two people who (in Mrs. Shipmet's own words) "had always been the best of friends, I'm sure—h'm!"

But Gwenda knew better than any, better than the delighted Chick, that Mrs. Shipmet's change of front was due to the fear that she would also lose Chick and the advertisement which the Marquis of Pelborough would bring to her boarding establishment. And, in truth, Chick had already composed, in his mind, the letter, announcing his forthcoming departure from Brockley.

Gwenda was obdurate. She had had the offer of a room in Doughty Street, Bloomsbury. A woman acquaintance of hers had a flat there, and the girl had accepted the offer gratefully.

"I've a wonderful room, Chick," she said enthusiastically after their greeting, "and Maggie Bradshaw has the most gorgeous baby! His name is Samuel, and you'd adore him."

They lunched in style at the Holborn Restaurant, and the meal was an unusually extravagant one for Chick.

"What happened after I left?" asked the girl. "Don't forget that I haven't seen you since Saturday; you were a dear to come all the way to Bloomsbury with me."

"What happened?" said Chick, trying hard to remember. "I don't exactly know, When I got back, they were all waiting up for me, and Mrs. Shipmet was awfully kind, and took me into the senctum and asked me if I would like a glass of wine. That was kind, too, although I don't drink wine. She must have thought I was a bit upset."

"Very probably," said Gwenda dryly, "And what did they call you?"

"What did they call me?" repeated Chick, "Oh, I think they called me 'my lord' or something. It was very embarrassing, because all the people I didn't like were the most friendly. Even Mr. Fred came down and said it was an honour to be hit in the jaw by me, which, of course, is stupid."

He looked at the girl thoughtfully,

"Gwenda, I must leave Mrs, Shipmet. She wants to give me her best bedroom, and I really can't afford it. Couldn't I come to your place?"

The girl's eyes danced with laughter.

"You might come and live with the infant Samuel," she said solemnly. "Margaret talks of taking another boarder."

Chick nearly leapt out of his chair in his excitement.

"That would be fine," he said. "And are you really working, Gwenda?"

She nodded.

"I am playing the part of Lady Verity. Chick," she said suddenly, "Mr. Solburg wants to see you."

Chick looked a little uncomfortable.

"I suppose he thought it was awful nerve on my part to call him up last Saturday and ask him to give you that engagement," he said. "I don't know what made me do it."

"I know," said the girl softly. "It was because you're the kindest boy that ever lived, and I got the engagement, too."

She did not tell him that Miss Moran, who had had the part which had been taken away from her, had been stricken with influenza, and that accounted for Solburg's change of front.

"I want you to promise me something, Chick."

"I'll promise you anything, Mrs.—Gwenda," said Chick. "When can I come to Doughty Street?"

"As soon as you like," she answered. "This is what I want you to promise," she went on. "Don't do anything that Mr. Solburg asks you until you have seen me."

Chick stared at her.

"What could he ask me, Gwenda?"

"I don't know," said the girl, "but you promise."

"Of course I promise," said Chick. "This has been a tremendously exciting day for me. Do you know what happened this morning?"

She shook her head.

"I was offered a partnership!"

"With Mr. Leither?" she said, trying to keep a straight face, for she had seen Mr. Leither, and knew the trials which Chick had undergone at the hands of his employer.

"It's a fact," said Chick. "You wouldn't believe it, would you? I thought I should astonish you. I never thought that Mr. Leither was such a kind soul. He's always been a little strict with me, and only the other day, in his joking way, he told me a little boy could do the work better than I. And yet he offered me a partnership right off, without any expense to myself."

"Wonderful," said the girl. "And did you accept?"

Chick shook his head.

"No," he said. "I didn't think I was up to the job. You see, I don't know very much about this insurance business, and it rather bores me. Under those circumstances it wouldn't have been fair for me to accept Mr. Leither's offer."

"Why do you think he offered it to you?" she asked.

Chick considered,

"I suppose it is because I had come into this title," he said, "and he thought that I couldn't afford to keep it up. There's a tremendous lot of kindness in the world, Gwenda, in people whom you'd never suspect, too. It makes me go all choky when I think about it."

She looked at him long and earnestly.

"You make me go all choky at times," she said quietly. "Now eat your lunch, and afterwards we'll go over to Doughty Street and interview Maggie."

Maggie proved to be a tall, attractive, red-haired girl, who smoked cigarettes all the time and had a grievance against Fate. She was not completely attired when Chick made his appearance, but Chick was seldom embarrassed. Even the unusual sight of a pretty lady in a pink dressing-gown did not so much as surprise him. He had the trick of accepting what he found, which is half the secret of happiness.

"Maggie, this is Mr. Beane," said Gwenda, to Chick's astonishment. He had almost forgotten that his name was ever Beane.

"How are you?" said Maggie carelessly. "Take a chair, Mr. What's—your—name—Mr.—er—"

"This is the gentleman I spoke of, Maggie. Do you think he might have the bed-sitting-room on the next floor?"

The house in which Maggie Bradshaw lived was divided into two maisonnettes, and Maggie had mentioned casually that the people below her—a middle-aged couple—had a room to spare, but could not offer board. Chick would take this room and board with Maggie. Not an ideal compromise, but one which had its advantages.

"If he can stand the society of two old married ladies," said Maggie humorously, "to say nothing of that kid of mine, he can come."

A queer little sound made her turn her head and groan.

"I'll bring him," said Gwenda. She ran out of the room and came back nursing a small red-haired baby, who was chewing as much of his hand as his mouth could accommodate. He jerked his eyes round in the queer way that babies have, first to the window and the fascinations of the bright light, then to Chick, and Chick grinned and held out his arms.

"You like babies, eh?" said Maggie. "Well, that's one satisfaction."

"Like them?" said Chick, holding the infant Samuel scientifically. "Good gracious, yes! Everybody likes babies!"

"Then I'm a freak," said Maggie Bradshaw, "for I loathe them."

Chick nearly dropped the child in his amazement.

"You don't like other babies?" he said incredulously.

"I don't like any of them," said Maggie. She fumbled in a yellow box, produced a cigarette, and puffed a curl of smoke in the air. "I suppose I'm an unnatural mother. Judging by your face, I'm a monster," she smiled. "A baby to you is just a lovely little creature to amuse and pet. To me he is one large piece of iron roped to my ankle."

The baby's soft cheek was against Chick's ear, and suddenly the child chuckled, a cooing little laugh, as though he had understood the woman's speech and was enjoying the humour of it.

"Mrs. Bradshaw is joking," smiled Gwenda, to whom this view was no new one.

She liked the girl. They had played together in the provinces, and Gwenda had been one of the witnesses of Maggie's wedding to a temperamental young actor. The marriage had not been a success. Mr. Bradshaw was touring Australia, and sending very occasional money for the support of his family. They had not understood one another; they both admitted that. They also admitted at their last interview that the marriage had been a mistake, and at the end Mr. Bradshaw had wept and made an impressive exit to Australia. Mrs. Bradshaw might have made as imposing an exit, but for the bit of iron.

"I'm not joking," said Maggie, She took the baby from Chick's arms, smiled in his face, but the infant Samuel was scrutinizing her, his head first on one side and then on the other, with a wholly expressionless face. "You think because I feed Sam and look after him, and dress him as well as I can, and don't beat him or drop him out of the window, that I'm necessarily fascinated, but you're wrong, Gwenda, my love. I've got to play the game with him, but I can see him wearing me out and making an old woman of me."

The infant Samuel emitted a piercing yell, and then drew back his head and stared, as though he expected some startling result.

"Take him, Gwenda; the little beggar is hungry."

It was Chick who took the child. He had been a holder of babies ever since he could remember; the satin softness of their skins, the loveliness of their little wet mouths pressed against his cheek, the touch of their fairy hands, was unadulterated pleasure to him.

"When do you think of moving in?" asked Mrs. Bradshaw, coming back with a feeding-bottle.

"On Saturday," suggested Chick.

The woman nodded.

"Give him that, Gwenda," she said. "Look at the little glutton."

The infant Samuel was straining away from Chick, his little round arms outstretched, his fingers working convulsively.

"I'll show you your room, Mr. Beane."

The room was infinitely better than his room at Brockley, the position much more central—and there were Gwenda and Samuel.

On his way to the Strand he stopped at a telephone booth to ask permission from Mr. Leither to take extra time for his luncheon. That permission was readily, even playfully, given.

"He's a wonderful fellow, is Mr. Leither," said Chick, shaking his head in astonishment. "I think I've been judging him rather harshly, Gwenda." Gwenda did not answer.

Chick had never been at "the back of the stage" before. His interview with Mr. Solburg had taken place at the gentleman's office in the Strand. He was now to find him in his native element—a man of Jove-like power, before whom actors and actresses, many of whom were people of title (in the play), and one at least a sanguinary villain, who stopped at nothing and feared nobody (on the stage), trembled and grew confused.

He was sitting in the deserted stalls, watching three people talk at one another in inaudible tones. Chick would have lingered on the cold stage, lit only by one batten, to watch this rehearsal, but the girl led him by the arm through the pass-door into the stalls.

Mr. Solburg greeted him with no more effusion than on their last meeting.

"Sit down, my lord, will you?" he asked. And then, addressing the stage-fold: "You ought to be farther down stage, Mr. Trevelyn, when you make the speech about the baby, and you, Miss Walters, should be farther to the o.p. side...That's right. Not too far, please; there will be a window there with garden backing."

"Where's the baby?" whispered Chick, a little overawed.

"It is in the property-room, having its nose fixed," said Gwenda in the same tone; and Chick started violently, until he saw her twitching lips.

"Now go on from where Miss Walters comes in," commanded Mr. Solburg.

Miss Walters came in and was greeted by Mr. Trevelyn, but what they said to one another Chick could not hear.

"I wish they'd speak up," he whispered, and Gwenda smiled.

"They're only 'walking through' the parts," she said, "just to get their actions right."

"Never seen a rehearsal before, m'lord?" asked Solburg over his shoulder.

"No, sir," said Chick.

"This isn't a real run through," explained Solburg, half twisting round (they sat behind him). "We are just 'walking' a few of the scenes. Now, Mrs. Maynard, this is where you go on."

Gwenda was no more audible than her fellow-players. She was corrected twice by Mr. Solburg, to Chick's surprise and disgust.

"Cross to left down stage, Mrs. Maynard. No, no, down stage in front of Miss Walters. That's right. You ought to be near the door. Stop! Put a chair there, somebody, to indicate the door."

He took a cigar-case from his pocket and offered it to Chick.

"Don't smoke cigars? You're wise." Solburg was regarding the stage seriously and intently. "How would you like to be an actor, my lord?"

"Me?" said Chick in surprise.

"You," nodded Solburg. "Just a small but important part. I could get the author to write one in. You'd only have a few lines to say, and you wouldn't be on the stage ten minutes."

Chick was laughing softly.

"Do you like the idea?" asked Mr. Solburg, turning abruptly so that his good-humoured face was within a few inches of Chick's. "You'd be near your friend Mrs. Maynard, and the salary would be twenty—no, twenty-five pounds a week for eight performances."

"No," said Chick. "It's awfully kind of you, Mr. Solburg, and I guess the reason which prompts you. But I'm not an actor, and I should be keeping out of employment some person who was."

Solburg frowned.

"No, you wouldn't," he said. "But that's by the way. Will you think it over?"

Chick shook his head.

"I couldn't," he said definitely, and Mr. Solburg smiled.

"I think you're wise," he said. It was his pet tag, and usually he was sincere when he said it. "Only, if you feel like accepting another offer that's bigger, come to me and give me the chance of giving you as much."

"I shan't go on the stage," said Chick, "and I don't suppose anybody else will be interested in me to the extent of offering me so wonderful a salary."

Again Mr. Solburg looked round.

"My dear boy," he said, with a half-smile that made his strongly Hebraic face almost sinister, "they won't offer it for your good—they'll want to exploit you, as I do. That's frank, isn't it? Frankness is my best vice. They'll want you to appear because you're a nine days' wonder, a romance, and because the Marquis of Pelborough would look wonderful in the cast. That's why I wanted you—and because you're a good lad, too, if I may take the liberty, my lord!"

Chick nodded vigorously. He felt behind the offer a generosity and sincerity which deprived him of speech.

"Come into the theatre when you like," said Solburg. "I'll put your name on the door and stage-door. You can go on the stage when you like. Come to dinner with me one night, when I've got this production off my mind, and I'll point out to you every crook and mug who is likely to get at you. And, believe me, Lord Pelborough, they will come after you!"

"Thank you, I will, Mr. Solburg," said Chick gratefully.

"I think you're wise," said Mr. Solburg.

It was nearly four o'clock when Chick reached his office—he was in a panic when he saw the time by the post-office clock. But, bless you, if Chick had not returned until six, he would have earned no more than an indulgent smile. It is true that the ledger-clerk was a little disappointed that the new Marquis had returned from lunch perfectly sober, for he was a patron of the pictures, and was strong for a dissolute nobility.

Before he left that night, Chick informed the chief clerk that he was changing his address.

"Quite right," said that worthy man. "Ritz Hotel, I suppose? Eh—comrade?"

"Not exactly—comrade," said Chick gravely, and went back to Brockley to break the news.

Mrs. Shipmet, the good hostess of Acacia Lodge, was arrayed in her best, for she had had an important day. Hitherto her acquaintance with modern journalism had been restricted. She looked upon newspaper reading as a lazy practice, mostly indulged in by bad servants and out-of-work boarders. If she approved of newspapers at all, it was because they came in handy to line the larder shelves, or were very necessary for kindling the drawing-room fire.

And now the painstaking and reliable character of news collection was revealed to her. All day long she had sat in her "senctum" and had spoken with respectable young men, many of them, to all appearances, gentlemen, and these reporters had made notes in quaint wild scrawls, which Mrs. Shipmet knew at once was shorthand, and had treated her with the respect, and even reverence, which is due to important personages.

She had told all she knew about Chick—his manners, habits, recreations, tastes in literature, art and science. He was "more like a son" than a lodger, she told them all, and his accession to the title "had not altogether surprised her." She left the impression that that was the good fortune which was very likely to overtake anybody who was "more like a son" to her.

She saw Chick from afar off, and was at the door to meet him.

"Good evening, my lord," She would have curtsied, but wasn't quite sure how it was done in these days. "And did you enjoy your visit?" she asked tactlessly,

"I seldom enjoy funerals," said Chick, and the lady became appropriately sad.

"We've all got to come to it," she said, shaking her head mournfully.

"So I've noticed," said Chick, with a smile. "I want to see you, Mrs. Shipmet."

Mrs. Shipmet had her suspicions, which were soon to be confirmed. She led the way a little majestically to the "senctum."

"I'm going to other lodgings nearer my office," said Chick. "I have been thinking of this move for some time."

"Indeed?" said Mrs. Shipmet, implying her doubt. "I hope Mrs. Maynard hasn't persuaded you against your better judgment, Mr.—I mean, my lord?" Chick smiled.

"I don't see how I could be persuaded against my better judgment, Mrs. Shipmet," he said. "And speaking of Mrs. Maynard, she has sent you this cheque."

He laid an envelope on the table. Mrs. Shipmet sniffed at it. Though she had never seen a dishonoured cheque in her life, she always regarded payment by this instrument as "unsatisfactory." She looked her dissatisfaction.

"I can't expect your lordship to stay on in my humble dwelling," she said, with an asperity of tone which discredited her disparaging reference, "the more so as what I might term the chief attraction has departed and is no more seen."

It was a peculiarity of Mrs. Shipmet that when she was ruffled, her language took on a Biblical character. Chick's blue eyes fixed and held her.

"I was sorry Mrs. Maynard had gone," he said, "and if she had stayed, I don't think I should have thought of leaving. I hope you aren't cross, Mrs. Shipmet?"

She said something about having done her best for him; he had always had the best of everything, and it seemed rather hard that he should be dragged away.

"When are you thinking of leaving, sir—my lord?" she asked.

"Now," said Chick laconically.

He had not intended leaving for a week. Mrs. Shipmet wept, and Chick packed.

His landlady so far recovered, on his departure, as to ask his approval of a new business card she had drafted, at the head of which was to appear (in gold letters) the words:

"Under the distinguished patronage of
and highly recommended by
The Most Honourable
the Marquis of Pelborough, K.G."

"What is K.G.?" asked Chick curiously.

"Knight of the Garter," said the landlady.

"But I'm not!" protested Chick. "And what's all this stuff about 'Most Honourable'? Really, Mrs. Shipmet, I think you're very kind, but that Most Honourable makes me very uncomfortable. I've always tried to be honourable, but it is rather cheap, isn't it, boasting?"

It was explained to him that 'Most Honourable' was the customary prefix to his title, just as "Honourable" and "Right Honourable" go before the names of certain politicians, statesmen, and peers of lower rank. He approved the testimonial, striking out only the dignity to which he had not attained.

His fellow-guests brought him their autograph books, and he signed "Chick Pelborough" until it was pointed out to him that members of the nobility only signed their title-names, whereupon he flourished "Pelborough" under certain moral maxims which were favourites of his.

It was late when his taxi reached Doughty Street, and he began to wonder if the household was in bed. After much ringing, Maggie appeared, still in her dressing-gown.

"Hullo!" she said in surprise. "I thought you weren't coming for a week. Have they chucked you out?"

She showed the way up to her sitting-room.

"Gwenda isn't back from the theatre yet," she said. "They are having their first dress rehearsal to-night." She looked at Chick dubiously. "I'd better go and see the people downstairs about your room," she said. "You like Sam, don't you?" she asked suddenly.

"I'm very fond of little babies," admitted Chick, and she looked at him strangely.

Chick found it difficult to analyse his feelings in regard to Maggie Bradshaw. She was rather over-powering, a tall, strongly-built girl, with a big mop of red hair, about which he had spoken enthusiastically to Gwenda, without, however, evoking any very hearty response. She was good-looking in a heavy way. Her features were too bold. Too bold—that was the quality in her which checked his liking.

"Yes," she said thoughtfully, "you're a kind sort of kid—maybe...yes..."

She did not attempt to fill up the blanks in her speech, but went downstairs to Chick's new landlord.

She came back in ten minutes and handed him a key.

"Your room is facing the entrance," she said. "They've put your trunk inside, so you can't mistake your little cell. Do you want to see your new home? They won't be in bed for hours yet, and Mr. Worthing said he'd wait up for you."

She told him that his new landlord was a lawyer's clerk, and that his wife was inclined towards spiritualism.

"Otherwise, they're ideal people," she said, and went on to talk about Gwenda. Here she was fascinating to Chick. She was the first person he had ever met who knew his friend or was anxious to talk about her. Maggie knew surprisingly little of Gwenda's early life, as it proved.

"She's never mentioned her husband to me," said Maggie, "and, Heaven knows, I've spoken enough about my little bit of trouble. Sometimes I think Mr. Gwenda Maynard must be in gaol, she's so cheery."

Gwenda and she had met when they were both playing in the same touring show.

"That was when I met my doom," said Maggie grimly. "You think I'm heartless, Mr. Beane, and I suppose I am, but do you know what Samuel means? It means that I've had to turn down the best offer that I've ever had—to play my old part in Princess Zelia. It opens in New York next month, and there's a contract waiting for me to sign and steamer reservation already made. I've got to go and see Brancsome to-morrow and tell him that I'm engaged by Samuel and Co. to play the heavy mother in the great boarding-house drama 'Chained by the Leg.'" She laughed and threw her cigarette into the fire, and it was at that moment that Gwenda's key turned in the lock.

"Chick!" she said in amazement. "Whatever are you doing here?"

"He has been driven from home," said Maggie, looking at the clock, "and this is where Samuel gets his night-cap."

Chick helped the girl off with her coat and gave a resume of the events of the evening.

"So you told her you left because I'd gone, did you?" said Gwenda. "How lovely you are, Chick! Yes, it has been a trying night. Solburg made us do one scene over and over again until I could have screamed."

She drew a long sigh.

"Well, you're here, anyway. Has Maggie been discussing the duties and responsibilities of motherhood?"

"I'm sorry for Mrs. Bradshaw," said Chick.

"Be professional and call her Maggie," smiled Gwenda. "But you're sorry for everybody, Chick."

"I'm sorry for Samuel, of course," he confessed, "but I sort of see her point of view." He wrinkled his forehead in thought. "I wish one could buy babies," he said, "the same as you can buy cats and canaries."

"Don't make Maggie an offer, or she'll give him to you," warned Gwenda, bubbling with laughter. "Chick, you ought to run a creche! And talking of infants reminds me that Solburg has had a youthful reporter with him all the evening. Solburg is a good sort, and I think he was splendid to you this afternoon; but he has queer ideas about things, and he'll do almost anything for an advertisement. He always runs some stunt for the first night of a show."

"When is your first night?" asked Chick.

She shook her head.

"I shan't tell you, and I don't want you to know, so please don't read the newspapers for a day or two. I'd be scared to death if you were in front."

Mr. Solburg's passion for publicity was revealed the next morning. Chick, who had passed a restless night, owing to the strangeness of his surroundings, got up early and rang the bell of the upper maisonette before half-past eight.

To his surprise, Maggie was up and dressed.

"Rather a shock to see me without my dressing-gown, eh?" she laughed. "Come along up and have breakfast. Gwenda has something to show you."

The something was a newspaper wherein was announced that "for one night only the Marquis of Pelborough would make his first appearance on any stage" in the Society drama Tangled Lives.

"The Marquis is expected to be one of the guests assembled in the great ballroom scene."

Gwenda held the paper whilst he read the lines aloud.

"That is Solburg," she said viciously. "I knew he was planning something of the sort."

"But I'm not going!" said the indignant Chick. "Of course I shan't appear."

"Of course you won't," said Gwenda scornfully. "But everybody in the audience will be pointing out one or the other supers on the stage and saying 'There's the Marquis,' and that is all Solburg wants. The next day he will say that, owing to an indisposition, you couldn't appear. He'll have had his advertisement, and that is all that will matter. It is too bad."

How "bad" it was, Chick discovered when he turned up at Leither's. Although the hour was early, the office was besieged by reporters. Had Chick waited and seen them, his denial would have been printed. Instead, a warning—which was not intended as a warning—delivered by the ledger-clerk, who was waiting on the mat, sent him hurriedly to the nearest telephone station, there to call up Mr. Leither and implore him to get rid of the Press-men. Which Mr. Leither did, in his blandest manner, by admitting the truth of the paragraph. For Mr. Leither represented a category which was in direct opposition to the Shipmet school, and believed implicitly in the printed word.

"I'm sorry, my boy—my dear Pelborough," he said, when Chick had stolen furtively into the office, the first furtive act of his life. "Seemed true enough. Why shouldn't you go on the stage, my dear boy? It is a very respectable profession. I have had several good 'lives' from the stage. I negotiated one policy for ten thousand pounds."

"Mr. Solburg's won't be a good life, if I see him this morning," said Chick, with some heat.

"He never was a good life, my dear Pelborough," said Mr. Leither gravely.

Chick's position in the office was now an alarming one. As an insignificant dispatcher of "follow-up" letters and guardian of the day- book, he had found work which was well within his grasp, and did not make any very severe demands upon his abilities. But the day-book had been handed over to the ledger-clerk, and the addressing of envelopes had been taken in hand by the typist. There was apparently no work for Chick to do, except to sit still whilst Mr. Leither patted him from time to time, or respond when addressed as "my dear Pelborough." Many more people came to call upon the insurance agent than had ever called before. They spoke to Mr. Leither, but they looked at Chick. This did not bother the new peer. What did worry him was that when he discovered something useful to do, the thing he was doing was taken from his hands by his colleagues.

It was "Excuse me, I'll fill that ink-pot," or "Pardon me, let me change that blotting-paper," until Chick in despair was driven to drawing figures on his blotting-pad. Even then the office stood round and admired audibly.

He dined that night with Maggie alone. She was very serious, and he thought she had been weeping. It must have been her interview with Brancsome, the agent, and the refusal of the tempting contract. He remembered that and sympathized with her.

"Gwenda won't be home to dinner, of course," she said, and Chick wondered why she said "of course." Perhaps the rehearsals would be longer and more tedious today. He had intended, in spite of her admonition, discovering when the new play was to be produced, but the matter had slipped from his mind.

"You think I'm an awful creature, don't you?" asked Maggie for the third time during the meal.

"I never think people are really awful," said Chick. "When I was learning to box, the first thing I was taught was to have a very high opinion of the people I had to meet—and they were queer fellows, too. If I don't think badly of them, why should I think badly of you? It is a pity you don't love Samuel."

"Have some more potatoes," said Maggie almost roughly.

After the meal was finished and cleared away, Maggie came back to the little dining-room, where Chick had settled himself to read, and to his astonishment she was dressed for going out.

"Do you mind listening for baby? I shall be gone for an hour," she asked. "I don't suppose he'll wake until eleven, so don't go in to him, please."

Chick smiled.

"I'll listen with both ears," he said.

She went to the door, hesitated, and came back; then, before Chick could realize what she was doing, she stooped and kissed him.

"You're a good boy," she said, and was gone before he could find speech.

"Gosh!" said Chick at last, for nobody more attractive than a maiden aunt had ever kissed him.

He read his book—it was Prescott's Peru—stopping now and again to tiptoe to the door of Maggie's room (he afterwards discovered that he had really been listening at the kitchen door) and to creep back to his chair. It was nearly ten o'clock when he realized that Maggie had been gone a long time. And with that realization came a faint and fretful howl. He jumped up, located the sound, and went into the right room, to discover Samuel blinking strangely and making queer noises.

"What is the matter, old top?" asked Chick, picking him up in his arms. But Samuel continued to behave strangely. And then, looking round for a bottle, Chick saw the letter propped up against one of the ornaments on the mantelshelf. He carried the baby nearer and read:

"I am going to leave Samuel. Look after him. I must earn money—this flat has put me hopelessly in debt. Look after Samuel, please. I will send money. I shall not return for six months. Please look after Samuel; it breaks my heart to leave him. There is," (should be 'are,' thought Chick) "twenty pounds on my dressing-table. The furniture can be sold to pay the tradesmen. Look after Samuel. Maggie."

"My sacred aunt!" breathed Chick, and then his attention was violently jerked to Samuel. The little man was red in the face, and Chick laid him face downwards across his knees and rubbed his back. But Samuel was not appeased. A thin hair-raising shriek advertised his discomfort, and Chick snatched him up again. What should he do? He was certain Samuel was ill, and he could not go for a doctor. He found a shawl and wrapped Samuel tight. His landlady was out; Chick must take the child himself to discover a doctor—no simple matter in a strange neighbourhood.

Fortune was with him, for he picked up an empty taxi almost at the door. Under the influence of the taxi's jolting progress, Samuel's shrieks died to a whimper. Though the night was cold, and Chick had neither greatcoat nor hat, he was moist with fear.

A policeman directed him to a doctor's house, and suggested a hospital. The doctor was out, and Chick grew moister. Gwenda! She would understand. He directed the taxi to the Strand.

He got out of the cab at the stage door of the Strand-Broadway, and nobody stopped him as he went cautiously down the dark stairs to the door which he knew led to the stage. And now, dodging the heavy sets, he came to the wings, and Samuel howled piteously.

Thank goodness, there was Gwenda! The rehearsal was in full swing, all the lights were blazing, and she occupied the stage alone. What was more, she was looking in his direction, made up, too, with painted face and blackened eyebrows. He tried to attract her attention, and apparently succeeded, for she stretched out her arms, and her intense vibrant voice called:

"Give me the child! Give me the child!"

Chick could not know that she was appealing to the stage soldiers who had taken her stage baby.

As the elegant Mr. Trevelyn, sneering heavily, came through the canvas door to mock her, Chick bolted from the wings. Samuel had got his head clear of the shawl and was looking wide-eyed at the bright lights.

"Maggie's gone!" said Chick hoarsely, "and Samuel's swallowed something!"

He heard the gasp from a thousand throats, and turned his head to the footlights. Beyond them was a sea of pink faces and white shirt-fronts. It was the first night of Tangled Lives, and he had made his first appearance before an audience.

"Moses!" said Chick, as the curtain dropped.

III

A WRIT OF SUMMONS

Had the eminent author of Tangled Lives foreseen that at the conclusion of his third act there would arrive on the stage, a little blinded by the glare of the lights, more than a little worried for the child of tender years he bore in his arms, no less a personage than the Most Honourable the Marquis of Pelborough, who, having arrived, would blunder into the very thrill of a carefully devised finish, he could not have written words that better fitted the situation when Chick stumbled on to the stage of the Strand-Broadway Theatre, holding the infant Samuel in his arms. For these were the lines:

Lady Verity (appealingly): Give me the child! Give me the child!

Count Robing: You shall never see him again! Ha, ha, ha!

(Enter Flemming hurriedly: he bears a child in his arms.)

Flemming: You lie! The child is here!

(Curtain.)

The eminent author, it is true, did not suggest that the mother of the child had bolted, or that the infant himself had swallowed a foreign body, as Chick, obtruding a vital fact into the realms of dramatic fiction, stated so definitely. Let the curtain of the Strand-Broadway fall; let the dramatic critics gather together in the bar, puzzled by the "comedy finish" to a tragic scene; let Mr. Solburg, that important manager, stroll to the back of the stage, shaking with internal laughter, and realizing that he has a big story to give to the newspaper men the next morning, and let Chick be hurried back to Doughty Street for a feeding-bottle and the wherewithal to fill it, whilst an aged dresser hushes the infant, and then let Chick's diary bridge a gulf.

Saturday 30th.—Became a marquis.

Monday 1st.—Buried my uncle.

Wednesday 3rd.—Appeared on stage; adopted baby.

Thursday 4th.—Salary raised to £5 a week.

Four dramatic days in an amazing week.

Hitherto Chick's life had run smoothly, if not normally. The work of an insurance clerk with a limited income is governed by a ready-made routine. His uncle's endless petitions to the House of Lords that the ancient Marquisate of Pelborough should be revived in his favour. Chick had regarded so indulgently that his attitude was almost one of indifference. It was the mild contempt of youth for the foibles and fads of the aged. And lo! a miracle had happened. The Lords had endorsed the claim of Dr. Beane, and the old man had been literally shocked to death, leaving an earnest youth to the enjoyment of the title.

On the night of his involuntary appearance in drama Chick could not sleep. He turned the matter over in his mind. He was a marquis, a peer of the realm, a descendant of kings and great warriors. He had an uneasy sense of responsibility without the slightest idea of how that responsibility could be met.

His landlord, the lawyer's clerk, had given him permission to read any of the books which filled half a dozen shelves in the dining-room.

At three o'clock Chick turned on the light and padded softly into the little dining-room in search of knowledge and guidance. Perhaps there was a book about lords. There were, in fact, half a dozen, but they were novels. He skimmed through several of these and discovered that there were two distinct brands. There was one kind which was old and stately and held his head high, and there was another which indulged in betting and behaved abominably to his lady friends. Chick carried the books back and renewed his search.

He found what he wanted in a well-worn encyclopaedia, sitting on the edge of his bed. Under "Marquis" he discovered that he ranked nearly as high as a duke.

"Je-hos-o-phat!" said Chick aloud.

"The mantle is scarlet, with three and a half doublings of ermine."

What mantle, he wondered? And what was a "doubling"? He was thrilled to read that "one of the earliest creations of this title was that conferred upon Charles, Earl of Steffield, who was created Marquis of Pelborough by Richard III."

He put the book back on the shelf and went to sleep, and was awakened by a little maid-servant, who brought him a cup of coffee at half-past seven. With daylight came a sense of the problems which he had dismissed the night before.

Gwenda was up and his breakfast was being laid when he rang the bell, and it was she who admitted him.

"Good morning, Chick! Have you seen the newspapers?" she asked, when he sat down to breakfast.

Chick started guiltily.

"No, I haven't. They haven't said anything about my bringing Samuel to you?" he demanded hoarsely.

"They haven't," said the grim Gwenda, "but they will!"

"How is Samuel?"

She smiled. "He slept like a young angel. Chick, what are we to do with him?"

"I told you last night, Gwenda," said Chick doggedly. "I'm going to adopt him till his mother comes back."

"And what about this flat?" asked Gwenda, with great patience.

"I'll pay all her bills, and we'll keep the flat going." Chick was very definite and business-like this morning, thought the girl. "I have enough money to do that."

But the adoption was to prove a bigger and more complicated business than he had thought. It meant the engagement of a nurse, and the nurse must also act as housekeeper, chaperon, and friend of Gwenda's, or the dream menage he had planned tumbled to pieces. Gwenda put no obstacles in the way, as well she might, for the position was an awkward one for her. It involved the adoption of Samuel by her, and not by Chick at all.

The gods were very good to Chick that day. The first visit at a servants' registry produced Mrs. Orlando Phibbs. It even produced her in the flesh, for Mrs. Phibbs was on the premises when the girl called. At first sight Gwenda was not impressed, Mrs. Phibbs was big and majestic. She had large and imposing features and a double chin, and she listened to Gwenda's requirements, rather haltingly stated, with a calm detachment which was very chilling. And then Gwenda had an inspiration. She told the whole story of Maggie and Samuel, and the ultroneous adoption by Chick, and as she progressed, the ponderous dignity of Mrs. Phibbs relaxed and a broad smile humanized her forbidding face.

"My dear," she said briskly, "I think this is my job."

She was the widow of a doctor, and had been a nurse in her youth. Her husband—this she said with the greatest calmness—had drunk himself to death, leaving a number of "debts of honour" which gave her infinite satisfaction to repudiate, four tickets in the Calcutta Sweepstake, and a house so cleverly mortgaged that the doctor would undoubtedly have ended his days in prison had his fraud been discovered in time. She revealed these details on their way back to the flat.

"I'm not a decayed gentlewoman, and don't think of me as one," Mrs. Phibbs warned her. "I'm troubled with a sense of humour and an occasional 'go' of rheumatism."

Samuel, who had been left in the care of his self-appointed guardian, adopted Mrs. Phibbs with acclamation.

And Mrs. Phibbs was truly wonderful. She settled herself in the room of Samuel's fugitive mother, took control of the girl whom Maggie had employed, and ordered Chick to give notice to his landlord and occupy the room which had been originally designed for him.

"Propriety!" said Mrs. Phibbs scornfully. "I've a son in the Army who could eat that boy! What is his name, by the way?"

"The Marquis of Pelborough," said Gwenda.

Mrs. Phibbs stopped her work.

"The Marquis of—oh, yes! I read something about it in the papers. He is the boy who inherited the title from an uncle. Phew!" Mrs. Phibbs whistled shrilly but musically. "An interesting household, Mrs. Maynard. Your husband doesn't live here?"

Gwenda shook her head. "I think it would be best if I told you about my marriage," she said, and evidently the explanation she gave for her husband's absence was wholly satisfactory. "Chick—Lord Pelborough—doesn't know, and I don't want him to know," she said. "I've never told anybody but you, and it is strange that I should take you into my confidence."

Chick was exactly an hour and a half late in reaching his office. He had telephoned Mr. Leither, and that obliging man had told him to take the day; but Chick was beginning to feel conscience-stricken, and had resolved that this irregularity of conduct must cease forthwith. He went so far as to seek an interview with his employer and to suggest that this lost time should be deducted from his wages, but Mr. Leither pooh-poohed the suggestion.

"You take these things too seriously, my dear Pelborough," he said genially. "By the way, I have raised your salary to five pounds a week. It is wholly inadequate "—he shrugged his shoulders—"and I must lighten the work for you, Pelborough, I really must. After today your desk will be in my room. I can't have you out there with the clerks—that will never do."

Chick heard of this new arrangement with dismay, and endeavoured to discover what his duties would be. Apparently they began and ended by his looking as ornamental and important as possible, and interviewing possible clients.

"There's one thing I'd like to speak to you about," said Mr. Leither, in some discomfort of mind. "What about clothes?"

"Clothes?" said the puzzled Chick.

"I have the best tailor in the world," said Mr. Leither extravagantly. Chick thought that he was not a good advertisement for that excellent tradesman, but said nothing. "Suppose you go along and order half a dozen suits. A dress-suit—have you got a dress-suit, Pelborough?"

"No, I haven't," admitted Chick.

"You ought to have." Mr. Leither shook his head. "What about shirts and boots and things? My dear Pelborough, you really must dress up to your station. Now, look at me." Chick looked at him, and thought he had never seen a man upon whom the ingenuity of tailor and cutter were so patently wasted. "Suppose I came here dressed like a ragamuffin—not that you are a ragamuffin, my dear Pelborough; that is a little figure of speech—what chance should I have of inspiring confidence in 'lives'?"

It was a new thought for Chick, and he carried his trouble to Gwenda, for now he went home to lunch.

"I think he's right," said the girl. "But, Chick dear, you must buy your own clothes. You cannot be under an obligation to Mr. Leither."

"Of course I'll buy my own clothes," said Chick in surprise. "He wasn't suggesting that he should pay for them."

"I rather think he was," smiled the girl.

The question of clothes was to come into greater prominence than Chick or the girl supposed or imagined.

The following morning a letter reached him, readdressed from Brockley—a large white envelope and bulky. It was addressed to "The Most Honourable the Marquis of Pelborough, etc." What those etceteras meant were revealed in the contents of the communication.

"To Our Right Trusty and Well-Beloved Charles, Marquis of Pelborough, Earl of Steffield, Viscount Morland, Baron Pelborough in the County of Westshire, Baron Slieve, Master of Kollochbach, etcetera.

"Greeting. WHEREAS Our Parliament for arduous and urgent affairs concerning Us the State and defence of Our said United Kingdom and the Church is now met at Our City of Westminster. We strictly enjoining command you upon the faith and allegiance by which you are bound to Us that considering the difficulty of the said affairs and dangers impending (waiving all excuses) you be personally present at our aforesaid Parliament with Us and with the Prelates Nobles and Peers of our said Kingdom to treat and give your counsel upon the affairs aforesaid. And this as you regard Us and Our honour and the safety and defence of the said United Kingdom and Church and dispatch of the said affairs in nowise do you omit. Witness Ourself at Westminster...etc...etc..."

"What does that mean?" he gasped. They were at breakfast, the three, and Samuel, in a bright scarlet dressing-gown was sitting in a baby-chair in the background, chewing a spoon. "I don't know any of these people."

"Which people?" asked Gwenda.

"This Earl of Steffield, and Viscount Morland, and Baron What's-his- name..."

But Gwenda was helpless with laughter.

"Chick, you silly dear, you're all those people," she said. "They're your secondary titles."

"Gosh!" said Chick. "Am I really?"

"Of course you are. When you grow up and you have children, you will give the second title to your son. He will be Earl of Steffield."

"But does this mean I've got to go to the House of Lords?"

Gwenda nodded. "I was wondering how long it would be before you were summoned. Yes, Chick, you are now one of our hereditary legislators."

"H'm!" said Chick. "I'll drop in this afternoon and get it over."

She was still laughing.

"Oh, Chick, you can't drop in at the House of Lords and get things over," she said, dropping her hand on his shoulder and shaking him gently. "The thing is to be done with ceremony. You had better write and say that you will take your seat next Monday, and I'll find out what you have to do."

"But couldn't I just call in, and say 'How do you do?' and come away?" said the worried Chick, "I don't want to waste any time. I've been rather unfair to Mr. Leither, and we've got a man coming on Monday afternoon who is pretty certain to take out a big policy, and Mr. Leither will want me to tell him all about the schedules."

She explained that the introduction of a new Lord in Parliament was something of a ceremonial, and that night, when he met her at the stage-door to bring her home, she gave him particulars which terrified him.

"I've been talking to Mr. Solburg," she said, "and really Solburg is much nicer than I thought he was. He hasn't said anything to the Press, Chick, about your appearance in the third act of Tangled Lives. He said the play is going so well that it doesn't want any extra advertisement. You'll have to get an hour off to-morrow and lunch with Mr. Solburg."

The lunch was at a club in Mayfair of which Mr. Solburg was a member, and the beauty of the room, the smartness of the lunchers, and the general air of luxury which prevailed, struck Chick dumb.

"No, I shouldn't advise you to be a member here, my lord," said the frank Mr. Solburg. "You're pretty safe so long as you have no money, but there are men and women in this room who would find a way of pawning your title."

He pointed out one or two notorieties. Very respectable persons they seemed, thought Chick, and was amazed to discover that they lived on the border-line of rascality.

"That fellow over there works the American liners," said Mr. Solburg. "He's the son of a lord, and an 'honourable', but he's the decoy duck that brings the other birds to the slaughter."

"But why are you a member of this dreadful club?" asked Chick, astonished.

"They don't bother me," said the comfortable Solburg.

"They would bother me," said Chick, "and this is the place I should certainly avoid if I had money— which, thank Heaven, I haven't."

"I think you're wise," said Mr. Solburg.

After lunch he drove him in his big car to make a call on Stainers, the famous theatrical costumiers.

"We can do the robe," said Mr. Stainer, who was of Mr. Solburg's nationality. "Real ermine, Mr. Solburg. It was used by "—he mentioned the name of a great actor manager—"but the coronet we have to hire from Fillings of Bury Street, and they'll want a deposit."

"Make me responsible," said Solburg, "but get a good coronet, and see that it fits his lordship."

With due solemnity Mr. Stainer measured the size of Chick's head, and that night robe and coronet were delivered at Doughty Street, and Chick tried them on before an admiring audience.

The coronet had been made for a larger head than Chick's, but Gwenda, with folded paper and a few quick stitches, managed to make it fit. Chick surveyed himself sombrely in the glass, His scarlet mantle trailed on the ground, his big ermine cape smothered him, but the sight of the coronet on his head, with its pearls and its strawberry leaves, hypnotized him.

"Gosh!" he said at last.

It was a word which adequately expressed his emotions.

"I look like a king, Gwenda. I shan't be mistaken for anybody like that, shall I?" he asked in alarm.

"Don't be silly, Chick. Of course you won't."

"But am I to walk through the streets all dressed up?" asked Chick in horror. "Of course I could go by bus or take a taxi, but they would laugh at me," protested Chick. "Couldn't I go in, and carry this thing in my hand and my robes over my arm, just to show 'em that I'd got 'em?"

"You dress at the House of Lords," smiled the girl. "Chick, you're being crazy."

Gwenda took complete charge of the arrangements. That afternoon she went to the House of Lords, and after passing the scrutiny of numerous officials, having interviewed the Yeoman Usher, and the Secretary to the Great Chamberlain, and the Usher of the Black Rod, and the Sergeant-at-Arms, and the Gold Stick in Waiting, and divers other high but very courteous officials, she secured the interview she wanted, and came back to Chick, flushed with excitement.

"Chick, you're to be introduced to the House by two Lords," she said, "and you can 'robe'—that is what they call it—in a special room, and you have to walk up the floor of the House and take the oath and shake hands with the Lord Chancellor."

"You're pulling my leg, Gwenda," said Chick, going pale.

"And Monday will be such a good day," she went on enthusiastically. "There is to be a big debate on the Child Workers Bill, and everybody will be there to see you."

Chick closed his eyes and breathed heavily.

"And here are the names of the people who will introduce you—such nice men. Chick—Lord Felthinton and the Earl of Mansar. They've read all about you, and they say they'll be delighted to do anything for you."

"Phew!" said Chick, looking helplessly from side to side.

"Rubbish!" said the practical Mrs. Phibbs. "Anybody would think you were going to an execution, Chick." (At his earnest request she had adopted this style of address,)

"Couldn't it be put off for a week?" said the agonized Chick. "We're awfully busy on Mondays."

"You're going on Monday," insisted Gwenda firmly. "Now, Chick, don't let us have any argument about this, and I think you ought to wear a Court suit. I'm going to ask Mr. Solburg about it."

The week passed all too quickly, but as the fatal day came nearer, Chick grew more and more resigned.

On the Sunday night he sat reading with Gwenda and the watchful Mrs. Phibbs. Samuel had retired for the night, and the long silence was broken only by the rustling of Chick's newspaper and the click of Mrs. Phibbs's knitting-needles. There was something in Gwenda's pose that was unexpectedly comforting to Chick. He watched her for some time over the top of his newspaper. He thought she was the most beautiful woman in the world, and certainly Gwenda Maynard was pretty. Her face had a delicacy of moulding which he had never seen in other women's faces. Her eyes were big and shadowy, and held a mystery which to the boy was insoluble.

"Gwenda," he said, "I've been thinking."

She raised her head from her book.

"I've been thinking about the importance of everybody except me," he said.

She put down her book.

"It is rather good at times to be impressed by a sense of one's own nothingness," she said, "but not for you, Chick. You are going to be a big factor in life."

He shook his head.

"I was reading the political news," he said. "I've never read it before, and never realized the power of the Government. Why, Gwenda, it can do anything! It could shut up your theatre or—or—"

"What makes you think all this, Chick?" asked the girl.

"I don't know, only it seems so ridiculous that a fellow like me should have the nerve to go into Parliament, and that's what it amounts to."

She laughed, stretching out her hand to his and gripping it in her cool palm.

"You'll be a big man yet, dear," she said. "You'll make and break Governments like that!" She snapped her disengaged fingers.

"Goodness?" said Chick fearfully. "I hope not!"

Chick faced the day of days a little wanly. He would not have had any breakfast, but Gwenda insisted, and he absolutely refused any lunch—he said it would choke him.

The coronet and robes were packed in a suit-case, and Chick insisted upon travelling to the House of Lords by bus. He said it was less conspicuous. The girl had received from one of his lordly sponsors a ticket admitting her to the gallery, to watch the ceremony, and she went with him.

He was reminded of a great cathedral he had once visited. He could not remember where or in what circumstances, but the place had left just such an impression as was now revived. He felt it would not be decent to talk above a whisper in these high vaulted corridors, broad and spacious. The stone walls were decorated with pictures of historical events, at every half a dozen paces was a marble pedestal surmounted by the bust of a dead-and-gone Parliamentarian, and now and again a life-sized statue of some statesman who had made or mangled history. It was as though he moved through a large and splendid tomb.

The feet of hurrying men sounded hollowly as they crossed or recrossed the marble floor of the big lobby. The sing-song voice of an attendant wailed unintelligible names; there was a loud whisper of sound, for here the members of the Commons interviewed their constituents.

The entrance to the House of Lords opened from this lobby, and lay at the end of a broad vestibule, the walls of which were also covered by historical paintings.

Chick's heart was in his mouth as he approached the first of many policemen—there seemed hundreds of these courteous men.

"Lord Pelborough? Yes, my lord, I will show your lordship the way."

Chick clung on to the battered suit-case in which the borrowed vestments of his nobility were packed, and Gwenda and he followed the officer until they came to another policeman, who took them in charge and finally piloted them to where the sponsors were waiting.

Chick regarded them with awe and reverence. One was tall and bent, a man of forty-five, with a keen, intellectual face. He wore an eye-glass and was fashionably attired. Chick regretted bitterly that he had not followed Mr. Leither's advice and arrayed himself in something more striking than a blue serge suit. The second was young, plump and rosy, and had a tiny moustache.

"This is the Marquis of Pelborough," said Gwenda.

The elder man held out his hand. "I'm very glad to meet you. Lord Pelborough," he said, with a little smile. "I've read a lot about you."

"Yes, sir—my lord, I mean," said Chick huskily.

"And this is the Earl of Mansar." He introduced the rosy young man, who grinned amiably.

"It's an awful fag coming down here all dolled up, isn't it?" he said. "But, bless you, these old devils are so blind they wouldn't notice you if you came in your pyjamas!"

"Take Lord Pelborough to the robing-room, Mansar. The Lord Chancellor takes his seat at three. You've got about ten minutes."

Chick was led away as one to the scaffold, but under the cheering influence of the volatile Mansar, who discoursed eloquently, and without stopping to take breath, upon the weather, the horrible condition of the roads, and the mistake of adopting a Parliamentary career. Chick began to take an interest.

What followed was like a dream. He was dimly conscious of being draped in his long scarlet robe, and of Lord Mansar and an attendant fixing the coronet.

"Keep it straight, dear old thing," murmured his lordship. "It's inclined to go a bit raffishly over your right eye. That's right!"

Chick was led to the lobby. The girl had disappeared.

Lord Felthinton fixed his eye-glass and reviewed the new peer with approval.

"As a matter of fact. Lord Pelborough," he said, "you should be introduced by two marquises; but there isn't a marquis in the House today, and you'll have to be content with the escort of inferiors."

Chick dimly remembered that Gwenda had told him that Lord Felthinton was one of the richest landowners in England, and during the time of waiting he tried very politely to turn the conversation to land, about which he knew nothing more than that it was the substance on which houses were built. His mouth was dry, and when he spoke his utterance was thick and sounded like that of somebody else speaking.

An official came through the swing-doors, an elderly gentleman who wore a chain about his neck and was dressed in knee-breeches and Court coat. He murmured something and Felthinton nodded.

"Come on, Pelborough," said Mansar. "Buck up! Have you got the summons?"

Chick produced it from his trousers pocket with a trembling hand.

"Off we go," said Mansar cheerfully.

That walk up the red-carpeted floor was the worst part of the dream. Chick was dimly conscious that to the left and right of him were men who were clothed in the garments of civilization. He was horribly conscious that he was fantastically attired. He stood before the table, a peer on either side of him, and signed his name with a trembling hand, and repeated that he would "bear true allegiance...heirs and successors..." and then he was led to a bewigged figure sitting on a broad divan, and the figure solemnly rose, took off his three cornered hat, and shook hands with him.

The next thing that Chick really remembered was being in the robing-room with the Earl of Mansar, and that young man was smiling broadly.

"Dear old thing, you were wonderful!" he said ecstatically. "You were simply amazing."

"I was," said Chick. "I amazed myself to such an extent that I don't know whether I'm alive or dead."

"You're alive all right. Get your nightie off, put the strawberry leaves into the bag. Come along, and we'll listen to this debate."

"But I'm not going back again," said Chick in alarm.

"Yes, you are," said Mansar calmly. "Your young lady has gone into the gallery, and I told her that I was bringing you back to listen to the spouters."

Chick mopped his wet brow.

"I've an awful lot of work to do," he said.

"Come along," said Mansar, grasping him by the arm.

This time their entry into the House was unnoticed. Mansar piloted him to a leather bench to the right of the Lord Chancellor, and Chick, all unwittingly, found himself supporting the Government. He did not know that he was supporting the Government, and it would not have worried him much if he had.

Now he was calmer he had a better opportunity of examining the House. It was a beautiful chamber, he thought, all gilt and crimson. The people who occupied the benches did not seem as if they were made to match. They were, in the main, elderly men, and their attention was concentrated upon a very stout, tall gentleman who stood by the table and expounded the views of the Government upon a Bill which was evidently under discussion.

Presently he sat down, and another rose. Chick noted mentally that, however violently these men might oppose one another's opinions, they invariably referred to each other as "the noble lord." Once or twice the wigged figure on the divan—which he was to learn was called the Woolsack—interposed in the debate, and there was an exchange of heated courtesies. They addressed him of the divan as "My Lord Chancellor."

Once Chick looked up at the gallery and caught Gwenda's eye. Her face was glowing with pride, and he smiled up at her.

Then through a fog of words, through the drone of the prosy and the fire of the eloquent, came an understanding of the subject which was being discussed, It was an amendment to a Bill which raised the age at which children could be employed, and Chick forgot the House of Lords, forgot the girl in the gallery, forgot his own nervousness and embarrassment, and listened intently, nodding to every sentiment which he approved, shaking his head violently when a very pompous gentleman, who sat behind him, insisted that the children of the working classes were better employed in a factory than wasting their time at school in a vain endeavour to assimilate knowledge which could not be of any use to them in after-life.

Then there was a pause. The last speaker sat down, and the Lord Chancellor threw a glance from left to right. It was at that moment that Chick decided that he would go out and wait for Gwenda. He rose and instantly found himself the focus of all eyes.

"Lord Pelborough." said the Lord Chancellor in sepulchral tones, and Chick turned to him quickly.

"Yes, sir—my lord, I mean," he said.

"—has the floor."

Chick looked at the floor and then at the figure on the divan.

"You've got to make a speech!" hissed Mansar's voice, and Chick blinked.

So it was compulsory for a new member to speak? He did not know that by rising and nodding in his friendly way to the Lord Chancellor he had sought the opportunity.

"As a matter of fact," said Chick, "I was going."

There was a low murmur of "Order! Order!" at this breach of the rules of debate.

"But," Chick went on, rubbing his chin nervously, "I quite agree with the stout gentleman over there." He nodded to the representative of the Government who was in charge of the Bill.

"The noble lord refers to the Under-Secretary of State," said the Lord Chancellor.

"Thank you very much, sir—Lord Chancellor, I mean," said Chick. "I didn't know his name, but I quite agree with most of the things he said. I'm quite sure he must be a gentleman with boys of his own."

"The noble lord will be interested to learn that I am a bachelor," said the smiling Secretary, as he rose.

"You surprise me," said Chick earnestly, "but I can assure you that what you have said is perfectly true."

The House did not laugh, it stared in silence, and Chick, blissfully unconscious of the hundred conventions he broke, of all the rules of debate he outraged, of all the ancient customs which he was treading under foot, went on in his easy conversational tone, his hands in his pockets, his pink face turned to the taciturn Chancellor.

He had never spoken in public, but the vocal paralysis which comes to the amateur orator did not affect him. At first his speech was halting, his sentences inclined to jumble, but presently he forgot that he was in the Supreme Legislature, forgot everything but that these ordinary-looking men were listening and wanted to hear what he had to say. Chick had lived amongst the people and had been a witness of their struggles and heroism. He had fought with weedy, ill-nourished boys who had acquired men's voices and men's vocabulary. And he knew what education meant, and why the public schoolboy spoke another language from the child thrown out on to the world to fend for himself and gain his education at street-corners. He had strong views formed in secret and never before expressed.

"The difference between the illiterate general labourer and the skilled artisan is the two years you snip from his schooling," was one of the phrases he used, and one afterwards employed by the educationists as their watchword.

Gwenda watched and listened dumbfounded. Here was a Chick she had never suspected, eloquent and convincing.

Suddenly he realized his position and faltered. The tremendous setting of the House overwhelmed him, and he stopped.

"That's all," he said huskily and sat down.

Amidst a murmur which was half approval, half dissent, something happened—a bell rang, and the members rose and moved out of the House. Chick found himself detached from Mansar and moving toward the lobby.

"Yes or no, my lord?" asked an official at the barrier.

"No, thank you," said Chick hastily. "I never drink."

He thought that the refreshments were provided, and followed into the lobby indicated by the attendant's hand. A lot of men came into the room, and they were talking. Two or three, who seemed surprised to see him there, came and spoke to him, but mostly they were concerned as to whether the Government would or would not be defeated on the amendment. Most of them thought it would be a close thing. Presently they all, for no reason at all, trooped out of the lobby and back to the House, and Chick found himself following sheepishly.

He caught sight of Mansar, who took him by the arm.

"This is going to be a close thing, old chap," he said, "and your speech was a corker!"

"Which is close? What is it?" asked the mystified Chick.

"Hush!" said Mansar.

Two men walked to the table, there was an exchange of words, and suddenly a roar of cheering.

Mansar sat open mouthed.

"The Government is defeated by one vote," he said. And then, a horrible suspicion seizing upon him: "You didn't vote for the age limit to be reduced, did you?"

"No," said the indignant Chick. "I haven't voted at all."

A light dawned upon Lord Mansar. "Which way did you go? To the 'Aye' lobby or the 'No'?"

"I don't know which," said Chick. "A man asked me 'Yes or No?' and I said 'No.' I thought he was offering me a drink."

"And you went into the 'No' lobby!" said Lord Mansar heatedly. "You spouted in favour of the Government measure, and you voted for the infernal amendment! Confound it, Pelborough, your vote defeated the Government!"

IV

SPOTTING THE LADY

Lord Pelborough (C.U.) said that he could not agree with the noble lord (Lord Kinsoll) when he said that children were better occupied in a factory than in school. He spoke as a father. It was nonsense. (Order, order.)

"The Lord Chancellor: The noble lord is not in order. The term he employed is not a parliamentary expression.

"Lord Pelborough apologized to Their Lordships' House. He would not like to see his son in a factory.

"If Their Lordships' House agreed to this amendment, they would have reason to be ashamed. (Order, order.)"

Chick glared, fascinated, at the paragraph. It occurred in the Parliamentary Report of The Times newspaper.

"Did I say all that?" he asked hollowly.

Gwenda nodded.

"All that and more," she quoted. "Chick, you were delicious! I was so excited up there in the gallery, that I thought I should faint!"

"I felt like fainting too," admitted Chick ruefully. "Fancy their reporting me! Why—why it almost makes me real! Gosh!"

In another part of the newspaper he might have read in the summary of proceedings a more extensive reference to himself. The writer retold the romantic story of the young insurance clerk who had inherited a great title, and who had neither estate nor private income, who, in fact, remained a working man.

There were other diligent students of politics that morning.

Chick, getting to the office on time, was greeted by the socialistic head clerk with something like enthusiasm.

"Splendid, my lord, splendid!" he whispered, and made grimaces in the direction of Mr. Leither's room, thereby indicating that another body blow had been delivered at the employing classes.

"Er—yes," said Chick. "Good morning."

Mr. Leither, so far from resenting this attack upon his kind, and apparently abandoning all his plans for engaging the "ragged little boy" of whom Chick had heard so much, to do his work, and to do it better, was both tolerant and approving.

"A very excellent speech, Pelborough," he beamed. "I didn't realize my prospective partner was an orator. You tickled 'em, my boy, you tickled em!

"I didn't see any of them laughing, sir," said Chick.

That morning, at his earnest request, he was given some work to do. It suited Mr. Leither well enough that he whom he termed his prospective partner, should go back to his outer office. He had found on his arrival that a long-distance call had been put through and urgent instructions left that he should call on Babbacome Jarviss, M.B.E., a man for whom Mr. Leither had every respect. For Mr. Leither had made much money from him.

The "M.B.E." which followed the name of Mr. Babbacome Jarviss had a certain significance. Mr. Jarviss had made hundreds of thousands, nay, millions, of fuses, shell-cases, bombs and divers other articles employed in war. He had sold the British Government blankets and sheets, boots, butter and bacon. He had rushed to the aid of the American Government with beds, belts, packing-cases and barrels. He had succoured France with leggings and horseshoes, and comforted Italy with coal tar, potatoes and mosquito netting.

Mr. Jarviss often admitted that he had practically won the war. And his reward had been the very last class of the most-generally-bestowed order.

It is true that Mr. Babbacome Jarviss had acquired in the course of the war a large and noble edifice in the Georgian style, standing in its own park-like grounds. That he who began the war as a contractor in a small way, celebrated the armistice driving round his estate in a splendid motor-car. It is beyond dispute that he made large, some say excessive profits, and had a cash balance of something over a million after he had bought his Georgian home, standing amidst delightful scenery.

As a matter of fact, he found some difficulty in getting his name put forward for an M.B.E., for he was without friends.

Mr. Jarviss had a wife who drove about the country-side in motor-saloon lined with pink crepe-de-Chine, which was Mrs. Jarviss' idea of extreme gentility. The third member of his household was Minnie Jarviss, his daughter and heiress. Minnie was a highly-coloured young woman with a weakness for purple raiment. She was not pretty. When she smiled she looked like a Beauty of Labrador; when she did not smile she looked like nothing on earth. She had high cheek-bones and a broad face, her hair was lank and mouse-coloured, but since it is ordained that no woman should regard herself as being entirely without attraction, Minnie prided herself upon a mysterious quality called "charm." It had nothing to do with the golden lucky pig with ruby eyes, or the four-leafed clover in emeralds or even the diamond "13" that dangled from her bracelet. She wasn't quite sure what it was. She had heard people say of girls who were without good looks: "Oh yes...but she has charm!" and had arrived at the conclusion that "charm" was Nature's invariable compensation for plainness.

Her father had dreams for her and bought Hatterway Hall from the last of the Hatterway family with the idea of giving her opportunities which Wimbledon had denied. He gave a great ball in her honour and invited the local gentry. By the oddest coincidence, the local gentry were engaged, or ill, or travelling abroad, and, "whilst thanking Mr. Babbacome Jarviss for his kind invitation," regretted their inability to accept the same.

Mr. Jarviss was regretting his expensive purchase when chance and a powerful motor vehicle carried him to the village of Pelborough, some fifty miles distant. The name had a familiar ring and he knew why when the landlord of the "Pelborough Arms" old him the story of Dr. Beane's amazing accession to the peerage.

"Marquis of Pelborough," said Mr. Jarviss thoughtfully, "and hasn't a cent! H'm!"

He drove home by the shortest route, went to the room which the furnishers had stocked with brand-new books and had christened the library, and sought information from back numbers of newspapers.

"In the employ of Mr. Leither, the well-known insurance agent," he read, and whistled.

There had been times during the war when it had not been expedient to tender for contracts in his own name. Mr. Leither, in consideration of one-half per cent commission, had been his agent in these transactions, and in consequence was under some obligation to him. He put a telephone call through to London, but by this time Mr. Leither had already left his office. The call next morning was a trifle too early, but he had not long to wait before his sometime agent came through.

"Yes, he's here," said Mr. Leither, lowering his voice; "in fact, he's in the next room, Mr. Jarviss."

"What's he like?" asked Jarviss.

"Oh, he's—well, he's like anybody else," was the unsatisfactory reply.

"Young?"

"Oh yes."

"Married?"

"No, good heavens, no!"

Mr. Jarviss considered deeply.

"Could you get him up here for a couple of days, Leither?"

"Yes, I could," replied the other after cogitation. "I could send him up on insurance business..."

"Well, send him today," instructed the plutocrat, "and listen, Leither, you might tell him the tale about me, my money and what I'm worth, see!"

"Certainly," said Leither, not quite sure yet what was behind all this.

"There's a couple of hundred thousand pounds for my son-in-law."

"Oh!" said Leither, understanding, "I get you."

"And five per cent commission for anybody who introduces the business, eh?" said the magnate jocularly.

"I get you, Mr. Jarviss...yes...yes...I understand. I'll pack him off, if not today, to-morrow."

Mr. Jarviss hung up his receiver. He had paved the way, a million and charm must do the rest. Especially heavy was the obligation laid upon charm. He reread the morning newspaper.

"Bit of a speech-maker, too," he said with satisfaction.

Chick had other matters than legislation to occupy his mind. Samuel, that amazing infant, had shown an embarrassing affection for him that morning. He had nursed the baby for a quarter of an hour before he went to work, and Samuel strenuously resisted the attempts, first of Gwenda, and then of the enticing Mrs. Phibbs, to take him away from his custody. Possibly Sam had developed a sense of social value. Mrs. Phibbs suggested, as much.

"He warns a Marquis to nurse him, does he?" she demanded of the squalling child, but Sam was not in the mood for humour. His wail pursued Chick down the stairs, and on returning to lunch, he was alarmed to discover that the baby had hardly stopped whimpering since.

At the sight of Chick, the child's head parted in a smile.

The Marquis of Pelborough sat at the window with his charge, and all that time Samuel behaved like a Christian. But on the first attempt of Mrs. Phibbs to relieve the lordly nursemaid, Sam emitted a yell which attracted the attention of everything living and hearing in Doughty Street. All these exhibitions of friendship and peevishness might be excused on the score of inaccurate dietary, but in the evening Sam was more fretful and even Chick could not wholly pacify him.

Gwenda and Mrs. Phibbs held a consultation, after the discovery of small red spots on Sam's fat chest, and a doctor, hastily summoned, but somewhat tardily obeying that summons, took one glance at the little spots which had multiplied into a hundred, said "Measles" simply and cold-bloodedly, adding that it might be German measles, but there was no reason for worrying.

Gwenda received the tragic news on her return from the theatre.

"It's terrible, isn't it?" said Chick in an awe-stricken voice.

"I don't know that it's very terrible," smiled Gwenda cheerfully. "All children have measles."

"Ought we to get a nurse?" asked Chick.

"Rubbish!" It was the practical Mrs. Phibbs, entering at that moment, who supplied the answer. "What do you want a nurse for?"

Nevertheless, Chick did not sleep soundly that night. He experienced all the responsibilities and fears of parenthood, and saw the hair-raising possibilities of his guardianship, as he had never done before.

On the second day of Samuel's attack, when the most encouraging reports came from the doctor, without any visible or substantial reason, Chick arranged to lunch with Gwenda in the Strand. She had to attend a rehearsal of a touring company which was taking Tangled Lives on the road.

"I'm going into Gloucestershire," said Chick without any preliminary, "and I shall be away for two or three days, Gwenda."

She nodded.

"That's very good news, Chick. I think you ought to take a little holiday. What is the occasion?"

"One of our clients," said Chick, with comical importance, "wishes to be supplied with particulars of a new insurance policy which has lately been issued by the 'London, New York and Paris' Company, and Mr. Leither wants me to go up and tell this gentleman all about it."

"But will it take you two or three days. Chick?" said the girl, looking at him quickly, but thinking rather of Mr. Leither. "Who is the man?"

"He's a gentleman who made a lot of money in the war, a very generous man," recited Chick.

"Who told you all this?"

"Mr. Leither," nodded Chick. "Why, I'm told that this Mr. Jarviss is going to settle two hundred thousand pounds upon his son-in-law!"

"Oh yes," said Gwenda softly, "and who is his son-in-law?"

"I don't know," said the innocent Chick, shaking his head. "I expect he's some lucky fellow—that is," he added, "if the girl is nice."

Gwenda looked at him curiously.

"Suppose the girl wasn't nice. Chick?"

"She must be nice, or he wouldn't want to marry her," said Chick gravely.

Gwenda looked down on the tablecloth, and twiddled with the wedding-ring on her finger.

"I wonder what qualities you regard as being nice in a girl?" she asked—a fatal question, as she ought to have known,

"Well—" hesitated Chick, "if she's like you, Gwenda; if she's pretty and has a lovely mind..."

"Yes, yes," said Gwenda hastily. "I know what you mean. Not like me. Chick, but like you think I am. Well, when are you going?"

"I was going this afternoon," said Chick.

She nodded.

"Perhaps, Chick," she said after a long silence, "this son-in-law of Mr. Jarviss is marrying her because Mr. Jarviss is giving him two hundred thousand pounds."

Chick stared.

"You don't really mean that? Do you know them?"

"I don't know them," said the girl, "but I know people."

Chick shook his head.

"I shouldn't think so, Gwenda I suppose there must have been cases like that; but, after all, any man would be willing to marry any nice girl, whether she was rich or poor. The big thing is to get the right girl, isn't it?"

Gwenda bit her lips. "I suppose so," she said.

Chick had an interview with his employer before he left.

"Now, my dear Pelborough," said Mr. Leither, with the inevitable slap on the back—Chick was prepared for it now, and braced himself to meet the assault—"you're going to have a very good time in my dear friend Jarviss's house. What a man he is, Pelborough!" he went on ecstatically. "What a host! What a generous friend! Two hundred thousand pounds for his son-in-law!"

"I hope he deserves it, sir," said the Marquis of Pelborough.

"I'm sure he does," said Leither. "What a lot one could do with two hundred thousand—a million dollars, ten million francs at the present rate—£10,000 a year invested at five per cent. All for the son-in-law!"

"What is his name?" asked Chick interested.

Mr. Leither coughed.

"Well, I don't know that there is a son-in-law, yet—in fact, I don't know whether Miss Jarviss is engaged. What a wonderful girl she is!"

Now Mr. Leither had never seen Minnie or he would have turned the conversation then and there.

"What eyes!" he apostrophized. "What a dainty little figure of a girl..."

"She must be very pretty," said Chick, when his superior had exhausted his superlatives. "Shall we insure her too?"

Chick arrived at his destination to find that Mr. Jarviss himself had done him the honour of meeting him. The honour went no further.

Mr. Jarviss was the kind of man who felt that he was losing three points if he admitted that any other individual in the world was his superior. Therefore his manner to Chick was brusque, and he ventured upon no courtesy of title. His conscious role was that of "rough diamond," a role which goes with "pot luck," and "taking people as you find them!"

"We haven't made any preparations for you, old man," he said; "you'll have to pig in somehow."

"Certainly," said Chick, having visions of sleeping over a stable. "I thought Mr. Leither had wired you I was coming."

"Oh yes, he said you were coming. What do you think of the car, eh?"

They stood at the top of the slope running down to the station road, by the side of which three or four cars were parked.

"I like it very much," said Chick. "There are a lot of people who don't like Fords, but I'm told they are—"

"Not that one," said Mr. Jarviss annoyed, "the other one, that big one! The chassis alone cost me three thousand!"

Chick made appropriate but genuine sounds of wonder and amazement.

"I want you to meet my daughter," said Mr. Jarviss as they drove up the hill which Hatterway Hall crowned. "She is a very nice girl."

"So I'm told," said Chick politely. "And engaged to be married, too, I congratulate you, Mr. Jarviss."

Mr. Jarviss turned to look at him.

"It may seem an indelicate moment to approach that subject, when a young lady is standing on the threshold of her life," Chick went on, blissfully unconscious of anything save that he was doing his duty, "but don't you think it would be a wise provision for her to take out an insurance policy? There is one in particular which I can recommend." He fumbled in his pockets. "It insures against illness, accidents and death. It has also the advantage," he prattled on, "of insuring the life of the first child for the period of nine years."

"Oh, it does, does it?" breathed Mr. Jarviss, recovering himself. "What makes you think that Minnie is engaged?"

"I understood so," stammered Chick, realizing that he had made an error. "I'm awfully sorry if I've let out Mr. Leither's secret."

"If it was anybody's secret it would be mine." growled Mr. Jarviss.

"I am sure it would," murmured Chick.

"She's a very nice girl, is that girl of mine." repeated the proud father, shaking his head, as though he were a little overcome by the thought of her virtues.

"Yes, I am told so." Chick was in a hurry to remove the memory of his solecism. "Very pretty, if I may be allowed to say so. It must be rather jolly, Mr. Jarviss, to be the father of a very pretty girl."

"Well—you wouldn't call her pretty at first sight," said Mr. Jarviss hurriedly. He also was anxious to remove any wrong impression. "She's got what I should call 'charm'."

"Ah!" said Chick wisely.

"And charm is better than looks."

"I'm sure it is," said Chick, nodding. "And most good-looking people are charming, aren't they?"

He smiled benevolently upon his impatient host. "I suppose when I've a family I shall be modest about my children; it's the Chinese custom, isn't it? I read something in the paper about it the other day."

"What this country wants "—Mr. Jarviss was not interested in China—"are unions, if I may employ the term, between the strong healthy daughters of the people and the proud and effete aristocracy."

"I'm sure you're right," said Chick earnestly. "I'm rather a democrat, Mr. Jarviss, and in my heart of hearts I've never recognized aristocracy, except the aristocracy of genius. I've often thought, as I've gone into the country, what a pity it is that all these beautiful girls are condemned to live their lives in little villages, away from the opportunities—"

"I'm not talking about beautiful girls who live in villages," almost snarled Mr. Jarviss. "I'm talking about my daughter."

Chick smiled politely.

"You will have your joke, Mr. Jarviss," he said, "which reminds me that I have brought all the schedules you wished to see, and Mr. Leither thinks that Schedule 'A' of the policy which the new London and Paris Company are issuing will just suit your case."

"I don't want to talk about insurance. I'm interested in discussing marriages between the aristocracy and what I might call the wealthy, the very wealthy," he said emphatically, "middle classes. I'm going to give two hundred thousand pounds to the young gentleman who marries my daughter. How's that for a nest-egg?"

"I think you're very generous," said Chick warmly. "It is one of the most generous gifts—marriage portions is the word, isn't it?—I've ever read about. But, of course, you know your son-in-law, and I'm sure you would not take the risk of putting all that money in the hands of a spendthrift, Mr. Jarviss. I'd rather like to meet him."

"I hope you will," said Mr. Jarviss grimly, as the car drew up before the door of Hatterway Hall.

He piloted his guest into a big oak-panelled hall, and a girl who was sitting in a picturesque attitude reading a book, rose with a start and tripped to meet him.

Chick regarded her with interest. Probably a friend of the family, he thought, and mentally noted that emerald green does not suit a too-blooming countenance.

She smiled, first at Chick and then at her father.

"A foreigner," thought Chick, blinking.

"This is my daughter. Lord Pelborough," said Mr. Jarviss, and Chick's hand, which was half-way out, stopped dead, his jaw dropped, and he peeked forward in his short-sighted way.

"Your—your daughter," he stammered.

"This is Minnie. Minnie, I hope you'll make Lord Pelborough's visit a comfortable one."

"Why, of course I will, papa," she said with that arch smile of hers.

Chick blinked again.

Whilst three footmen piloted, escorted or carried Chick's bag up to his room, she slipped her arm in his with girlish confidence and led him through a great big pillared room, which reminded him of the approach to the Lords' Lobby, into a drawing-room which had been furnished as a compromise between the conflicting tastes of Minnie and her mother. There must have been six hundred articles in the room, ranging from an oxidized-silver fire set to a purple cushion on a pink settee, and they all said "Hullo" at once, and Chick was almost deafened.

Dinner was a meal which he will remember all his life. Mr. Jarviss belonged to that order of hosts who believe that the beginning and end of hospitality consists of filling your guest with food.

"Now, come on. Lord Pelborough, you must have another bit of this pheasant, I insist." Or: "Mother, Lord Pelborough is eating nothing!"

"John, give Lord Pelborough some more lamb."

Chick made valiant efforts to present a clean plate, but every time he succeeded a new meal was placed in front of him. He rose somewhat unsteadily from the table, feeling like that grotesque figure which is employed to advertise somebody's pneumatic tyres.

"Now, my boy, go and smoke your cigarette on the terrace."

"Thank you, I'm not smoking," said Chick.

"Well, take your coffee out on to the terrace."

"Isn't it rather cold?" asked Chick in surprise, but apparently in preparation for his arrival (though this was not the case) that portion of the terrace to which he was invited had been enclosed by glass and was centrally heated.

"Are you coming, sir?" asked Chick.

"I'll be along presently," said the diplomatic Jarviss. "You run away, my boy."

Chick was incapable of running anywhere. He waddled into the superconservatory and sank with a sigh of relief into a large divan chair. The "terrace" was untenanted, but from nowhere in particular came Minnie Jarviss, and sat charmingly on the arm of his chair. Chick rose.

"Oh, please don't get up. Lord Pelborough," she smiled. "I'm quite comfortable."

"Let me get you a chair," said Chick.

"You're a very naughty boy," said Minnie charmingly; "now sit down where you were."

Chick, out of sheer politeness, obliged her. When her arm fell carelessly upon his shoulders, he winced. When he felt the whole weight of her leaning towards him he shivered.

"You are a funny boy," she said less charmingly than before. "Why don't you keep still?"

"Perhaps if I got you that chair you would prefer it?" said Chick, looking round desperately in the hope that the lady's mother or father would appear to relieve him from an embarrassing situation. But the lady's mother was playing patience in the large and vociferous drawing-room, and the lady's father was in his library, hoping for the best.

Chick tried his own best to turn the conversation into the ways of insurance. He was worried because he had not had an opportunity to discuss Schedule "A" with her father, and endeavoured to interest the girl in the fascinating possibilities of the policy he had outlined on the way from the station.

"Don't be silly, silly, silly!" she said, tweaking his ear, an operation which made Chick shrink back into the chair. "I'm not going to be married yet awhile, at least I don't think so."

"I thought you were engaged, Miss Jarviss?"

"Not yet," she said playfully. "Mr. Right hasn't come along yet, and if Lord Right has come along, he hasn't asked me."

"Is he a lord?" asked Chick, interested.

But she wouldn't tell him. She asked him to guess. She gave him three guesses, in fact, and to be on the safe side, he started with the Lord Chancellor. Apparently that noble lord was unknown to the Jarvisses, for she asked him if he was the horrid man who put all those dreadful income taxes upon the profited classes.

"That's one guess," she said: "two more."

But Chick gave it up.

"I think you're silly," said Miss Jarviss, "but perhaps you're so rich that you don't want two hundred thousand pounds."

"Me?" said Chick in amazement. "Nobody wants to give me two hundred thousand;" and then the horror of the situation dawned upon him, and he could have swooned. He got up, pale with consternation and amazement.

"I—I wouldn't marry anybody," he almost squeaked, "not if they had millions and millions of pounds! I think it's a dreadful idea, marrying people for money. I wouldn't marry the most beautiful woman in the world—for money."

"I didn't ask you," said Miss Jarviss defiantly, "I didn't ask you, you conceited devil, so there! A man like you ought to be poisoned! Coming here giving yourself airs...without a penny in your pocket...upsetting a girl..." She wept her way to the comfort of her mamma.

The next hour contained sixty agonizing minutes. When he met Mr. Jarviss again that great man was even more brusque, was in fact rude.

Chick crept up to his room that night miserable, and meeting the girl in the corridor, she fixed him with such a basilisk glare that he bolted into his room and locked his door.

The next morning when they brought his tea, it had a funny taste; it was like tea and yet it was not like tea, and he remembered all the stories he had read of women's vengeance. Hell, he knew, had no terrors like a woman scorned. He left his cup half empty.

The interview after breakfast with Mr. Jarviss was conducted mainly by himself. That gentleman sat glumly behind his solid oak table and grumbled his replies in monosyllables.

When the train pulled out of the station, Chick was a very grateful young man. He knew he had failed his employer, but even that did not worry him so much as the increasing fear which the peculiarly tasting tea had aroused. He was feeling strange too; there was a singing in his ears, and his head buzzed with queer noises. His throat was parched, his lips were dry, and he went hot and cold alternately.

"She's poisoned me!" murmured Chick aghast, and added as he recalled his responsibilities, "I wish I'd taken an insurance myself!"

A week later a large angry man stalked into Mr. Leither's office, and, without knocking, flounced into the room where that amiable and untidy man was sitting.

"Why, Mr. Jarviss, this is an unexpected pleasure!" said Leither in surprise.

"Pleasure be blowed!" growled Jarviss. "That infernal pup of yours, Lord What's-his-name, by gad, the young brute...!"

Mr. Leither's eyebrows rose.

"I haven't seen him since his return. Of course you know—"

"Know! I know more about him than I want to know, Leither," said the infuriated man.

Mr. Leither's jaw dropped. The vision of a five per cent. commission faded in the dim distance.

"Didn't he give her his pledge?" he asked romantically.

"His pledge!" roared the other. "No, my daughter is ill! Where is he now?"

Mr. Leither shook his head.

"He's in bed—with German measles," he said.

Mr. Jarviss staggered back.

"So that's how she caught it!" he wailed.

V

CHICK, WAITER

Gwenda Maynard turned into the Park. The crocuses and the daffodils were out, and the first tender green of spring was showing against the dingy brown of the lilac bushes, but none of these pleasant sights brought her to the loneliness of Hyde Park on a chilly afternoon in March.

Her problem was an unusual one. She had the care and responsibility of two children. From the first of these, Master Samuel Bradshaw, aged eleven months, she was soon to be relieved, for his mother had sent her a frantic cable on her arrival in New York, begging her to devise some method by which the child could be sent to her. Gwenda proved her capability by discovering a nurse who was returning to the United States on the Aquitania, and Samuel's box, so to speak, was already packed.

The second of the children had no frantic mother to demand him—for which Gwenda was secretly glad—and into what was a guardianship she had drifted, although Chick was her senior by eighteen months.

He was a responsibility, because by the oddest trick of fortune this youthful insurance clerk had inherited a great title—and nothing else.

Gwenda was looking to the future, and the future she studied was Chick's. She had few illusions; five years spent on every variety of stage, from the "fit-up" company to the more decorous society of a West End theatre, had left her faith in men and women an attenuated thing. Five years of struggle, of fierce, unrelenting battle against forces as grimly determined and merciless, had brought to her the cold, early morning sanity of view which comes to those who have wakened from dreams.

Her friends said that the circle of gold on her finger stood for a tragedy, but the closest of them had received no hint from her as to what that tragedy was. She never spoke of her husband, but some people believed that he was not very far away. She conveyed the impression that he was somewhere in the background, and there were managers who believed that they knew him.

Chick never asked—but he wouldn't. He accepted her with her mystery, her secrets, and all that went before, and was content to worship and adore her in his own clean way. Chick's love was like rock crystal, shaped and unchangeable. Crystal clear and transparent, it was part of his life, and he never disguised it.

With this Gwenda was content and grateful. She gave the boy all that he needed, but was desperately conscious that she must give him more than he recognized as necessary.

She looked at the watch on her wrist. It was three o'clock, and her appointment was for half-past. But since she did not know the house, and might experience some difficulty in finding it, she changed her direction and walked towards Knightsbridge. She walked slowly, and was so engrossed in her thoughts that the half-hour passed like five minutes. It was a little after the time when she pressed the bell of a flat in Knightsbridge.

A man-servant opened the door and showed her into a big and smoky room, evidently a man's study, and an out-of-door man's at that, for the walls were covered with trophies of hunt and stalk.

She had hardly time to look around when a young man came in. He smiled broadly as he took her hand.

"Will you talk here, or would you rather go into the drawing-room? My sister is dressing."

"Here will do very well, Lord Mansar," she smiled. "You didn't mind my 'phoning you yesterday—I haven't upset your arrangements for today?"

"Not a bit," said the Earl boisterously, which was not true. He had forgone a hunting fixture and a hunt ball, but this she could not know. "You want to speak about our young friend the Marquis—Lord Pelborough?"

She nodded.

"You understand his position," she said. "I almost said social position," she smiled. "Chick is employed by an insurance agent, and he receives a salary of five pounds a week."

He nodded.

"And yet there isn't a man in this town," she went on quietly, "who is a kindlier gentleman than this boy."

"I liked him," said Lord Mansar, nodding.

"I don't know much about nobility," the girl went on, "but I feel that Chick has a responsibility to you and to your kind. I'm not afraid of Chick falling into bad hands, because his natural honesty will keep him clear of anything questionable, but attempts will be made to exploit him, and, indeed, Mr. Leither, his present employer, is doing something of that sort already. Now, Lord Mansar," she said earnestly, "can you suggest any method by which Chick could take a place which would be creditable to him and to the order he represents?"

Mansar rubbed his chin, and frowned. He was not used to problems of any character, and this was so remarkable a problem that for a moment he was confounded.

"It's a question of money," he said at last, "and really I can't think of any way by which Pelborough can make good. He cannot go into any of the Services, because he hasn't been prepared. Anyway, the Services are not paying propositions."

He looked at the girl thoughtfully.

"He might marry well," he said, and wondered whether he was committing a faux pas, but Gwenda only nodded.

"I have thought of that," she said.

Lord Mansar was silent.

"Have you any suggestion you could offer?" he said at last. "Because, frankly, I have none."

"The only idea I had in my mind," said the girl, hesitating, "was that you might possibly help him by— well, by bringing him out."

"Bringing him out?" said the puzzled Mansar.

"You might help him to meet the right people," said the girl desperately.

"Oh, I see!" A light dawned upon the Earl of Mansar, and a broad smile illuminated his cherubic face. "I'll arrange that with all the pleasure in life, Mrs. Maynard. I'll tell you what I'll do. I'll get him an invitation to a dance. You know Mrs. Krenley?"

"I'm afraid I don't," laughed Gwenda.

"I thought everybody knew her," said Mansar, in surprise. "She knows all the best people in London. I'll get her to send an invitation to Pelborough. I don't know what good those people can do him," he added a little ruefully; "they haven't been very serviceable to me. But you may be sure, Mrs. Maynard, I will do whatever I can. His lordship is no relation to you, I presume?"

Gwenda shook her head.

"I dare say you find it difficult to understand how I come into the business at all," she said quietly. "I am, as I explained to you before, engaged at the Broadway Theatre. Chick and I became acquainted by reason of our staying in the same boarding-house; there is no other relationship, actual or prospective," she said emphatically, and Lord Mansar nodded.

To those people who troubled to think about the matter at all, the Honourable Mrs. Krenley was something of an enigma. George Krenley was the son of one poor peer and the brother of another who, if anything, was slightly more impecunious. He had married, before the War, a member of the ultra-smart set, who brought to her husband no other dowry than was represented by an expensive wardrobe, the reputation of being the best bridge player in London and a most expensive circle of acquaintances. Yet after a few years of their married life the Krenleys were acknowledged as the leaders of the smartest society in the Metropolis. They leased a magnificent house in Bickley Square, they entertained largely and generously, and maintained a mansion in Somerset, and did all this apparently on the six hundred a year which Krenley drew from his mother's estate.

Two mornings after Gwenda had interviewed Lord Mansar, Mrs. Krenley sat in her boudoir, smoking a cigarette and looking thoughtfully at a letter which lay on her lap. She was a good-looking woman of thirty, and somewhat of a contrast to her stout, plain husband, who was sitting on a low divan amusing her brother with a pack of cards.

"Do you know Pelborough?" she asked, looking up from the letter.

Gregory Boyne, who was a florid edition of his sister, shook his head.

"Pelborough?" he said slowly. "I seem to remember the same. Yes. He's the shopwalker Marquis, isn't he? The fellow they were talking about the other day at the club?"

"He has no money," grunted Krenley, shuffling the cards. "Why do you ask, Lu?"

"Mansar wants me to invite him to our dance on Friday."

Boyne's lips curled. "We don't want that kind of chap here," he said. "Why, the fellow's a hooligan! You'd be the laughing-stock of London, Lu."

She was looking thoughtfully at him, tapping the letter on the palm of her hand.

"Our people might be interested to see him," she said. "It would give them something to talk about Besides—"

"Besides what?" asked Krenley huskily. His voice at this early hour of the morning was invariably husky.

"If I wrote and told Mansar I could not invite the boy, I hardly know what excuse I could make," she said. "It isn't like a dinner, where every place is fixed. One more or less at a dance doesn't really matter."

"Write to him telling him point-blank that we don't want the bounder," said her brother carelessly, and he heard her laugh.

"Would Mansar come?" she asked significantly, and Boyne twisted in his chair to face her.

"I hadn't thought of that," he said. "I don't think we'd better choke off Mansar."

"And he doesn't want much choking off," interrupted Krenley. "You've got to play that fish with a master hand, Lu."

Mrs. Krenley nodded.

"That is what I think. How much did he lose last time, Bob?"

"Seven thousand," said her husband promptly. "It's a flea-bite to him. If I had known that he was getting scared, he'd have lost more. No, I should write him a nice polite little note, if I were you, Lu, telling him to bring along his Marquis. I should choose that night for a real big coup. Mansar's worth a million if he's worth a penny, and he's the kind of fellow who'd honour any cheque he signed—even if he was drunk when he signed it," he added significantly.

Chick had heard the news without enthusiasm.

"It will be wonderful for you. Chick," said Gwenda, her eyes shining. "You'll meet all your own kind of people."

They were at breakfast when she had received the letter from Lord Mansar enclosing Mrs. Krenley's invitation to Chick.

"I don't like parties very much," said Chick disconsolately, "but if you think I ought to go, Gwenda—why, there's nothing more to be said. What time does it begin?"

"At ten o'clock," said Gwenda, reading the invitation.

Chick frowned.

"At ten o'clock at night?" he said incredulously. "That will be keeping them up late, won't it?" He thought awhile. "I'd better go half an hour before," he said. "It would look more polite."

"You'll go about half an hour late," said the girl decisively. "Can you dance, Chick?" To her amazement he replied in the affirmative.

"The instructor at the Polytechnic is very keen on our dancing," he said apologetically. "It helps in the footwork."

"The footwork?" she repeated.

"Yes," and Chick explained. He had been to dancing lessons at the Polytechnic—apparently everything was to be learnt at the Polytechnic—and dancing is a useful accomplishment in a boxer.

"And did you really dance with real girls?" asked Gwenda, her eyes bright with laughter.

"Yes," admitted Chick. "I never looked at 'em, but I spoke to one or two."

Gwenda laughed.

"You're the queerest boy in the world, Chick," she said. And then, more briskly: "What are we going to do about your dress-clothes?"

"Dress-clothes," said Chick, panic-stricken. "Have I to dress up?"

She nodded. "Haven't you a dress-suit?" she asked in dismay.

Chick had nothing so grand.

After business hours that day she met him, and they made a tour of those emporia which make a feature of ready-to-wear clothing. It was surprisingly easy to fit Chick. It almost seemed as if the reach-me-down tailors of the world had decided that the standard shape, length, and breadth of dress-clothing should be based upon Chick's physique.

Although the dance did not begin till ten, Chick was dressed at half-past five. Dressing for a dance, he discovered, involved a larger outlay than he had imagined. There were shirts and studs, silk socks—or socks that had the appearance of silk—patent shoes, and a crush hat (the latter begged by the practical Gwenda from the wardrobe mistress at the theatre), and a very extra special white silk scarf.

For three hours Chick sat on the edge of the chair in the little flat, awaiting the hour of his trial with the pained expression of one who was anticipating the hour of his execution, and when at last he reached the big door of the house in Bickley Square and saw the footmen, the stream of beautiful ladies and most elegant men passing through the portals, he had an urgent desire to run home.

He strolled along the pavement, wondering exactly what he ought to do. He thought there should have been a ticket or some tangible proof of his bond fides. If he could have walked up the steps and presented a square of pasteboard to the foot-man, he would have felt more comfortable. Half of his troubles ended when Lord Mansar descended from an electric brougham and, catching him by the arm, whisked him into the house. Before he knew what had happened, Chick found himself bowing stiffly to a beautiful lady and holding her jewelled hand.

"Glad to meet you, Lord Pelborough," she said sweetly. "I've heard so much about you."

Chick, who had prepared a little speech expressing his thanks for the invitation, was almost immediately dismissed as Mrs. Krenley welcomed another guest.

"Now, Pelborough, what are you going to do?"

Mansar took his arm and led him into the big ballroom, which was filled by two-stepping couples, Mansar's cheeks were a little flushed, for he had dined remarkably well.

"I'll just sit down," stammered Chick, "and look at the dancing. What time can I go?"

Mansar laughed.

"My dear old thing, you're not here yet, and if you run away before you've made a few useful acquaintances, I'll never forgive you. Come along." He seized Chick's arm and hurried him to a queer-looking man who offered him a limp hand.

"This is Lord Pr-sh-n-m." (It might have been "Mir-kr-sh," or some such name; Chick never remembered.) He was a Cabinet Minister, and a very important person. He was so important that he didn't look twice at Chick—indeed, it is doubtful if he looked once. He was a thin-faced man with pale eyes and a heavily-wrinkled forehead.

From him Chick was led to Mr. "Sesewsur" (or it might have been Mr. "Snigulun"). Chick made a most heroic effort this time to catch the name, but did not succeed. Every person he met seemed to be attached to a title which defied the ear, titles which were jumbles of consonants and vowels and nasal sounds.

"And now, old thing," said Lord Mansar, patting him on the back, "I'll leave you. I'm going up-stairs to play. Do you play?"

Chick smiled and shook his head.

"I used to be able to play 'God save the King' with one finger," he began, and Mansar departed in a tempest of laughter.

Chick found a chair and sat down. He enjoyed the music and the movement, and nobody troubled him. People looked curiously at the forlorn figure, and wondered who he was, and what excuse there might be for his presence. But nobody, not even the unrememberable ladies and gentlemen to whom he had been introduced, came near him. After a while he got a little bored, and followed the heated dancers from the room, being curious to know where they went. He discovered a buffet, and a footman with a large tray handed him a glass containing liquor of a golden hue. It looked rather like ginger ale, and tasted like cider, but at the first gulp he spluttered. It was a frothy, gaseous drink that went up into his head and gave him a tingling, suffocating sensation in his nose.

"Is that alcohol?" he gasped.

"No, sir, champagne," said the footman.

Chick nodded. He did not like to hand back the glass, but he had no intention of drinking the fiery potion. After awhile he managed to slip the glass on to a side-board, and strolled away guiltily.

All sorts of people were going upstairs. At first Chick did not like to follow them, because he thought they might be personal friends of the hostess who had the run of the house, but after awhile he summoned up courage to explore the upper floor.

In a big saloon above the ballroom some thirty people, men and women, were gathered round a green baize table, in the centre of which was a small roulette wheel. He watched, fascinated, whilst real money, though not in very large quantities, was thrown on one of the numbered squares or little oblong spaces inscribed with foreign words.

"Gambling!" said Chick in amazement, and looked uneasily at the door, through which at any moment, he felt, a detachment of police might enter. He was to learn later that a mild flutter at roulette was one of the attractions of Mrs. Krenley's parties.

After awhile even this thrill passed, and Chick strolled out on to the landing, where it was cooler than in the heated room. He stood with his back to the wall, his hands clasped in front of him, wondering how he could get the crush hat and the overcoat which he had so confidingly handed to a footman on his arrival.

He felt very lonely, very "out of it." He was a stranger in a strange land, and did not speak the language of these gay people, who addressed one another by their Christian names. He had almost made up his mind to make a furtive inspection of the footmen in order to discover the custodian of the hat and coat, when a door at the farther end of the landing opened, and a tall, florid man came out. He looked round and beckoned Chick, and Chick, most anxious for diversion, obeyed the summons with alacrity.

"Go down to the butler," said Mr. Gregory Boyne, "and bring up half a dozen quarts of Pommery—tell him it is for Mr. Boyne. Hurry!"

"Certainly," said Chick, and went down the stairs more cheerfully than he had come up, for at least he had found a momentary occupation. He was being useful, and he felt more in the swing. They were treating him as an equal, he thought, making him one of them.

He found the butler in the buffet-room, a stout, imposing man.

"Six bottles of Pommery, sir? Certainly. For Mr. Boyne, I think you said."

Chick nodded.

"I will send a waiter up with them."

"Don't bother," said Chick; "I'll take them."

The butler looked at him knowingly.

"All right, sir," he said, with a smile. And Chick went up the stairs, now happily deserted, with three large bottles under each arm.

He knocked at the door, and after awhile he heard a key turned, and it was opened by Boyne.

"Come in," he said. "You had better stay here and open these bottles."

The room was a comparatively small one. Under a silver electrolier was a round green table, and seated about it were five men. Mr. Boyne, when he returned, was the sixth.

"Now open a bottle quick," said Boyne in a low voice, "and see that that gentleman's glass is kept filled."

Chick peered at "that gentleman," who sat half turned to him, and to his amazement he discovered it was Mansar.

"And look here, waiter," said Boyne in the same tone.

"Eh?" said the startled Chick.

"Don't interrupt, confound you!" snapped Boyne. "You must serve Mr. Krenley and myself from that bottle." He pointed to a large magnum on the sideboard. "It is ginger ale. You understand?"

"Excuse me," began Chick, anxious that he should not be admitted under any false pretences, and realizing that he had been mistaken for one of the hired waiters. "I should like to say—"

"I know what you'd like to say, but you'll get a tenner extra; all you have to do is to keep your mouth shut and that glass full."

"Yes, sir," said Chick feebly. Suddenly he had realized the enormous discredit of being mistaken for a waiter, and he prayed that he could elude the gaze of Lord Mansar. His lordship, however, was fully occupied and wholly absorbed in the game.

The bright pink which Chick had seen in his cheeks was now a brick red, his voice was thick, and his actions a little unsteady. Chick refilled the glass at his elbow and stood behind him, watching.

They were playing a game with which he was not familiar, but which he afterwards learnt was chemin de fer. A half an hour's observation produced several convictions in Chick's mind. The first and the most obvious of these was that Lord Mansar was losing very heavily, the second, that he lost most heavily when he held the bank; the third, and not the least startling of his discoveries was that whenever Lord Mansar took the bank, the cards were shuffled and handed to him by either Mr, Krenley or Mr, Boyne.

The game was played with one pack of cards, and Chick noticed that as Lord Mansar, at the end of a very unsuccessful bank, picked up a nine of clubs, which had been his undoing, he left the wet impress of his thumb on the white surface of the card, for he had been handling, a little unsteadily, a glass of champagne immediately before. When it came round to his turn to be banker again, by an odd coincidence the card he turned was a nine of clubs, which had not the wet imprint of his thumb. Chick drew a long breath.

"My luck is diabolical," said his lordship, with an unsteady laugh, as he affixed his signature to an IOU for eighteen hundred pounds. "How much have I lost, Boyne?"

"Oh, not a great deal," said Boyne soothingly, as he added the IOU to a number of others. "We'll have a settling-up when this is finished, and you can give me a cheque."

"How much have I lost?" insisted the young man, with drunken gravity.

"Play on," smiled Krenley. "I've lost as much as you, Mansar. You've got as many of my IOU's as you have of Mansar's, haven't you, Gregory?"

Mr, Boyne nodded, and the game went on.

Chick was watching so intently that once Boyne had to kick his foot to remind him that Mansar's glass was empty.

"I'm finished," said Mansar, after a further disaster. He rose shakily from the table, put his hand to his hip pocket, and took out a cheque-book. "How much is it?"

"Twenty-seven thousand pounds," said Boyne, who had been totalling up the IOU's on a piece of paper.

"What?" Lord Mansar stared at him.

"Twenty-seven thousand pounds," repeated Boyne calmly. "You've had a lot of bad luck, old man."

The shock half-sobered Mansar. For a moment he looked at the other, then he sat down again at the table.

"I see," he said quietly. "Will somebody give me a pen and ink?"

They handed him a fountain pen, and rapidly he wrote the cheque.

"Thank you," said Boyne. But before his hand closed on the slip of paper it was snatched away. He turned round, open mouthed, to see the "waiter" calmly tearing the cheque into shreds. Mansar saw it, and recognized the young man.

"Why—why, Pelborough," he stammered, "what the devil are you doing?"

"I'm tearing up a cheque," said Chick, with his queer little smile.

"But my dear chap, that's outrageous. You ought not to—"

"I'm tearing up your cheque, Lord Mansar, because you have been cheated."

"Oh, indeed?" It was Boyne who spoke. "That's a pretty serious accusation to make, but I suppose that a guttersnipe—"

"Hold hard," said Mansar. "He wouldn't make that charge without some reason. What do you mean, Pelborough?"

"I don't know anything about this game," said Chick, "but I think you are under the impression that you played with one pack of cards. As a matter of fact, it has been played with fourteen, to my knowledge."

"What do you mean?"

"Every time it was your turn to be banker—that's the word, isn't it?" said Chick, "that fellow "—he pointed to Boyne—"changed the cards. He took a new one from his pocket and passed the old one to that fellow on his right. I'll bet he has still some packs in his pocket."

There was a deadly silence, which Boyne broke.

"You don't believe—" he began.

"Let me see your pockets," said Mansar.

"Do you know what you re asking?" It was Krenley who interrupted. The other two men were silent, and Chick had long since recognized that they were the mere padding of the party, probably confederates of Boyne.

"I know what I'm asking," said Mansar. "Lord Pelborough has made a charge that is a very easy matter for you to meet."

"And do you seriously expect me to turn out my pockets?" sneered the florid man.

"That is exactly what I expect you to do," replied Mansar quietly. "If Lord Pelborough is mistaken, I will give you a cheque for the amount I have lost, and offer you every reparation that a gentleman can offer to one whom he has grossly insulted, for I am inclined to associate myself with Lord Pelborough."

"If you expect that I am going to allow you to search me, you've made a mistake," said Boyne furiously.

"Take off your coat."

It was Chick's cool voice.

Boyne looked at him for a moment, and then, with a roar of rage, sprang at the slim figure. He was a head taller than his intended victim, and almost twice as heavy. But Chick was a scientist—probably the greatest fighter at his weight in England. He took that queer dancing side-step of his, and brought his left and right to the body. Boyne staggered, and before he could recover himself, Chick's smashing left struck him on the point, and he went down with a thud that shook the room. Chick bent over him and put his hand in his pockets, and there before the startled gaze of Mansar he produced, like a conjurer extracting articles from an apparently empty receptacle, pack after pack, neatly and dexterously bound together by rubber bands.

Chick went downstairs with Mansar, and Mrs. Krenley followed them into the night.

"You've behaved disgracefully to my brother, Lord Mansar," she said, lowering her voice that the waiting chauffeur might not hear, "and as for the street arab you have brought with you—"

"Mrs. Krenley,"—Mansar's voice was like ice—"the word of this street arab will be sufficient to drive you out of decent society."

Mrs. Krenley went back to her desk with a pained expression on her face. Upstairs, attended by his brother-in-law and his satellites, Mr. Boyne also had a pained expression, and with better reason.

VI

A LESSON IN DIPLOMACY

The Most Honourable the Marquis of Pelborough sat on the edge of a bed, sewing a button on his shirt. The threading of the needle had occupied fully ten minutes, and there had been certain interruptions which necessitated the concealment of the garment under his pillow, for Chick Pelborough was in some awe of his housekeeper, and was not less panic-stricken at the possibility of Gwenda Maynard detecting him in this act of repair.

It was Sunday morning, and the church bells were ringing; but Chick was an evening churchgoer.

Doughty Street, on Sunday mornings, was usually a place of desolation and silence, except for the occasional feeble wail of a milkman, or the hoarse and mysterious cries of newspaper sellers. Therefore the advent of a motor-car, which stopped at the door, was something of an event. Chick looked out of the open window, saw that the car was too large for a doctor's, and wondered who was the tall and smartly-dressed gentleman who alighted. He returned to his occupation, whistling softly a tune he had heard at a dance. And as he sewed awkwardly and laboriously, his mind was busy with his future.

The future was really beginning to worry Chick for the first time. He was a clerk earning five pounds a week, and had accounted himself comfortably placed, until the death of an expensive uncle had saddled him with an ancient title. He knew that a marquis clerk in the office of an insurance broker was something of a social monstrosity, and every day brought a new sense of discomfort. And Gwenda expected something better of him, too; that added to his distress. He felt that he was disappointing the pretty actress who was striving so wholeheartedly to put him on his feet.

In the course of those Sunday morning reparations Chick did most of his serious thinking, and of late his thoughts had centred round and about Gwenda Maynard. He wondered what her husband was like, and found it almost impossible to think of her with a husband at all. She had been distrait and absent-minded lately, and he wondered why. There was something on her mind, Chick knew. Perhaps it had to do with a letter which had been sent on to her from the theatre—a letter in a blue envelope. It had come at breakfast, and at the sight of the writing Gwenda had gone white. Chick felt it was from her husband, and his heart was hard against the man who could hurt her.

He put down his shirt, biting off the cotton in the approved style, and, still with his attention on the locked door, poured some water in a basin and began to wash his two silk handkerchiefs. He was in the midst of it when a knock came to the door.

"Chick!" said an urgent voice.

"Yes, Gwenda?"

Chick hastily squeezed the water from the handkerchiefs, threw them under the bed, wiped his hands imperfectly, and unlocked the door.

"Why do you always lock your door on Sunday morning?" asked Gwenda, and her eyes, roving to the bed, saw the shirt and, what was more damning, the threaded needle which Chick had stuck in the pillow.

"Chick, you've been sewing on buttons!" she said accusingly. "You know Mrs. Phibbs or I will always do that for you."

"I'm sorry, Gwenda, really," said Chick incoherently, "but the button came off, and I didn't want to trouble—"

"There is somebody to see you," said Gwenda, cutting short his explanation.

"To see me?" said Chick in surprise.

"Lord Mansar," said the girl.

Chick gaped.

"Put on your coat, Chick. And whatever have you been doing with your hands?"

She walked across to the bed, picked up the handkerchiefs, and shook her head.

"Really, Chick, you're incorrigible," she reproached him, "Do you want me to go to Lord Mansar and tell him you can't see him because it is washing day? Now wipe your hands, turn down the collar of your coat, and brush your hair."

The Marquis of Pelborough meekly obeyed.

Lord Mansar rose, as they came into the room, and offered his hand.

"I'm an awful rotter not to have come before," he said apologetically, "but the fact is, I was so heartily ashamed of myself that I couldn't have seen you even if I'd been willing. Besides, I didn't know your address until yesterday."

"Chick enjoyed the dance, Lord Mansar," said Gwenda. "It was awfully nice of Mrs. Krenley to have him there."

"Oh, very nice," said Mansar grimly, a hard little smile on his cherubic face. "Didn't Pelborough tell you?"

"He only told me he had a very pleasant evening," said the girl, in wonder. "What happened?"

Mansar told her the story of that night, and did not minimize the extent of his own folly.

"So you see, Mrs. Maynard," he said, "Chick's introduction to Society was not attended with the happiest circumstances."

"But, Chick," said the girl in amazement, "you did not tell me!"

Chick was very red and more than a little embarrassed.

"I had a letter from Mrs. Krenley yesterday," said Mansar. "She was full of excuses and explanations, and begged me to go there again and bring you, Chick. I should imagine there's something preparing for you, something with boiling oil in it. Now, Mrs. Maynard "—he looked at the girl with a light of amusement in his eyes—"you asked me to do something for Pelborough."

"Did you, Gwenda?" gasped Chick, in amazement, and it was her turn to flush,

"Yes, Chick," she said quietly. "I saw Lord Mansar and asked him if he would find an opening for you. You can't stay in your present job very much longer; it is not the position you should be occupying."

Chick had already reached that conclusion, but he said nothing.

"An idea occurred yesterday to me," Mansar went on. "I was lunching with Sir John Welson, who is one of the Under-Secretaries at the Foreign Office. And I think I can find you a job, Pelborough—Chick you call him, don't you?" he smiled at the girl. "Well, I'm going to call you Chick, too, and, by Jove, you're the most wiry Chick that was ever served up on a Park Lane table!"

The joke amused him immensely, and when he recovered himself he went on: "The only thing that may lose you the job is that you have one very unfortunate deficiency—at least, I'm afraid you have— otherwise I could get you an appointment as an extra Foreign Office Messenger without any difficulty."

Chick's jaw dropped. "I don't think I'd like that." he said. "It would mean wearing a uniform, or something, wouldn't it?"

"Not exactly," said the other drily. "I'm not referring to the gentlemen in buttons who run errands. A Foreign Office Messenger is a sort of King's Messenger."

"That would be splendid, wouldn't it, Chick?" said the girl, her eyes shining.

Chick scratched his head thoughtfully.

"It means about four or five hundred a year, travelling expenses, and a pretty soft time," Mansar went on, "only—and here I come to the big drawback—you'd have to speak French and have a knowledge of some other language."

The girl's hopes faded.

"Of course, you could learn, but it would take you some months—" began Mansar.

"I can speak French," said Chick.

Gwenda stared at him.

"Really, Chick," she said, "you're the most surprising person."

"And I know quite a lot of Spanish," said the amazing Chick almost guiltily.

"Wherever did you acquire these accomplishments?" asked the girl.

"At the Polytechnic," said Chick in a tone that suggested that he had explained everything.

The next afternoon he met Lord Mansar by arrangement in Whitehall. He sent a note to his office explaining that he would not be able to attend that day, and Mr. Leither, who had lured several possible clients to the office on the understanding that they would meet the marquis clerk, was pardonably annoyed.

It was a busy morning for Chick and for the girl. From nine o'clock, when the big stores open, until lunchtime, Chick had tramped and ridden on omnibuses round London submissively with Gwenda. He had tried on ready-made morning suits, he had stared with horror at the reflection of himself in a top hat, he had tried on gloves which bothered him, and had fought with collars which threatened to choke him, and he went back to the flat with a flushed and triumphant Gwenda, a parcel under each of his arms and a hat-box dangling by a string from his finger.

"There's too much clothing about this marquis business, Gwenda, isn't there?" he asked doubtingly.

"Clothing maketh the man," quoth Gwenda.

"It maketh a marquis, anyway," said Chick, without enthusiasm.

Arrayed in a costume which he firmly believed drew down upon his head the derision and contempt of all civilized people who wore soft hats and soft collars, he met Mansar, and was relieved to discover that that young gentleman, too, was similarly, if not so newly, attired.

"You'll like Welson," said Mansar, as they were sitting in a large and solemn waiting-room, their cards having been taken into the sanctum of the Under-Secretary. "He's a queer old devil, but really not half a bad sort. He's by far the most important man in the Foreign Office."

"What does he do?" asked Chick.

Mansar was nonplussed.

"I'm blessed if I know," he said. "What do any of these johnnies do? They just sit round and fund papers and things, and conduct the foreign politics of the country."

"I shouldn't have to do anything of that, should I?" asked Chick, in alarm.

"I don't think so," said Mansar gravely.

A few minutes afterwards they were shown into a very high-ceilinged room with a very large marble mantelpiece, an enormous desk, and a comparatively small old man, who peered up at them over his glasses as they entered.

"Hallo, Mansar!" he said. "Sit down. Is this your friend Lord Pelborough?"

Chick offered a large glove at the end of his arm—it didn't seem like his—and solemnly shook the hand of the Under-Secretary.

Sir John scrutinized him keenly, and then, taking a large form out of a large drawer—everything seemed overgrown at the Foreign Office—proceeded to fill up particulars.

Chick gave his name in a hushed voice and his place of residence.

Presently Sir John's pen poised over the column which was headed "school."

"Eton?" he asked, looking up.

"Yes, thank you, sir," said Chick gratefully. "I lunched quite early."

"Sir John wants to know where you were educated," said Mansar gently, and Chick gave the name of a school which was wholly unfamiliar to the Under-Secretary.

"This is not a very remunerative post: your lordship quite understands that? Nor is the position a permanent one," said Sir John, leaning back in his chair and taking off his glasses, the better to see the candidate. "But it is unnecessary to tell you that your office is a very important one."

He opened another drawer and took out a small book,

"Here are some instructions which you had better digest," he said. "And now, sir, I do not think that we shall be in need of your services for a week. You had better report for duty on Friday."

He rang a bell, and his secretary came in.

"Show Lord Pelborough Major Stevens's old room."

In this simple way did Chick pass into the service of his country and become a cog in the wheel of Foreign Office administration.

It was a sad blow for Mr. Leither when Chick broke the news,

"I am sorry, very sorry, Pelborough," he said, shaking his head. "After all these years of association, it seems almost a tragedy to lose you. The Foreign Office, I think you said?"

Chick nodded.

"Yes, sir."

"H'm!" mused Mr. Leither. "You will be brought into contact with some very important people, Pelborough, some very important lives, Pelborough," he said. "Never forget that there is a half-commission waiting for all the business you introduce."

Very handsomely he paid Chick up to the end of the week, and would have given him a bonus on account of future business, but this Chick would not hear of.

The Lord of Pelborough left the insurance office with a little sigh of relief, boarded a passing bus, and went home to break the news to Gwenda.

He had not failed to notice that morning that Gwenda was more preoccupied than usual, and not so ready as she generally was to enter whole-heartedly into his affairs. He thought that the cause of her trouble was revealed during the evening meal, but in this he was mistaken.

"Chick," she said suddenly, without any preliminary, "I am giving up my part in the play."

"What?" said the startled Chick, "Giving up your part?" She nodded. "But I thought the play was a great success? The papers all praised it."

"It is a success," she said quietly, "but I—I am leaving. And I'm a success, too, I suppose, but I'm tired of the part."

Chick patted her hand.

"Poor old girl!" he said sympathetically. (He had never done such a thing before.) "That means that you'll have to start those wretched rehearsals all over again?"

"If I get a job," she said. "It is very difficult to get on in London, you know. Chick, and if I hadn't had the influence of the Marquis of Pelborough,"—she smiled—"I don't think I should have got this,"

Chick frowned and turned a troubled face to her.

"What win you do if you can't get a job in London?"

"I shall have to go in a touring company," she said.

"That means you'll leave the flat?" said Chick, in dismay.

"For a little time. But you'll be able to afford to keep it on; you'll be quite a moneyed man." She tried to smile, but failed dismally.

"Phew!" said Chick, and leant back in his chair. "That's dreadful news!"

"Anyway," she said, with an attempt at gaiety, "I shan't be leaving London just yet. And you're not to worry about it. Chick. I'm almost sorry I told you."

"I had to know sooner or later," said Chick. "Gwenda, you always leave your engagements suddenly, don't you? That nice Jewish gentleman told me. Aren't you well?"

She laughed as she rose. Passing him, she dropped her hand on his shoulder, and he took it in his and pressed it to his lips.

"Don't do that, Chick!" she cried, and snatched her hand away.

He stared at her in amazement.

"I'm sorry," he said and went very red. "I—I didn't mean anything, Gwenda."

"Of course you didn't. Chick." Her face was white and her lips were trembling. "It was just silly of me. You want some more tea," she said, and took the cup away from him.

But Chick was not to be deflected from his indiscretion.

"You know how I love you, Gwenda," he said simply. "It was only love that made me do that."

"I know, Chick," she said, not looking at him. "You love me—as you would love a sister."

Chick rumpled his hair.

"I suppose I do," he said, but there was doubt in his voice. "But never having had a sister, I can't exactly compare things. I love babies, too, but it isn't the same kind of love. Gwenda," he asked suddenly, and he never knew why he asked the question, "where is your husband?"

It was so unlike Chick—Chick the reticent, the delicate, the tender, to ask a question which well might have been brutal.

"My husband?" she faltered. "Why—why. Chick, do you ask that?"

"I'm blessed if I know," said Chick, "only I've thought a lot about him lately. I woke up in the middle of the night with a scared feeling that maybe he'll come along and take you away one of these days."

"Don't let that worry you," she said, after a long interval of silence. She stood by the table, twisting the plain gold band about her finger absentmindedly. "And now let us talk about something else."

The week that followed was one of great anxiety for the Marquis of Pelborough. He reported for duty on Friday, according to instructions, and expected to be immediately taken into the Under-Secretary's room. He found that reporting meant no more than signing a book; he did not even go to his room, being informed by a uniformed messenger that his services were not required for that day.

Another letter came for Gwenda that week, and Chick, going into the dining-room one day, saw her hastily conceal a blue paper she was reading, and there were tears in her eyes. He did not ask the cause, pretending not to have noticed the occurrence, but he was worried for the rest of the day.

Although he was not expected to make any length of stay at the Foreign Office, he discovered that there was no objection to his occupying the very small room of his predecessor. The furniture consisted of one chair and one table, a fender, a pair of tongs, a poker, a coal-scuttle. It was a nice quiet room for study, Chick discovered, and he tackled with the outward appearance of ferocity, the intricacies of the Spanish grammar.

One day Gwenda met Lord Mansar in Bond Street. His car was passing her when she caught his eye. He signalled her to wait, and came running back.

"How is Chick getting on?"

"That is the very question I was going to ask you," she smiled.

He thought she looked a little pinched, and less pretty than usual.

"I think he'll be a success," said Mansar. "I was talking to Sir John Welson yesterday."

"What does Sir John think?"

Mansar hesitated.

"Well, frankly, he thought that Chick was rather callow."

"In fact, rather a fool," suggested the girl, with a little smile. "They're all wrong about Chick; there is nothing of the fool about him."

"Of course, he isn't subtle—" began Lord Mansar, but she shook her head,

"You are quite wrong there, Lord Mansar," she said quietly. "Apart from the fact that there's nothing quite so subtle as honesty, he has a fund of shrewdness which sometimes amazes me. You never quite know what is going on in his mind. I've seen him manoeuvre our housekeeper, Mrs. Phibbs, into doing things she didn't want to do, and I used to think that it was just his transparent simplicity which moved her. I don't think so now."

She was on her way home when Mansar had met her, and now he insisted upon driving her to Doughty Street.

Gwenda did not accept services readily, but she was a little tired, a little dispirited, and for the moment was eager for the society of somebody who would take her out of herself.

"I saw Chick the other day in Whitehall," Mansar said, as they were driving along Piccadilly, "looking as solemn as an owl and carrying a great leather portfolio under his arm. He looked as though he had been entrusted with the secrets of the Cabinet!"

Gwenda laughed.

"There was nothing more startling in his portfolio than two Spanish grammars," she said. "Chick bought it as a compromise between a leather bag and a satchel."

Mansar took his leave of her reluctantly. Gwenda had an appeal beyond her visible charm; her sincerity and her sane, clear outlook on life had made a greater impression upon the young man than he cared to admit even to himself.

"I hear you have left the stage?" he said at parting.

Gwenda nodded. "I left on Saturday. That doesn't necessarily mean that I am leaving the stage," she said, and changed the subject.

That same evening Chick was unexpectedly detained at the Foreign Office. To his terror, he was summoned to Sir John Welson's room at the moment when he had put away his grammars and his sheets of notes, and was preparing to go home.

Sir John also was on the point of departure.

"How are you shaping, Lord Pelborough?" he asked.

"Very well, sir," said Chick respectfully.

"Studying the gentle art of diplomacy, I hope?" said Sir John, who was in a good humour. "Well, my boy, the art of diplomacy can be summed up in a sentence. Always make your opponent feel that he's getting the best of you. That is the beginning and end of diplomacy. By the way, I want you to stay on until eight o clock to-night. The Minister may have some important dispatches to go to Paris."

Chick was thrilled. The fact that his travelling kit consisted of the clothes he wore and a top hat did not worry him. Later he learnt to keep in his room a travelling bag, ready packed. Fortunately, the Minister decided that the Paris trip was unnecessary that night, and Chick was released, a little disappointed, at a quarter to eight.

He had sent a wire to Gwenda, telling her that he might not be home that night, so he did not hurry home. It was nine o'clock when he turned into Doughty Street, his portfolio under his arm, his tall hat rakishly on the side of his head—it was dark, or Chick would never have dared such secret raffishness—his mind fully occupied with the recitation of a hundred Spanish idioms which he had committed to his memory during the past few days.

When he came to the house, he was surprised to see the door open and Mrs. Orlando Phibbs standing in the doorway with a shawl over her shoulders.

"Hallo, Mrs. Phibbs!" said Chick, in astonishment. "Are you looking for anybody?"

"No, Chick," she said in a low voice; "only Mrs. Maynard has a visitor."

"A visitor," said Chick, startled.

"I don't think I should go up. Chick," she said, putting her hand on his arm. "She asked me to go out. He's said terrible things to her."

Chick's blood went cold.

"Who is it?" he asked huskily.

"Mr. Maynard."

Mrs. Phibbs became a blurred vision to Chick, and the street for a second swung and swayed.

"Mr. Maynard!" he said, after a long pause. "Her—her husband?"

Before she could reply, there was a sharp little scream from the head of the stairs, and, without waiting for another second, Chick raced up the stairs. He came into the dining-room to see Gwenda leaning against the table, her face drawn and white, her eyes red with weeping. He saw her quick breathing, and saw, too, that she was rubbing a reddened wrist.

Once in a boxing contest Chick's opponent had deliberately fouled him, and his heart had been cold with the desire for murder. So he felt now as he looked on the visitor. He was a man of forty-five, hollow-cheeked and unshaven. His crooked mouth was twisted in a sneer, his deep-set eyes were fixed on Gwenda, and for the moment he did not notice Chick.

"If you think you're going to live in luxury whilst I'm starving, you've made a mistake, Gwenda—" he said. He stopped suddenly and surveyed Chick. "Who's this?" he growled.

"This is Lord Pelborough," said the girl breathlessly.

He whistled. "A lord, eh! And you told me you had no money! Now, look here, my girl, you've got to find me the fare to Canada and give me a little to start on—"

"What is the matter, Gwenda? Is this—your husband?"

She could not speak.

"Oh, Chick, Chick!" she sobbed, and dropped her head on his breast as his arm came round her.

"Husband!" laughed the visitor. "That's good."

Gwenda drew away from the boy and shook her head.

"He is my brother," she said simply, and the smile that dawned on Chick's face was seraphic.

"Your brother!" he said softly, and looked at the ill-favoured man almost benevolently.

The girl dried her eyes and took greater command of her voice.

"He's just come out of prison," she said. "He's my half-brother. If you want to know why I'm always throwing up my engagements, there's the reason." She nodded at the man. "For ten years he has dogged me, following me from theatre to theatre, and the only peace I've had was when he was in prison."

"Now, look here, Gwenda—" began the man threateningly, but Chick put up his hand.

"I don't think you had better use that tone," he said gently. "Gwenda, I'd like to talk to your brother."

She shook her head.

"It's no use, Chick," she said, with a helpless gesture.

Chick's brain was working rapidly. Suddenly, and without another word, he left them and went straight to his bedroom. In a little cash-box that he kept in a drawer were fifty pounds which he had taken from the bank to meet the emergency of sudden travel. He opened the box, took out the money, and, slipping it into his portfolio, snapped the lock. Then he came back with the portfolio under his arm.

He heard a murmur of voices before he turned the handle of the door, and caught the word "Mug," and smiled to himself, for Chick had a very keen sense of humour.

"I want to talk to your brother, Gwenda; would you mind going into your room?"

She looked at him.

"What are you going to say, Chick?"

"If you don't mind," he urged, "I should like just a few minutes' conversation with Mr, Maynard. You see, I haven't much time," he said apologetically. "I have an important dispatch which I am taking to Berlin." He touched the portfolio. "I came back to get my money. Do you think a hundred pounds will be enough for the journey?"

She could only stare at him dumbfounded.

"Will you go to your room, Gwenda?" he asked again, and she nodded.

When she had gone, Chick motioned to a chair,

"Sit down, please, Mr. Maynard," he said. "I am sorry your sister has had this trouble. Is there anything I could do to induce you to go away?

"You could give me the money," said Mr. Maynard, with his crooked smile.

"That I couldn't possibly do," said Chick firmly. "Why should I help a man like you? If I gave you money, you would only come back again next week for more."

"I'll swear to you—" began the man, and again Chick raised his hand. He had at times the dignity of an archbishop.

"Please don't swear," he said, "and please don't get angry," he added, as the man's face darkened. "I dislike intensely talking about myself, but I feel that it is only right that I should tell you that I am a light-weight amateur champion—you could get confirmation of this at the Polytechnic—and I am supposed to have the most punishing left of any man of my weight. I hate telling you this," he said awkwardly, "but it will save such a lot of unpleasantness if I do. You, of course, have just come out of prison, and you're not in condition. It would be rather like striking a child. What I am going to suggest to you, Mr. Maynard, is that you go away for three days and think over my offer to you, which is that I will allow you a pound a week so long as you do not bother Mrs. Maynard."

The man would have interrupted him, but Chick went on: "A pound a week until you find some honest employment. Now, what do you say?"

Chick placed his portfolio on the table.

"I should not be willing to help you to get to Canada," Chick went on, "even if I could. As a matter of fact, the hundred pounds in that portfolio is all I have in the house, but that is beside the point, Mr. Maynard. I like the Canadians, and I do not see why I should inflict a man of your character upon Canada. Will you accept my offer?"

"No!" snarled the man violently.

"Then I must consult Mrs. Maynard," said Chick. "Will you excuse me for about ten minutes?"

He left the room and found the girl pacing up and down in a condition bordering upon hysteria.

"Sit down, Gwenda." His voice was unusually soft. "Is this the man who has been bothering you all these years?"

She nodded.

"Is that the reason you have left your engagement?"

She nodded again.

"And is he the explanation of your sadness, Gwenda?"

"Yes, Chick," she said in a low voice. "He has been my nightmare for years. I had a letter from Dartmoor the other day, saying he was being discharged, and that he was coming to see me. I haven't slept since."

"I understand," said Chick gently.

"What are you going to do. Chick?" she asked. "Are you going to Berlin? And, Chick, there wasn't a hundred pounds—"

"I know," he replied, to her amazement.

"Have you made a suggestion to him?"

He nodded. "Yes, I have," he said after awhile, "but he hasn't accepted it, and I didn't expect he would."

His ears had been strained to catch one sound since the moment he left the room, and now he heard it.

"Sir John Welson told me today that you must always let the other side think they're getting the best of you, Gwenda," he said. "I have an idea that your brother is gone."

When they went back to the room they found it was the case. Mr. Maynard had gone, so also had Chick's portfolio, with fifty pounds and two Spanish grammars.

"You see, dear," said Chick that night, as he sat by her side at the table, his hand on hers, "if I'd given him money, he'd have come back. As he stole the money, he won't come back. He can't go anywhere near you for fear I shall be with you. Maybe he'll go to Canada and be killed," he added hopefully.

VII

THE FIRST DISPATCH

The Marquis of Pelborough was not a very earnest student of the newspapers, except of those pages devoted to sport, and more especially to the fistic art. There was probably no greater authority in England on the relative merits of light-and feather-weights than this mild young man, of whom the great "Kid" Steel had said, in his own simple way: "Dat guy's gotta foot like a fairy an' a punch like de kick of a broncho."

Chick, as a rule, merely glimpsed the pages containing the troubles of the hour (and "news," as it is understood in Fleet Street, is only trouble in some form or other), but one morning his attention was arrested by a "scareline" to a long paragraph, and he read:

"Following upon the arrest by Inspector Fuller of a number of men who are believed to be a dangerous gang of international burglars, a widespread conspiracy, having as its object the issue of forged French and Belgian bank-notes, has been brought to light.

"The head-quarters of the forgers is in Brussels, and the police have forwarded to the Foreign Office a number of original documents which leave no doubt as to the existence of the plot. The names of the chief movers in this conspiracy are not the least important of the discoveries made by Inspector Fuller."

"Gosh!" said Chick. "I wonder who they are?"

He was beginning to identify himself with the Foreign Office, and the fact that the incriminating documents were actually within the walls of that building gave the news vital importance in his eyes. Did he but know, he was to be almost as interesting a figure to the leaders of this easy-money movement as they were to him.

There are certain features of English public life which have been for all time an insoluble mystery to the foreigner. Few, indeed, are they who can appreciate the subtle difference between the accolade of knighthood and the patent of baronetcy. The older titles of the aristocracy have their exact significance, however. A marquis is a marquis all the world over, as a certain M. Lihnfelt knew.

There is a pretty little hotel situated on the boulevard of the Botanical Gardens (to Anglicize the cumbersome title of that thoroughfare) and very near to the Rue Pierre, and in this hotel lived, in comfort, this same M. August Lihnfelt. He had no apparent occupation, and was associated with one of those Government services which President Lincoln once described as "livings for which one does not work."

He was a tall, broad man, with a large bushy beard, and he wore in the lapel of his invariable frock-coat a splurge of crimson which was generally believed to indicate his possession of the Order of Leopold, but which, in point of fact, suggested no more than that he had at one period of his chequered career earned the gratitude of a Balkan Prime Minister, who had bestowed upon him the most minor of the least considerable decorations which the Bulgarian Government award for small services rendered.

One day there came to him, in his ornate sitting-room, a code telegram from London, which took the colour out of his face and made the big hands that held the telegram shake a little. For an hour he sat stroking his beard and staring at the disturbing message, and then he rose and, telephoning for his hired car, drove into Brussels.

He descended at the flower-decked portals of a famous cafe, and, although the day was warm enough to invite him to a table in the open, he strode into the dark and somewhat musty interior and, choosing a place at the far end of the room, ordered an aperitif.

He was joined a few minutes later by Monsieur Bilet, a small thin man with fierce moustachios, and they talked of the weather and the opening of the racing season, and of the new opera, until the waiter had satisfied their needs, and then Monsieur Lihnfelt, without a word of preliminary, produced the telegram from his pocket and placed it on the table.

Monsieur Bilet read and understood.

"Apparently Henri was not content with making two thousand good francs a week," said Monsieur Lihnfelt, without heat, "and he must have mixed himself up with those American people he wrote to us about."

Monsieur Bilet nodded and twisted his ferocious moustachios.

"I always felt Fertelot was the better of the two," he said, tapping the cablegram, the sender of which, it was clear, was that same Fertelot. "What shall we do?" he asked. "Is it to be Germany?"

The bearded man shook his head.

"There is time yet, and the Brussels police will not act until all the documents are placed in their possession."

To be a successful breaker of the law requires just that amount of calm and sense of diplomatic values which Monsieur Lihnfelt possessed.

"Suppose they communicate by telegram?"

Monsieur Lihnfelt stroked his beard and smiled.

"In that case, my dear Bilet, the railway stations will be watched, and we at this moment are under police observation."

He cast his eyes round carelessly. From where he sat he could see through the big open windows the whole length of the pavement before the cafe.

"No," he said, "we must rest." He beckoned the waiter, who evidently knew him. "Philip," he said, "are there any telegrams for me?"

"I will see, m'sieur."

He came back in a few minutes with a blue paper.

"I thought so," said Monsieur Lihnfelt, when the waiter had gone. "I telegraphed to Fertelot to communicate with me here."

He opened the paper.

"All documents are to go to Minister of Interior by Messenger, either today or to-morrow," ran the dispatch.

Lihnfelt put the telegram away.

"Fertelot is admirable," he said. "I agree with you, Bilet, he is the man who should have been in control. Henri is a beast and a fool."

At one o'clock the next morning he was awakened from a dreamless sleep—for men of his calibre practise, for the comfort of themselves, the doctrine of fatalism—and when he had read the third telegram, he dressed, left the hotel quietly and went in person to Monsieur Bilet, who lived, in a more magnificent style than he, at another hotel.

It was not unusual for Monsieur Lihnfelt to call, even in the middle of the night, and the porter took him up in the elevator to the fifth floor.

Monsieur Bilet, after a little persuasion, opened the door and received him, revolver in hand.

"I have to be careful," he explained as he locked the door behind the visitor and put back the revolver under his pillow. "What has happened?"

"Read this."

Monsieur Bilet blinked himself awake and read the telegram with an impassive face.

"The Foreign Office Messenger leaves for Brussels to-morrow afternoon. The Marquis of Pelborough has been warned for the service."

"The Marquis of Pelborough?" said Monsieur Lihnfelt thoughtfully. "Then the Government regard this dispatch as of the highest importance, if they choose a member of their aristocracy as its bearer."

They looked at one another.

"Who is he?"

Monsieur Lihnfelt shrugged his shoulders.

"He is an aristocrat," he said, "and the English aristocracy is different to ours, Jules. At the moment we are safe. I called on my friend at the Bureau of Police this evening."

"Yesterday evening," corrected Monsieur Bilet, who was a stickler for accuracy. "Well?"

"From his attitude and his manner I am sure that no telegram has been received. He even discussed with me the news of the conspiracy," said M. Lihnfelt. "You remember the particulars of this arrest in London were published in the Independance."

He sat down in the big arm-chair at the end of the bed and pondered silently.

"It is worth the risk," he said at last.

"What is worth the risk?" asked Monsieur Bilet impatiently. "It seems to me that our course is indicated, my dear Lihnfelt. There is a train for Cologne in the morning, and from Cologne it would be simple to work our way to Bavaria and so to Switzerland. It will be necessary that you should sacrifice your beard, though it pains me to suggest as much."

Monsieur Lihnfelt rose.

"There is also a train for Ostend in the morning," he said significantly, "and there we have six industrious friends, who have no more desire to spend the rest of their lives in prison than you or I, and, believe me, my dear Jules, your talk of beards and Switzerland is so much nonsense, for they would find us and bring us back. We can only be convicted if the personal letters, as I presume they are, written by me to Henri are not covered."

They looked at one another.

"Very well," said Bilet after a while. "I am in your hands."

On the boat that left Dover for Ostend on the following afternoon was a very happy little party of three. Chick, the proud bearer of his first dispatch, would never have dreamt of inviting Gwenda Maynard and her chaperon to share his adventure, but when he had gone to his chief's room to receive the precious packet (so covered with red sealing-wax that it was little short of miraculous that space had been found to write the address), Sir John Welson had made the suggestion himself.

"You can take your time with this. Lord Pelborough," he said. "We shan't want you for two or three days. Why don't you take your sister across—that pretty lady I saw you with in Piccadilly the other day?"

"She's not my sister, sir "—Chick blushed to the roots of his hair—"and, besides, when I'm on duty—"

"Don't worry about that," smiled Sir John. "You follow my advice, and take your sister, or aunt, or whoever the lady is. You will find Brussels delightful."

It is not customary for the head of a great Government Department to proffer such advice, but Sir John Welson had learnt from Lord Mansar something of the young man's story. He had previously read in a newspaper, but in a casual, uninterested way, about this insurance clerk who had inherited an empty title, but now Chick was becoming a real person to him.

The doors of a diplomatic career were, of course, closed to him, and the opportunities which the Foreign Office offered were very few. What could be done for this impecunious Marquis puzzled Sir John, and it puzzled his chief, the Foreign Minister, to whom the story had been told. Chick, did he but know, had been the subject of an informal discussion at a Cabinet meeting, one of those topics which arise when the serious business has been disposed of, and the members linger to gossip before they go their several ways.

In complete ignorance of his growing importance, no less than the sense of hopelessness that the discussion of his career aroused. Chick, with his portfolio under his arm, made his way to the nearest telephone and called up the house in Doughty Street. His flat was not connected, but the tenants in the flat below, who were in telephonic communication, had kindly offered the use of their phone whenever an emergency arose, and this seemed to be such a case. Fortunately Gwenda was home, and she listened in astonishment to Chick's proposals.

"Go to Brussels?" she said. "How could we, Chick? There isn't time to get ready. Besides—"

"I want Mrs. Phibbs to come, too," said Chick's eager voice. "Sir John Welson told me that I could take you, that it would be a good opportunity!"

In the end Gwenda succumbed, and there followed a rush period of packing and preparation which eventually resulted in the appearance of that happy little trio on the broad deck of the Princess Clementine.

Mrs. Phibbs, who had the gift of accommodating herself to all circumstances, might have been preparing for such a trip for years. But Gwenda was frankly excited. She was like a child in her eager interest, for she had not crossed the sea before.

"It is all too wonderful, Chick. I feel as if I am dreaming."

Chick beamed. A queer figure he made, and an object of curiosity to the other passengers, for he had clung literally and figuratively to his polished silk hat and his smart swallow-tail coat, and Gwenda, who had a dim idea that this was the conventional uniform of Government officials, had not even questioned the propriety of his making a sea voyage in that garb.

Never before probably had a King's Messenger, wearing the silver chain and the silver greyhound of his office—he had tucked this out of sight inside his waistcoat—escorted so happy a party.

Their united capital totalled twenty-five pounds; it seemed a great deal of money to Chick.

His eyes were fixed on the sea, his heart was peaceful and contented, for he felt that he was on the way to achievement. The future troubled him also, and there was some elusive thing which, amidst the chaos of uncertainty, worried him more than anything else.

"What is the dispatch you are carrying—" began Gwenda, and checked herself, "Oh, Chick, I'm so sorry! I ought not to ask that question."

Chick beamed again. He had no doubt about the contents of that precious package.

"I don't know for sure, Gwenda." He dropped his voice lest the secret should be carried, by the south-westerly breeze that followed them, to the unconscious criminals. "It is about the bank-note forgeries, I think."

She nodded, having read the newspaper account of certain arrests.

An hour later they made Ostend. Chick's passport spared him the formality of a Customs inspection.

"The train for Brussels, milor," said an obsequious official, "is on the left. It will leave in half an hour."

"Thank you, sir," said Chick, rather awed by the sight of so much gold lace.

He found a carriage and put Gwenda and Mrs. Phibbs inside, stacked their limited baggage on the rack, and went to the buffet in search of tea for them. He was trying to push his way through the crowd before the counter, when a hand touched him lightly on the shoulder, and he turned to meet a smartly dressed young man, who removed his hat deferentially.

"Pardon me, milor," said the new-comer in perfect English, "you are Lord Pelborough, aren't you?"

"Yes," said Chick in surprise,

"I have been sent by the Minister of Finance to meet you. I am the Baron von Ried."

"Awfully glad to meet you," said Chick awkwardly. "If you can tell me how I can get some tea—"

The young man smiled.

"Don't worry about that, please," he said. "We have tea prepared for you at the Hotel Splendide."

"In Ostend?" said Chick in surprise.

"Yes. The Minister is in Ostend; he asked me to intercept you and bring you along. He is most anxious to receive your dispatch without delay."

Chick scratched his chin.

"I'm glad I met you," he said, "I have some friends here; if you don't mind, I'll tell them."

"We have already notified them," said the Baron. "They have gone to the 'Splendide'."

Chick looked at him dubiously.

"I think you are mistaken," he said, and accompanied the other back to the carriage where he had left Gwenda. To his amazement, she had disappeared, with Mrs. Phibbs and the baggage.

"Do you see?" smiled the Baron.

"I see," said Chick, relieved.

Hugging his precious portfolio, he stepped into the taxi-cab by the side of his conductor, and the little car bumped and bobbed across the cobbled roadways about the station and reached the smoother streets of Ostend.

They sped quickly through the town. "Isn't that the 'Splendide'?" said Chick. He thought he had seen the name on a great white building.

"Oh, no, that is the Ostend 'Splendide'. We are at the Mariakerke 'Splendide'," explained the other. "It is not such a magnificent building."

The cab was following the road which runs past the racecourse toward Nieuport, and presently it stopped at an isolated building.

It did not look like an 'Hotel Splendide'; indeed it looked very much like what it was—the hastily patched wreckage of a house which had been sadly damaged by British guns in the course of the war. Chick stepped out and looked at the unprepossessing building with amazement.

"This way, milor," said the Baron, and, after a moment's hesitation, Chick followed him into an untidy passage. The street door was slammed behind him, and the Baron opened a second door.

"Will you step in?"

"Wait a moment," said Chick quietly. "What is the game?"

"Will you step in?" said the other, and his voice was no longer suave.

"I think I'll step out," said Chick, and turned.

In a minute the man was on him, his arms flung round him, but Chick was a past-master in avoiding a clinch. He shook the astonished assailant from him. Once, twice he struck, and the Baron tumbled on the floor, but before Chick could reach the door, he was overwhelmed by four men, who rushed into the room and flung themselves upon him.

In the meantime Gwenda had had an adventure of her own. Chick had scarcely left the carriage before an amiable-looking man, with a large moustache, had opened the door. He took off his hat, and his tone was of the utmost humility.

"Are you accompanying the Marquis of Pelborough, madame?" he asked.

"Yes," said Gwenda in surprise.

"He has met the Minister and has gone to the 'Hotel Splendide', and he sent me along to bring you after him," said the man.

"He has gone?" said Gwenda incredulously.

"Yes, madame." Monsieur Bilet's eyes had seen the wedding-ring on the girl's finger. He beckoned a porter.

"Place madame's baggage in the car," he said.

Gwenda was in a dilemma. She realized that if Chick had met the Minister, she would be an embarrassment to them, and it was quite feasible that he had gone off, though it was hardly like Chick to go without an explanation.

She left the carriage, and was driving from the station at the very moment when Chick had come back with the Baron to discover she was gone.

The man with the large moustache gave the driver directions, and the taxi was turned in the direction of Knocke, which is in the opposite direction to Ostend.

Fortunately Gwenda had a strong bump of locality. As the boat came in, she had noticed that Ostend lay to the south of the harbour, and a passenger had pointed out the hotels on the front. To reach the 'Splendide' they must turn to the right and not to the left.

She tapped at the window, and the driver stopped.

"Where are you going?" she asked.

"To Knocke, madame," he said.

"I want to go to the 'Splendide'," she said, and be seemed surprised.

"Monsieur told me to take you to the 'Grand Hotel', Knocke," he said. And then, with a shrug of his shoulders and a "Madame knows best," he turned his car. As he did so, she caught a fleeting glimpse of Chick and a sallow-faced smiling young man flash past the end of the road, and again she leant out of the window.

"You can follow that cab," she said. She was amazed when the cab did not stop at the very obvious entrance of the 'Splendide', but continued.

Her driver would have turned into the hotel, but she stopped him.

"Continue following that cab," she said, and the philosophical chauffeur, who in his life had had many strange commissions, kept in the track of Chick's car. The taxi, however, was much slower than the car which carried Chick, which was soon out of sight. Here, however, the trailing presented no difficulty, because there was only one road, and, except in the little villages through which they passed, no side-roads.

They came out of Mariakerke and saw the car standing in front of a dilapidated house. At once the girl knew that something was wrong. Chick was carrying dispatches, she realized, and dispatches which might mean the exposure of men who certainly were desperate, and assuredly would not hesitate to take the most extreme measures to prevent their falling into the hands of the authorities. Again she lent out of the window, and this time her voice was urgent.

"Do not stop," she said, in a low voice. "Pass that cab and continue until the road turns."

"It is as madame desires," said the chauffeur, who scented a romance and saw in 'Madame' an ill-used wife who was dogging the footsteps of her erring husband.

The road took a turn and the cab stopped.

"Where are you going, Gwenda?" asked the older woman. "If there is any trouble, I'd like to be in it, too."

Gwenda shook her head.

"No. If we both go, there will be nobody to carry a message to the police. I want you to go straight back, find a police-station, and tell the police what has happened. I'm quite sure Chick has been abducted."

"What are you going to do?" asked the woman.

"I'll watch." said Gwenda. She waited until the taxi had turned out of sight, and then followed on foot. She saw that the car that had been waiting before the house had also turned, and arrived at the bend in time to see Mrs. Phibbs pass it.

Presently three men came out of the house, closing the door behind them. One she recognized as the man who had invited her to leave the carriage and go to the hotel, the other was a tall, bearded man, and the third was one who had evidently been in an accident, for he kept a handkerchief to his eyes, and he walked with a limp.

She stood in the shadow of a broken wall and watched them. And then her heart leapt, for one man carried in his hand the familiar brown-leather portfolio. He stood for a moment by the side of the car, trying to fit it into an inside pocket, but the case was too large. He said something to the man with the big moustache, and they looked at the case. Then the man with the damaged eye went back into the house and came out with a bag, which he opened. Into this the portfolio was thrust, and then the car drove off.

She waited until the car was a speck in the distance on the long white road, and then she made her cautious way to the house.

At some time or other it had been the villa of a prosperous member of the Belgian bourgeoisie, and the garden, like those of so many such villas, was small and was enclosed in a brick wall, breast-high. She picked her way over a chaos of brick and battered stonework, for she trod the site of another villa which had almost entirely disappeared under gunfire. The back of the house was, if anything, more ugly than the front. The "garden" was a mass of weeds, and the one door leading to the kitchen was closed, and probably locked.

She looked round to see if she was observed, and then, lifting her skirt, she climbed the wall and moved toward the house. The door, she found, was fastened, but the window, looking into a neglected kitchen, which had evidently not been used since prewar days, was wide open. With some difficulty—for she was not dressed for such violent exercise—she climbed through the window into the room. There was no sound, and she opened a door leading to a gloomy passage. She heard two men talking, and crept along the passage until she came opposite the door of the room whence the sound emanated.

Very carefully she turned the handle and opened the door a few inches. The two men, who were standing in the centre of the room, had their backs to her, but Chick, a dishevelled figure, his battered top-hat still on his head—it had probably been thrust there by his derisive captors—sat in a corner on the floor, his arms and his legs tied, and a stick of wood between his teeth, the ends being tied behind his head.

Chick saw her and raised his eyes, and at that moment one of the men turned. He looked at the girl and gasped.

Before she could speak, the two men were on her, a big hand was laid on her mouth, and she was flung violently against the wall. Chick grew apoplectic in his attempt to release his hands, but apparently they did not intend treating her as they had served him.

"Madame will sit down," said the shorter of the men. He spoke in French, with the guttural intonation of a Flamand. "If madame makes a noise, I will put something in her mouth to stop her," he added.

Gwenda was cool now. "Take the gag out of that gentleman's mouth," she said. "If you don't, I will scream! Quick! It is choking him!"

The man hesitated, then, bending over the helpless Messenger, he broke the string that held the gag.

"What has happened, Chick?" she asked.

"They have taken my portfolio," groaned Chick. "Oh, Gwenda, I'm such a fool!"

"You will not speak," said the short custodian sharply; he was evidently the person in authority, "unless you speak in French."

"What are they going to do?" she asked in that language.

"Madame, we are keeping you here for one hour, and then we shall say an revoir," said the other man. "You will not be hurt, you understand, but if you give trouble or if you scream, I shall cut your throat."

He said this pleasantly, as one who was promising a favour.

"They have the dispatch?" she asked. She dared not revert to English, for instinctively she knew he would have no hesitation in keeping his promise.

"Where is Mrs. Phibbs?" asked Chick, and she hesitated.

"She is waiting for me," she said at last, and then in French: "Chick, do you remember that song in Gilbert's opera about the man whose life was not a happy one?"

He frowned,

"Do you mean the pol—" He stopped himself and murmured "Good!"

This conversation had not escaped the notice of the jailers. There was a short whispered consultation, and suddenly they made a move toward the girl.

"If you scream, we shall kill you," said the man who had previously made this threat, and she submitted to the binding process. "Now, my dear," he said with a leer, "we must stop that little trap of yours."

First he replaced the gag in Chick's mouth, and with a handkerchief, which he took from Chick's pocket, he gagged the girl.

They whispered together. Chick saw them looking at the girl, and heard one use a phrase which turned his blood cold, and then they were silent, listening to the heavy rumble of a motor-car which passed the shuttered window. When the sound had died away, they talked together again, but this time not so secretly.

What their plan was, he was not to discover. There came the sound of a heavy footfall in the passage, the door was kicked open violently, and a man strode in, and at the sight of the brass buttons and the long-barrelled revolver in the police commissary's hand, Chick uttered a prayer of thankfulness.

Later Chick, a little dishevelled, had a consultation with the Chief of the Police.

"I fear that by this time they are on their way to Brussels," said the policeman, shaking his head. "We could overtake them in an aeroplane, but we haven't an aeroplane. We could stop the train and arrest them, but there, again, how shall we know your lordship's dispatches are intact?"

Nevertheless, a wireless was sent to Ghent on the off-chance.

Messrs. Lihnfelt and Bilet, accompanied by the chief of their Ostend office—it was afterwards discovered that Ostend was the distributing centre for forged bank-notes, and not Brussels—were examining the locked wallet as the train drew into Ghent. Their attempt to cut out the lock with the simple means at their disposal had not been successful.

"It does not matter," said M. Lihnfelt. "Perhaps it would be better if we disposed of the portfolio and the papers at one and the same time. We shall be in Brussels before our friends are released."

"What of Vazyl and Miguiet?" asked the damaged Baron. "And what of me, Lihnfelt?" He pointed to his injured eye.

"You shall be rewarded, my friend," said M. Lihnfelt. At that moment the train stopped and the carriage door was opened.

M. Lihnfelt, to whose credit it must be said that he was the first to recognize the inevitable, put up his hands. "There is no necessity for violence, m'sieur," he said to the chief of the waiting policemen.

It was late at night when Chick, with his precious packet, hacked with the ineffective knives of the conspirators, reached the house of the Minister of Finance, a magnificent palace—like chalet on the outskirts of Brussels, and the sympathetic Minister himself came down the steps to welcome the Messenger.

"You have been treated monstrously, milor," he said. "These villains shall pay. It is an act the most abominable!"

Chick unlocked the portfolio and handed the heavily-sealed package to the Minister, and that worthy gentleman examined it with a puzzled frown.

"And yet, milor," said he, "I cannot understand why these men should have taken the trouble, for they are not farmers. And if they were farmers, how could they be interested in swine fever?"

"Swine fever?" gasped Chick, and the Minister was equally astonished.

"Yes, m'sieur," he said. "It is a copy of your new regulations for dealing with the importation of hogs into Belgium."

Chick's jaw dropped.

"I—I thought it had to do with the forged bank-notes," he stammered, and the eyebrows of the Financial Minister rose.

"No, no, m'sieur," he said gently. "As to that, we received the particulars by post this morning. Your assailants were captured. We shall also capture the gentleman—this Monsieur Lihnfelt who is the organizer of the forgeries."

Chick smiled slowly. "I think you've caught them both, sir," he said.

VIII

THE OILFIELD

"No, thank you, Joicey," said the Earl of Mansar for the third time, and the stout, good-looking young man who was his companion began rolling up the large plan with a pained expression.

It was an interesting chart, with parallelograms and rhomboids of pink and green, and he had talked himself hoarse in an endeavour to persuade his sometime comrade into agreement.

"I dare say it is all right," said Mansar, tossing a cigarette into the extended palm of the Honourable Felix Joicey, "and I know that, so far as you are concerned, it is all right. There is a lot of oil in Roumania—though I've never heard that a gusher had gushed in the Doebnitz region—and as likely as not there is a fortune in the proposition."

"There are a dozen fortunes," said the enthusiastic Mr. Joicey, and Lord Mansar nodded.

"I'll take shares, I promise you that," he said, "but I will not join your board. The fact is, Joicey, I hate the crowd who are running the company, and that's flat—they couldn't go straight if they were fired out of a gun."

"Meggison isn't bad," suggested Joicey.

"Meggison isn't as bad as Glion, and that isn't saying much. But if you came to me and offered me a seat in the court of the Bank of England, I wouldn't take it if either of those fellows had an account at the Bank."

Mr. Joicey lit his cigarette and his expression was doleful. He had served with Lord Mansar in the Guards, and had given up his profession as a soldier to enter the Stock Exchange, and had been fairly successful.

"I'm pretty heavily interested in this," he said, puffing his cigarette thoughtfully, "and I don't think you'd run much risk. We want a good name on the board—a name that will impress the small investor. We have to put the property on the market, for we need big capital."

Lord Mansar drew in his lips and lifted his eyebrows, a grimace which says, "I'm sorry, but I can't help you," in most languages. Then unexpectedly he smiled.

"By Jove!" he said softly.

"What?"

"Do you know the Marquis of Pelborough?"

Mr. Joicey frowned. He knew most of the marquises and not a few of the dukes, but he did not know the Lord of Pelborough.

"Not the fellow whose uncle claimed an extinct peerage—the insurance clerk?" he asked, suddenly remembering.

Mansar nodded.

"That's the fellow. He has been working at the Foreign Office, but that job is finishing, and I'm sure I could persuade him to go on the board. A thousand a year, you said?"

Mr. Joicey rubbed both his chins and looked out of the window.

"At the Foreign Office? He must be a pretty smart fellow. Quite a boy, isn't he?"

"He looks young," admitted his lordship, "but he is no fool. He's the cleverest amateur boxer at his weight in England."

Here he touched an ex-heavy-weight public-school champion on a tender spot.

"I wonder if I've seen him?" mused Joicey. "The best of the light-weights is a lad I saw box at the Polytechnic gym. He beat young Herberts, the Eton middle-weight, and gave him ten pounds. 'Chick,' they call him."

Lord Mansar's eyes glistened.

"That's the fellow. Now, be a sportsman, Felix, and shove him on your board. Glion will fall on the neck of a real live marquis."

"I'll think about it," said Joicey.

Late in the evening, when Mansar was dressing for dinner, he learnt by telephone that the promoters had agreed, a piece of information which gave him a double pleasure, since it offered him the opportunity of breaking the news. And he was not thinking of Chick when he sighed.

The Marquis of Pelborough was sitting, in his shirt-sleeves, playing dominoes with his housekeeper, when Lord Mansar's rat-tat at the street door sent him in hasty search after his discarded coat. Gwenda was in her room, answering a letter which she had received from her late manager, asking her to return to the part she had dropped. Gwenda had a brother, now happily in Canada and unlikely to return, a blackmailing, weak and conscienceless man, who had dogged her footsteps through life and had brought to a summary conclusion at least three good engagements. With his passing there had been lifted from her heart a heavy load which she had borne in secret almost as long as she could remember.

A tap at her door, and Mrs. Phibbs came in.

"Lord Mansar?" said Gwenda in dismay. The least cause for her embarrassment was her unreadiness to meet a visitor at that hour. Mansar's attentions had been marked, and whilst she did not doubt either his sincerity or his honesty, it was distressing to her to find a man she liked very much developing, against her will and wish, another relationship.

"I was just on my way to dinner," apologized his lordship, "and I thought you would not mind my calling in to tell you my news."

"Chick has some news also," smiled the girl ruefully. "His work is ending at the Foreign Office."

Lord Mansar nodded.

"I know," he said; "Sir John told me a few days ago. He's tremendously well satisfied with you, Pelborough."

"I suppose he is, sir," said Chick a little glumly. "I was wondering whether the letter I carried to Madrid—"

"He is perfectly well satisfied with you," said Mansar, "but the man whose place you filled is returning from Egypt. Welson has put your name down for the next vacancy, and I think you could be sure of having a permanent appointment. But I think we can do better than that." He smiled, and gave the gist of his conversation with Joicey.

"And they have accepted you, Pelborough. I think it will be a good thing for you."

Chick's face did not display any particular enthusiasm.

"I am rather scared of it," he said, shaking his head. "I don't know what directors do, and I know nothing whatever about oil. Besides, it almost seems as though I were becoming a guinea-pig director."

Lord Mansar was startled.

"You're a queer fellow, Pelborough. I should not have thought you knew what a guinea-pig director was."

Chick smiled in self-depreciation.

"You hear so many things in the City," he said, excusing his own intelligence. "But if you think. Lord Mansar, that I shan't make a fool of myself, and it is a job that I ought to take, I'm most grateful to you for suggesting it."

Mansar was just a little disappointed. Chick disappointed so many people who were misled by his simplicity into believing that he was mentally deficient. He gave them the same shock that the modern child administers to its parents, for Chick was neither dazed nor impressed by the mechanical toys of life, and saw, through the tin and the paint, the curled spring which worked them. There is nothing quite so disconcerting as this, and Lord Mansar might be pardoned his twinge of annoyance when Chick received the news of his excellent appointment with such sang-froid.

In truth, Chick was too alarmed to be impressed, and too overwhelmed by the view of this strange land which he must prospect to be enthusiastic. Gwenda went down to the door with their visitor. She was conscious of the chilling effect of Chick's lugubrious face.

"You have been wonderful to Lord Pelborough," she said, "and please don't think that he isn't very grateful. Chick gets so overburdened by these opportunities which you give him that he is not quite—"

"I know—I understand," said Lord Mansar with a laugh, "I always forget that these jobs which a man like myself, who has never felt the need of a job, would so light-heartedly must be almost paralysing to a fellow like Chick. Besides, I am more than rewarded for any service I have given," he said meaningly.

He took her hand and held it a while, so long that she gently withdrew it. There was an awkward silence as they stood on the doorstep, then Lord Mansar blurted:

"Mrs. Maynard, would you think I was very rude if I asked you a personal question?"

"I can't imagine you being very rude," she smiled.

"Is your husband dead?"

She shook her head.

"Are you divorced?"

Again she shook her head.

"And is there any prospect of your being divorced?"

"No, Lord Mansar," she said quietly, and he held out his hand again.

"I'm sorry," he said, and Gwenda went upstairs feeling a brute.

Chick received his introduction to Mr. Glion the next morning at ten o'clock. The place of meeting was a large bare-looking room, furnished with a long table and half a dozen mahogany chairs. On the distempered walls were four big charts framed in oak, and these, with a carpet on the floor, constituted the contents of the room—with this reservation, that Mr. Bertram Glion was in himself both a furnishing and a decoration. He was an immensely stout man, who emphasized and underlined his rotundity by his passion for vivid waistcoats. They were invariably of silk, and usually figured fantastically.

Mr. Glion told his intimate friends with pride that he designed them himself, a handsome admission that the responsibility was not to be put elsewhere. His face was very broad and very red. It could on occasions be crimson, and here Nature had emphasized his high colour by endowing him with a small, white moustache and a pair of snowy eyebrows.

He was a very rich man, who had built up his fortune on the faith of a large number of shareholders, who were in consequence very poor.

The relationship between Mr. Glion and his shareholders is best illustrated by an hour-glass. Place the hour-glass in its correct position, and there is only room for sand at one end. In his philosophy there was no place in the world for rich shareholders and rich company promoters. One or the other had to acquire wealth, and it was Mr. Glion's design that he should be the one.

He sat at the farther end of the table, in a large, padded and comfortable chair, and on his right, less comfortably placed, was his friend and partner, John Meggison. Meggison could be described as a faded gentleman. Almost all the attributes of his gentility had faded just a little. He was a long-faced, taciturn man, who wore pince-nez and spoke with a certain preciseness. His worn and wearied expression may have been due to the fact that he had spent his maturity in a vain endeavour to adapt his sense of honour to the exigencies of Mr. Glion's business.

Mr. Glion pushed back his chair and rose breathlessly to his feet as Chick was shown in.

"Lord Pelborough, eh? Yes." He looked at Chick and said "Yes" again.

Mr. Meggison also looked at Chick and shook his head slightly. It was intended to be a signal to his partner that Chick would not do. It was one of his illusions that Mr. Glion was influenced by his judgment.

"Yes," said Mr. Glion again. "Sit down, Lord Pelborough."

Five minutes later Mr. Glion was waddling round the room with a long pointer, explaining to Chick, by means of the charts, maps and plans which hung on the wall, the potentialities of the Doebnitz oilfields. They were joined a little later by Mr. Joicey, who made up in enthusiasm all that he lacked in experience, and by lunch-time the four directors of Doebnitz Oil were seated about a table at Mr. Glion's fiat.

Chick came home to tea a very preoccupied young man, and hung up his tall hat, looking so sad and depressed that Gwenda was alarmed.

"Are you disappointed, Chick?" she said.

Chick rubbed his nose and looked at her blankly.

"Eh?" he said, rousing himself with a start, "I'm awfully sorry, Gwenda. Am I disappointed? No, I'm not disappointed, except with myself. It is such an enormous business, Gwenda. There's a million pounds being invested in the company, and my name is going on the prospectus, and I've nothing to do except to go to the office once a month."

She shook him gently by the shoulder.

"My dear soul, there are lots of people who would give their heads to get that kind of position."

"I suppose they would," said Chick dubiously. "But, Gwenda, do you know anything about oil?"

"Do I know anything about it?" she said in surprise. "No, of course I don't; but you needn't be an authority on oil to be a director of an oil company."

"I suppose not," said Chick.

He had a subscription to a library, and returned the next day with a number of volumes under his arm. Gwenda, reading their titles and noting that they all dealt with oil and its production, marvelled a little. She was beginning to understand Chick, and to know that behind that appealing helplessness of his was a very definite strength of purpose. The courage which had brought him again and again to the centre of the ring to take punishment from the hands of a man who he knew must surely defeat him, but which nevertheless held him doggedly to the end, was exactly the courage which made him spend three days and nights in the quietness of his bedroom confirming a suspicion which had been born of a quick glance between Glion and his partner.

It was during the luncheon, and Mr. Joicey was speculating upon the dividends which this undeveloped oilfield would pay. It was a glint from eye to eye that Chick saw, but it was enough.

A week passed, and he had exhausted the subject of oil, and had exchanged his books for the only geological survey of Roumania procurable. It was a small book, but it was in German, and for another three days Chick sat hunched up with a German-English dictionary by his side, puzzling over the queer Gothic characters and making elaborate notes in his sprawling hand.

The prospectus had been issued with what seemed to Lord Mansar to be indecent haste, and at the first board meeting which Chick attended Mr. Glion announced that subscriptions were "rolling in." Glion, who had seen the birth and death of innumerable companies, and had a very large experience of guinea-pig directors, drove to his handsome house in Hans Crescent after the meeting, and he was in a boiling rage.

"What is this fellow they've lumbered on to me?" he stormed to the meek Meggison. "The man is an infernal jackass. By Jove, for two pins I'd chuck him off the board!"

"He's young," murmured Mr. Meggison.

"Young—be blowed!" exploded Mr. Glion. "Business which ought to have taken us ten minutes he kept us fooling about with until six o'clock! Did you notice how he insisted upon reading the engineer's report? Did you hear what he said about the purchase price and who was getting the money?"

"He's very young," murmured Mr. Meggison.

"Young!" spluttered the rotund Mr. Glion. "He's got Joicey dissatisfied, and I'm depending upon Joicey to work the market."

At that moment Mr. Joicey, no longer enthusiastic, was walking with a gloomy Chick along the Thames Embankment. Chick's tall hat was on the back of his head, and his hands were thrust into his trousers pockets.

"You know a devil of a lot about oil!" said Joicey testily, for a man resents the disturbance of his placid optimism. "Where did you learn it all?"

"I read it up," said Chick.

"Oh, in books," said Mr. Joicey contemptuously.

"Yes," said Chick, "in books. Books told you there was such a place as Roumania. You've never been there, have you?"

Mr. Joicey admitted he hadn't.

"You made Glion awfully wild," he said after they had walked a few minutes in silence.

"Did I?" said Chick indifferently. "That's the fat red man, isn't it?"

"That's him," said the product of a great public school. "You rattled him a bit about the purchase price. Five hundred thousand pounds isn't too much to pay, if the property is anything like what I think it is."

Chick grunted.

"Who gets the money?" he asked after a while.

"The Southern Oil Syndicate," answered Mr. Joicey uneasily, for he knew that the Southern Oil Syndicate was another name for Mr. Glion and Mr. Meggison.

They parted at the point where the one-decker trams dive into a dark tunnel and climb their way up to Southampton Row, and at parting Chick dropped his bomb-shell.

"I don't think there is any oil in that property," he said. "Good-bye, Mr. Joicey."

He left the young man staring after him.

A fortnight later came another report from the engineer in charge of the boring operations, which Mr. Glion received philosophically.

"Of course we must put down another borehole, gentlemen," he said. "It is very disappointing, very." He passed his hand wearily across his forehead. "Others will reap the reward of our labours," he said virtuously. "We may not get oil for a month, or two months, or two years, but sooner or later our enterprise will be justified. We will now pass to the next item on the agenda."

"Wait a minute," said Chick. "In the prospectus you said—"

"Any discussion of the prospectus is out of order," said Mr. Glion in his capacity as chairman. "We will now pass to the next business."

The following afternoon Chick received a wire asking him to call at Hans Crescent. Mr. Glion was ill. He was very ill. In proof of which, there he was in his bed, dressed in resplendent pyjamas, which in all probability he had designed in the odd moments when he was not designing waistcoats.

"My doctor has told me to give up work at once," he said. "Sit down, Pelborough. Let them bring you some tea. Or will you have a whisky and soda?"

Chick would take neither.

Mr, Glion had not achieved success without a profound knowledge of human nature, and Chick listened fascinated whilst the white moustache wobbled up and down as Mr. Glion outlined his plan.

"I am getting a bit too old for this, Pelborough," he said. "Here, at the zenith of my career, I have the most wonderful proposition that any financier has ever handled, and Anno Domini has floored me! This company requires the direction of young men, full of the vigour of youth. You understand me?"

Chick nodded, wondering what was coming next.

"I have been talking it over with Meggison," Mr. Glion went on, "and we have decided to stand on one side and let you boys run the company,"

"But—but," stammered Chick.

"One moment." Mr. Glion raised his hand with a pained expression. "This is not a question of doing you a favour, my friend. I must be justified. People are watching the ravaging effect of—er—Anno Domini, as I said before, and are chuckling up their sleeves. They think I will fail, but they do not know that I have at my right hand and at my left,"—he gesticulated picturesquely toward the window and in the direction of a Louis Seize cabinet—"two young geniuses—should that be genii? I am rather hazy on the subject— who will carry the Doebnitz Oilfields to triumphant success."

And then he outlined his scheme, and Chick listened open-mouthed.

Mr. Glion had a hundred thousand shares. Chick had exactly five hundred, which had been presented to him to qualify him for the directorship. He would hand his shares over to Chick at a nominal figure, "say, a shilling—or even sixpence," suggested Mr. Glion, watching the young man's face, and was immediately afterwards sorry that he hadn't said half-a-crown.

And Joicey should become managing director and Chick chairman of the board. It is doubtful whether Chick would have fallen in with this arrangement if he had read the scathing article in a respectable financial paper that morning. Joicey had read it, and was indignant when he came in answer to Chick's wire urgent. They met in the bare board-room in Queen Victoria Street, and Joicey's enthusiasm carried the day. The next morning they received the transfer of two hundred thousand shares which had been held by Mr. Glion and the philanthropic Mr. Meggison, and, constituting themselves into a board, they accepted and acknowledged the resignation of the former chairman and managing director.

And then the trouble began. For months afterwards Chick never saw a financial newspaper without shutting his eyes and shivering. He leapt in a night to the eminence of a public character, and a bad character at that. An independent report of the Doebnitz property had reached London, and it was less flattering than the engineer's. The post-box was filled with the letters of anguished and despairing shareholders who had already paid fifteen shillings on every one-pound share, and Chick felt that he would grow grey unless something happened.

There was an informal meeting in the little sitting-room at Doughty Street, and to Gwenda's surprise Lord Mansar attended.

"I've been trying to get you all day, Chick," he said. "You can't imagine how sick I am that I have let you into this swindle."

Mr. Joicey, looking unusually haggard and baggy about the eyes, for he had had no sleep for three nights, put down the newspaper cuttings he had been reading with a groan.

"Well, you were right, Mansar," he said. "The infernal scoundrels! They have left us to hold the baby."

"I'll come on the board," began Mansar.

"No, you won't," said Chick quietly. "We've got into this trouble through our own stupidity, and we've got to get out as best we can. It doesn't affect me, because—"

"It affects you more than anybody," said Mansar quietly. "You are just making your start, Pelborough, and I thought it was a good start for you. It is going to be very bad for you to be associated with a swindle of this kind, and I hate myself for putting you into it."

"Is there no money in the company?" asked Gwenda, who was the fourth about the little table.

"That's the swindle of it!" said Joicey savagely. "There's over one hundred and fifty thousand pounds in the bank, and Pelborough and I have full control of it. It was the money in the bank that was the lure. The business looked so solvent that we didn't hesitate, did we, Pelborough?"

Chick said nothing. He had done a considerable amount of hesitating, but had been over-persuaded by his volatile companion.

"But I thought the capital was a million," said the girl.

It was Mansar who explained to her the mysteries of high finance—of shares allocated in lieu of purchase price, of money actually paid out to vendors.

"Mr. Glion has his whack," said Chick. "I wonder if we could get it back?"

Joicey laughed.

"Could you get back a lump of sugar that had been standing in a cup of hot tea for ten minutes?" he asked. "Could you extract the ink you dropped on blotting-paper? No, you'll never get anything back from Glion. The beggar isn't even insurable," he said bitterly, "otherwise we could get a policy on his life and kill him!"

"He isn't a good life," said Chick, shaking his head, his mind reverting to the days of his insurance clerkship. "I think he would come under Schedule H."

The discussion ended, as all previous discussions had finished, without any definite plan being evolved. Indeed, there was no other plan than the liquidation of the company.

More satisfactory were the little talks which Mr. Glion had with his confederate. They occurred in a room panelled in rosewood and illuminated by soft lights that shone through Venetian glass, lights that were fixed in solid silver brackets, for Mr. Glion's study had been arranged by a well-known firm of decorators and furnishers, and he had wisely refrained from putting forward those suggestions as to colour and shape which had made his waistcoats famous throughout the City of London.

"They seem to be in trouble," said Mr. Glion as he sipped a long glass of Moselle. "Did you see the Financial Echo this morning?"

"They weren't exactly nice about us," said Mr. Meggison in his pedantic way. "The things they say about that boy Pelborough—"

Mr. Glion shook with internal laughter. "There is such a thing in this world, my dear fellow," he said as he poured himself another libation, "as being too clever. It has been my experience that when you have dealings with a fellow who thinks he knows it all, you are on a good soft proposition."

There came a discreet tap at the door, and his butler entered, carrying a salver.

"A telegram?" said Mr. Glion, adjusting his glasses.

He opened the buff envelope and extracted two forms filled with writing.

Mr. Meggison, watching him read, saw first a look of astonishment and then a broad smile dawn slowly on his face.

"There is no answer," he said to the waiting servant, and chuckled, and his chuckle became a laugh so punctured with coughing that his companion was seriously alarmed.

"When you are dealing with a fellow who thinks he is clever," repeated Mr. Glion, when he had recovered his breath, "you are on something for nothing."

He tossed the telegram across to the other, and Mr. Meggison read:

"We have struck oil at 220 metres, a fine gusher. Evidently oil lies very deeply here. The prospects are splendid. All the local authorities are surprised that we have found oil at all."

It was signed "Merrit."

"What the dickens does that mean?" asked Mr. Meggison, surprised, and his friend began to laugh again.

"I will tell you what that means," he began, when again the door opened to admit the butler.

"There's a telephone call through for you, sir, from the Marquis of Pelborough. Will you speak to him?"

"Switch him through," said Mr. Glion, his face creased with good humour.

He winked at the puzzled Mr. Meggison.

"Lost no time, has he?" he chuckled. "Hand that telephone across to me, will you, Meggison?"

It was Chick's voice that greeted him.

"Yes, yes," said Mr. Glion indulgently, "How do you do. Lord Pelborough? Yes, I've read the papers...I'm very sorry...No, I'm out of that business for good. The state of my health makes it imperative that I should rest, and my doctor has forbidden me to interest myself in any company at all...Buy back the shares and take control? Nonsense!...You wait, my boy, for a year or two. You'll have wonderful news from Roumania yet."

He winked again at the other, and was unable to proceed for a moment.

"Oh yes, you bought them all right," he said, answering the anxious inquiry. "The fact that you and Joicey haven't paid for them makes no difference. You owe us exactly five thousand pounds. That's exactly two hundred thousand shares at sixpence. No, we're not going to press you for payment."

He listened, shaking his head, whilst the sound of Chick's urgent voice reached Mr. Meggison at the other side of the table.

"I'm sorry. Good night."

He hung up the receiver.

"That is one of the most transparent tricks in the world," he said.

The "phone rang again. He hesitated for a moment, then reached for the instrument,

"Oh, is that you, Pelborough? No, I'm sure Mr. Meggison wouldn't come back under any circumstances. He's not well at all. And by the way, Pelborough, where is Joicey now? In Roumania, is he?" He grinned broadly. "Thank you, that is all I wanted to know."

He put the receiver down.

"As I was saying, that is one of the most transparent tricks, and it has been played on me before, but never, I am happy to say, with success. The wire was sent by Joicey, of course."

"Why should he send it here and not to the office? That exposes the fake," said Mr. Meggison.

"Not necessarily," corrected Glion. "Merrit has had his orders to send his wires direct here. No, no "—he held up his glass and admired its amber contents—"they oughtn't to have tried it on an old bird like me."

Mr. Glion came down to breakfast the next morning in his most amiable mood. He might have continued the day in that cheerful frame of mind, but for a paragraph in the stop-press column of the financial paper.

"Valuable finds of oil have been made on the property of the Doebnitz OH Company."

This puzzled him, and it shook his faith in his own judgment. That faith was entirely dissipated in the afternoon when the figures at his club showed Doebnitz Oil at seventeen shillings a share and rising.

Mr. Glion was a man of resource and ingenuity. Ten minutes after reading the staggering information which the tape machine supplied, he descended from a taxi at the door of the office in Queen Victoria Street and went up to the board-room.

He passed through the outer office, where three clerks were busy opening telegrams from shareholders, cancelling their offers to sell, and discovered Chick sitting in solitary state in that same luxurious chair which had been Mr. Glion's. Chick beamed up at the visitor, and Mr. Glion ordered his face to smile.

"Well, well, my boy," he said, and offered a plump and purple hand, "you see, I've come as I promised."

The smile left Chick's face.

"As you promised, sir?" he said.

Mr. Glion nodded and sat down.

"As we agreed over the 'phone," he said. "I have come to buy back the shares you offered me, and very handsome it was of you, my boy. I promise you that you shall not lose on the transaction."

"I've promised myself that, too, sir," said Chick gently.

"Have you the transfers ready?" asked Mr. Glion, searching for his fountain pen.

"No, sir—and I am not selling."

The rotund Mr. Glion quivered with surprise and indignation.

"What, sir! After we had agreed that I should take over your stock?"

Chick went to the door and opened it wide.

"Good evening, sir," he said politely.

One of Mr. Glion's greatest assets was an ability to recognize defeat.

Sudden affluence affects different people in different ways. The Marquis of Pelborough had succeeded, through the death of his uncle, to a title which brought with it nothing more substantial in the shape of estate than one acre of waste garden and a brick cottage badly in need of repair. "Chick" Pelborough was less shocked by his accession to the title than he was by the acquisition to wealth.

"Your future is settled now, Chick," said Gwenda Maynard, at the conclusion of a family council, in which his housekeeper as by right participated. "You should buy a nice house in the country and take your place in Society."

"But I don't want to go into the country," said Chick, aghast at the prospect. "The country bores me, Gwenda. When I used to go to Pelborough to see the old doctor, I used to pray for the hour when I could leave."

She shook her head.

"Going to the country for a day to see a crochety old gentleman who bullied you is quite another matter to living in a beautiful house, with horses to ride and a car to drive. No, Chick, you've lifted yourself so far—"

"You have put me where I am, Gwenda," said Chick soberly, "If you hadn't been behind me, jogging my elbow, I should have made a mess of things. You don't want me to leave here, do you?" he asked, with a sudden sinking of heart.

"Here" was a little flat at seventy pounds per annum, no suitable abode for a man who had sold out his holding in a certain oil company for a hundred thousand pounds.

The possession of such an incredible sum terrified Chick. It took him the greater part of a week to get over the feeling that he had been engaged in a successful swindle, and for another week he fought with an inclination to restore the money to a gentleman who, believing they were worthless, had certainly tried to ruin him when he had transferred his shares to Chick's account.

Gwenda did not instantly answer his question. She wanted Chick to stay—she had never realized how much he was to her—but the position was grotesque. She had set out to establish the insurance clerk who had so unexpectedly fallen into the ranks of the peerage, and she had devoted her unselfish energies to his advancement. And now that he was fairly on his feet she shrank from the logical culmination of her plan, and she hated herself for her cowardice.

"I don't want you to go, you know that, Chick," she said slowly, "only it isn't right that you should stay."

"Gwenda is talking sense, Lord Pelborough," said the practical Mrs. Phibbs, nodding her imposing head. "People must work up to the level of their superiors. Why, you're scared to death of these flibbertigibbet Society folk, and that isn't right. If you don't go up, Chick, you go down. My husband surrendered at the first check, and found his way to the saloon bar. He was one of those people who liked to be looked up to, and naturally he had to descend pretty far before he reached the admiring strata."

Mrs. Phibbs very seldom talked about her husband.

"He is dead, isn't he?" asked Chick gently.

"He is," said that brisk woman, "and in Heaven, I hope, though I have my doubts."

"Besides, Chick," said Gwenda, "we shall have very little time together here. The play may run for another year, and now that I've gone back to the cast I shall be fully occupied."

Chick said nothing to this. A few days before he was passing down Bond Street on the top of a 'bus, and saw Gwenda and Lord Mansar coming from a tea-shop, and they had driven away in Mansar's car. And on the very next afternoon he had met them walking in Hyde Park, and Gwenda had seemed embarrassed.

And it hurt him just a little bit—a queer, aching hurt that took the colour from the day and left him forlorn and listless.

"We'll postpone our talk until to-morrow," said Gwenda, rising. "Mrs. Phibbs, I shall be late to-night. Lord Mansar is taking Miss Bellow and me to supper. You wouldn't care to come, would you, Chick?"

Chick shook his head.

"I'm going to the gym, to punch the bag, Gwenda," he said quietly, and she thought it was the prospect of leaving which had saddened him.

Chick did not stay long in the gymnasium. The spirit had been taken out of him, and his instructor watched his puny efforts with dismay,

"You're not losing your punch, m'lord, are you?" he asked anxiously.

"I'm losing something," said Chick, with a sigh. "I don't think I'm in the mood for practice tonight, sergeant."

He dressed and came out into Langham Place, and he was at a loose end. Even the cinema had no appeal for him, and he loafed down Regent Street without having any especial objective.

Nearing the Circus, he turned into a side-street that led to Piccadilly. And it was here that he saw the girl. To be accurate, he heard her first—heard a faint, frightened scream, and the thud of her frail body against the shuttered window of a shop.

It is a peculiarity of men who love ring-craft that they have a horror of quarrels, particularly street quarrels. Chick always went breathless and experienced a tightening of the heart at the sight of a street fight. But this was not a street fight. The man was a wiry youth, somewhat overdressed; the girl appeared respectable and, on closer inspection, very pretty.

"You'd do it again, would you?" hissed the man; and then, as his hand came back. Chick crossed the narrow road, no longer breathless,

"Excuse me," he said, and the girl's assailant suddenly spun round. He had no intention of spinning round, and he glared at the slim figure that had appeared from nowhere.

Chick backed slowly to the centre of the asphalted road, and Mr. Arthur Blanbury (for that was the name of the girl's companion) entirely misunderstood the significance of the manoeuvre. He thought this interfering stranger had repented of his intrusion. In truth, Chick needed exactly three feet of clear space on either flank. This Mr. Blanbury discovered. Without any preliminary remarks, he drove at Chick scientifically. Chick took the blow over his left shoulder, and drove left and right to the body. It was Mr. Blanbury's weak spot, and he drew off, unguarding his jaw. Chick's left found the point, and Mr. Blanbury went down, in the language of the ring, "for the count."

You cannot indulge in any form of fistic combat within a hundred yards of Piccadilly Circus without collecting a crowd or inviting the attention of an active and intelligent constabulary. A big hand fell on Chick's shoulder, and he turned to meet the commanding eye of a policeman.

"Suppose you come along with me, old man," said the constable; and Chick, who had more sense than most people who have found themselves in his painful situation, did not argue, but allowed himself to be taken to Marlborough Street Police Station.

"The Marquis of what?" said the station inspector humorously. "What are you charging him with—drunk?"

But here an unexpected friend arrived in the person of the girl. Until then Chick had not seen her face. It was a very pretty face, despite its inherent weakness.

But if she was a stranger to Chick, she was known to the station inspector, who raised his grey eyebrows at the sight of her.

"Hallo, Miss Farland! What do you want?" he demanded.

And Chick heard the story. She was a shop girl at an Oxford Street store, and her assailant had been her fiancé. It had been one of those sketchy engagements which follow chance meetings in the Park. He was very nice and "gentlemanly," and had treated her like a lady until one night he revealed his true character. She "lived in" with a hundred other girls, and it was possible, as he evidently knew, for her to slip down to a door which communicated with the warehouse and the living quarters alike—being an emergency exit for the girls in case of fire—and to open that door to Mr. Blanbury and his associates, to two of whom he introduced her.

Instead she had communicated with her employer, and the police had trapped the robbers, with the exception of Mr. Blanbury, of whom she had not given a very clear description, actuated possibly by sentimental motives. They had met by accident that night, and Chick had been a witness to the sequel.

"Very sorry, indeed, my lord," said the inspector cheerfully. "Go back, Morrison, and pull in that man."

Chick waited in the charge-room until they brought in the somewhat dazed young man, and after he had disappeared through the door leading to the cells, he escorted the girl to her shop.

She was grateful, she was silent, being overawed by the knowledge that her escort was a "lord," but her prettiness was very eloquent, and Chick went back to Doughty Street with his head in the air and a sense that the evening had been less dismal than he had anticipated.

He was so cheerful when Gwenda came in, after a prolonged farewell at the street door—it was not her fault that it lasted more than a second—that she smiled in sympathy, though she did not feel like smiling.

"I've been locked up," said Chick calmly, as he shuffled his patience cards.

"Chick!"

"I was arrested and marched to Marlborough Street," said Chick, enjoying the mild sensation. Then he told her what had happened.

"You splendid dear!" she said, squeezing his hand. "How like you to interfere! Was she pretty, Chick?"

She was not prepared for his reply or his enthusiasm.

"Lovely!" said Chick, in a hushed voice. "Simply lovely! She's got those baby eyes that you like so much, Gwenda, and a sort of mouth that you only see in pictures—like a bud. You wouldn't think she worked in a shop. I was surprised when she told me. Such a nice young lady, Gwenda—you'd love her."

"Perhaps I should, Chick," said the girl, a thought coldly. "I never knew that you were such a connoisseur of feminine charms. Did you like her, Chick?"

"Rather!" said Chick heartily. "She's not a big girl—she just comes up to my shoulder. Gwenda "—he hesitated—"couldn't I ask her to come up to tea one day? I know her name—Millie Farland."

"Certainly," said Gwenda, slowly removing her wrap. "Ask her to come on Wednesday."

Chick looked surprised.

"But that is your matinee day, and you wouldn't be home," he said.

Gwenda eyed him thoughtfully.

"No," she said. "Ask her to come on Sunday. Anyway, she wouldn't be able to come any other day than Saturday or Sunday, if she is in an Oxford Street store, and I want to see her."

Miss Millie Farland was a young lady who enjoyed the fatal experience of publicity, which is a poison that has before now driven inoffensive citizens to commit violent crimes. It is possible to reform a drunkard and cure a dope fiend, but let the unbalanced mentality of unimportant people confront their names in print, and their cases are for ever hopeless. Never again will they be happy until they have once more tasted the fierce thrills of press notices.

Miss Farland had figured in a warehouse robbery. She had given evidence at the Old Bailey. She had seen herself described as a "heroine," and her actions eulogized in a paragraph which was headed "Pretty Girl's Smart Capture of Warehouse Thieves."

She had been photographed entering the court and leaving the court. She had been similarly portrayed at the local cinematograph theatre, and now a marquis had fought for her in the open street! A real lord had got locked up for her and had walked home with her!

There were fifty girls sleeping on her landing at Belham and Sapworth's and fifty on the landing below. None of them went to bed that night ignorant of the fact that the Most Honourable The Marquis of Pelborough had fought for her in Regent Street.

She went down early in the morning to get the newspaper, never doubting that the amazing adventure would occupy a considerable amount of the space usually given up to such drivelling subjects as meetings of the Supreme Council and silly and incomprehensible speeches by the Prime Minister. She had in her mind's eye seen such great head-lines as "Marquis Rescues Beautiful Shop-Lady from Brutal Attack," for Miss Farland had no illusions about her own charms.

And there was no mention of the matter—not so much as a paragraph!

"I expect he kept it out of the papers," she said at the 8.30 rush breakfast. "Naturally, he wouldn't be mixed up in a scandal, and probably he didn't want my name mentioned. He's awfully genteel! The way he took off his hat to me was a fair treat!"

"You'll be a marchioness one of these days, Millie," said an impertinent apprentice, and Miss Farland, who ranked as a "senior," scorned to answer the lowly girl.

To a buyer, a lady who, by virtue of her high position, occupied a room to herself (apprentices sleep four in a room, "seniors" two), she admitted that she had felt a queer flutter at her heart when his lordship had looked at her.

"I suppose we shall be seeing you in court again," said the buyer—"breach of promise and all that sort of thing."

Miss Farland thought it was unlikely. She and his lordship were just friends. Only that, and no more. Still, the prospect of standing in a witness-box and having her dress described and her coming in and going out photographed by a sensation-loving press, did not altogether displease her.

And then she received a letter from Chick. It was signed in his sprawling hand "Pelborough," and she was thrilled.

Before the day was over every member of the staff, from the engaging- manager to the meanest member of the outside staff, knew that she was invited to tea next Sunday, and that Lord Pelborough hoped that she was no worse for her alarming experience, and that he thought the weather was very changeable, and that he was "hers sincerely."

"That's what I liked about him—his sincerity," said Miss Farland to her assembled friends. "A man like that couldn't tell a lie. That's the wonderful thing about real gentlemen—they are always sincere."

So she went to tea, and Gwenda was very nice, but very disconcerting, because Miss Farland's first impression was that Gwenda was his lordship's young lady. As to Chick, he was his simple, friendly self, and discussed such matters as the weather and the Cup Tie Final (she was interested in neither subject) with the greatest freedom.

Presently she overcame her shyness and dispensed with the irritating little cough which prefixed her every sentence. She even addressed Chick by that name. Chick went red and choked over his tea, but he liked it. Gwenda neither went red nor choked, but she hated it.

It took away from the sweetness of the word and, on the lips of the girl, turned an endearing nickname into a piece of familiarity.

Chick saw her home.

"You will write to me, won't you, Chick?" Millie Farland had the prettiest pout imaginable. She had tried every one before her mirror, and this she now wore was undoubtedly super excellent.

"Write?" said the astonished Chick. "Oh—er—yes, of course I'll write—er—yes. What shall I write about?"

"I want to know how you are, of course. Chick," she said, playing with the top button of his coat.

"Is it loose?" asked Chick, interested.

"Of course it isn't, you silly boy," she laughed. "But you will write, won't you? I'm so lonely here, and you've no idea how happy I've been today—with you," she added, looking up shyly.

Chick had seen that slow uplift of fringed eyelid in a score of cinema plays, and yet he did not recognize it. She also had seen the movement and many others. The educative value of the cinema is not properly appreciated by outsiders.

"What did you think of her?" he asked, as soon as he got back to the fiat.

"A very, very pretty little girl," said Gwenda.

"Isn't she?" echoed Chick. "Poor little soul, she is so lonely, too. She loved being here—she asked me to write to her," he added.

Gwenda walked to the window and looked out. "It has started to rain," she said.

"I know," said Chick. "It was raining when I came in. What can I write to her about, Gwenda?"

She turned from the window and smiled.

"What a question, Chick!" she said, walking from the room.

"But really—"

"Write to her about oil," said Gwenda at the door, "and about boxing, but don't write to her about yourself or herself, Chick. That's the advice of—of an old married woman."

"Gosh!" said Chick. "But suppose she isn't interested in oil?"

But Gwenda had gone.

He tried the next day to write a letter, but discovered the limitations of correspondence with one whose tastes and interests were a mystery to him. Fortunately, Miss Farland saved him a great deal of trouble by writing.

She spelt a trifle erratically, and was prone to underline. Also she had acquired the habit of employing the note of admiration wherever it was possible. She had enjoyed herself immensely! She hoped he hadn't got wet! And wondered if he thought of her last night! She wanted to ask him a favour! She knew it was cheek! But she felt she must open her heart to him! A gentleman wanted to marry her! But she did not love him! Could marriage be happy without love? And so forth, over eight pages.

Gwenda saw him frowning over the letter, and wondered.

It was a little ominous, she thought, that Chick did not communicate any more of the letter than that it was from "Miss Farland."

The truth was, Chick felt that he was the recipient of a great confidence, and bound by honour to say no more about the girl's dilemma than was necessary. For Chick took these matters very seriously. He had a very great respect for all women, and, being something of an idealist, the thought that this pretty child might be hurried into matrimony with a man she did not love both depressed and horrified him.

Therefore, in the quietness of his room, he wrote, and found writing in these circumstances so easy an exercise that he had written twelve pages before he realized he had begun. And Chick's letter was about love and happiness, and the folly of marrying where love was not. He found he could enlarge upon this subject, and drew from within himself a philosophy of love which amazed him. There was one passage in his letter which ran:

"The social or financial position of a man is immaterial. It does not matter whether I am a marquis or a dustman. It does not matter whether you work for your living or you are a lady moving in the highest social circles: If you love me and I love you, nothing else matters."

He posted the bulky envelope, satisfied in his mind that he had set one pair of feet on the right way. He was staggered the next morning to receive a reply to his letter, although it could have been delivered only the previous night, and this time Miss Farland wrote seventeen pages. Chick's letter had been so helpful! She had never met a man who understood women as well as he did! On the seventeenth page was a postscript. Would Chick meet her that night, at half-past eight o'clock, near the big statue in the Park?

Chick kept the appointment and found her charmingly flustered. There was no necessity for him to take her arm as they walked up one of the deserted paths. She saved him the trouble by taking his. Curiously enough, she made not the slightest reference to the gentleman who desired to lure her into a loveless marriage. She talked mostly about herself and what the other girls at the shop thought of her. She admitted that she was a little superior to the position she held, and spoke of her father, who was an officer in the Army, and her mother, who was the daughter of a rural dean.

"A dean who preaches in the country, you know," she explained.

He escorted her back to Oxford Street. She reached her dwelling up a side-street which was never thickly populated, even in the busiest part of the day, and she stopped midway between two lamp-posts to say "Good night."

"You'll see me again, won't you?" she asked plaintively. "You don't know what a comfort your letters are to me."

And then she put up her red and inviting lips to his, and Chick kissed her. He had not either the intention or the desire, but there was the pretty upturned face with the scarlet lips within a few inches of his, and Chick kissed her.

When Gwenda returned home that night, Chick was waiting up for her—a very solemn-faced Chick, who did not meet her eye.

"Gwenda," he said a little huskily, "I want to speak to you before you go to bed."

Her heart went cold. She knew that Chick had gone to meet the girl. She had seen the voluminous correspondence which had passed, and she was afraid. She was determined, too. Chick should not sacrifice his future, his whole career, through the mad infatuation of a moment.

"What is it, Chick?" she asked, sitting down, her hands folded on the table before her.

"I'm afraid I've behaved rather badly," said Chick, still looking down.

"To whom?" asked Gwenda faintly. There was no need to ask the question at all.

"To Miss Farland," said Chick.

"Look at me. Chick!" Gwenda's voice was imperative. He raised his eyes to hers. "When you say you have behaved rather badly, what do you mean? Have you promised to—to marry her?"

His look of astonishment lifted a heavy weight from her heart.

"To marry her?" he said incredulously. "Of course not. I kissed her, that's all."

She was smiling, but there were tears in her eyes.

"You silly boy," she said softly. "You gave me a fright. Tell me about it, Chick."

He was loath to put the incident into words, and felt he was being disloyal to one whom he described as "this innocent child," but Gwenda's leading questions brought out the story bit by bit. She was serious when he told her of the letter he had written, though Chick could see nothing in that.

What was the letter about?"

"Well, it was mostly about love," said Chick calmly. "You see, dear, this poor child—"

Gwenda raised her eyes for a second.

"—has had an offer of marriage from a man who, I think, must be very wealthy, from what she tells me. Unfortunately, she doesn't like him a little bit, and she wrote to ask me what she should do."

"And did you tell her, Chick?" said Gwenda. "I suppose you haven't a copy of your letter?"

He shook his head, and she sighed.

"Well, perhaps there was nothing in it," she said. "What are you going to do, Chick?"

"I think I'd better write to her, when she writes again, and tell her that I can't see her," said Chick. "I don't want to hurt the poor girl's feelings, but at the same time I don't want to give her the impression that I'm fond of her. Of course I am fond of her," he added; "she's such a pretty little thing, and so lonely."

His resolution not to answer any more of her letters was shaken when she wrote, as she did the next day, an epistle which occupied both sides of fourteen sheets of large bank paper.

What had she done to offend him? She had trusted him! What had come between them?

"Don't answer it. Chick," warned the girl. And Chick groaned.

This letter was followed by others—some frantic, some pleading, some bearing pointed hints to the Serpentine and hoping he would never forget the poor girl who had loved him unto death!

"It's worse than the letters from the shareholders," groaned poor Chick. "Really, I think I ought to answer this one and tell her that I'm—"

"Unless I'm greatly mistaken," said Gwenda, "you'll have a letter to answer before the next week is over."

And sure enough, on the following Saturday morning came a typed epistle from Messrs. Bennett and Reeves, who were, amongst other things, according to the note-head, commissioners of oaths.

They had been instructed by their client, Miss Amelia Farland, to demand from the noble lord whether he intended fulfilling his promise of marriage to their client, and, if he did not so intend, would he supply them with the name of his solicitors?

Poor Chick, a crushed and pallid figure, collapsed into his chair, and Gwenda took the letter from his hand. There were many eminent firms of lawyers who would act for Chick, but she knew a theatrical solicitor, a shrewd man of business, who kept a watchful eye upon the affairs of Mr. Solburg, and to him she carried the letter and gave as near as possible an account of the relationship between Chick and the girl.

"Bennett and Reeves," he mused, as he read the letter. "They take on that kind of work. I'll write them a little note. I don't think your Marquis will be troubled with this action."

Some time after, Miss Millie Farland entered the offices of her solicitors, wearing just that expression of silent suffering which would have photographed so well had there been any photographers waiting in Bedford Row to snap her.

Mr. Bennett received her with every evidence of cordiality,

"About this action, Miss Farland," he said. "They are going to fight the case, and they have briefed Sir John Mason. But do you want this case to go into court? Because, if you do, it is my opinion that you haven't a leg to stand on. I've been making independent inquiries, and it seems that Lord Pelborough did nothing more than rescue you from a former lover of yours,"

"You have his letter," said Miss Farland severely.

"Callow essays on love and marriage," said Mr. Bennett contemptuously, "Now let us get down to business. Before we can go any farther in this action you must deposit an amount sufficient to cover the costs. That will be, let us say, two thousand pounds,"

Miss Farland rose. Afterwards, describing her action, she said that the man quailed under her glance.

"I see," she said bitterly, "there is one law for the rich and another for the poor."

"It is the same law," explained Mr. Bennett, "The only difference is that the poor pay in advance, and the rich pay afterwards."

Miss Farland, addressing a meeting of her sympathizers on Number One landing that night, expressed her determination to go through with the matter to the bitter end. Happily she was spared that ordeal, for an evening or two later, whilst she was strolling with a friend by the side of that very Serpentine in which she had hinted her young life might be blotted out, a small boy bather got into difficulties—and Miss Farland could swim.

The breakfast-room at Belham and Sapworth's crowded round her as she read the paper in the morning, and feasted their eyes upon a larger headline than she had ever received: "Pretty Girl's Gallant Rescue in the Serpentine. Modest Heroine Refuses to Give her Name until the Police Compelled Her."

Miss Farland drew a happy sigh.

X

COURAGE

The beauty of Monte Carlo has no exact parallel unless it be the beauty of the Cape Peninsula in the early spring.

The Marquis of Pelborough had never dreamt of such loveliness as he saw from his bedroom window at the "Hotel de Paris."

The days were sunny, and cool breezes tempered the heat of May. The season was over; many of the villas that dotted the hill-side were tenantless, and the more fashionable of the restaurants were shut. Nevertheless, though a few tables had been closed, the Casino was largely patronized, and Chick had been a fascinated spectator of play in which thousands of pounds had changed hands with every turn of the cards.

Gwenda was "resting"; a sore throat and a mild attack of influenza, which had given Chick the first clear understanding of what she meant to him, had compelled her to stop work. The hint which the doctor had thrown out about a more equable climate than that of Doughty Street, Bloomsbury, had been seized upon by Chick.

"Like where, doctor?" he asked.

"Oh—er—the South of France, or Torquay," said the man of medicines, who invariably offered these alternatives and left his patients to choose that which was most convenient to their pockets. Gwenda was all for Torquay; Mrs. Phibbs, who had never been farther abroad than Brussels, supported her as in duty bound, and prayed that Chick would not assent. He neither agreed nor disagreed. One evening he came into the flat and laid a bulging pocket-case on the table.

"I have arranged the passports and the tickets for Monte Carlo," he said masterfully. "The sleeping berths are reserved from Calais, and we leave on Sunday morning."

Gwenda was too weak to argue. Illness is a great disturber of sleeping routine. Gwenda had dozed through the days and had spent many wakeful and thoughtful hours in the night.

She had been weak with Chick, postponing the inevitable parting from sheer selfishness, she thought. Chick could stand alone now. Was there any time when he could not? Her mind went back to the days when they were fellow-sufferers at a Brockley boarding-house, she an out-of-work actress, he an insurance clerk without the faintest idea that his uncle's petitions to Parliament, that the ancient Marquisate of Pelborough should be revived, would be granted. And then suddenly the title had been revived and inherited by Chick, and she had taken in hand the management of his life.

But had he ever been helpless? She shook her aching head. Chick was surprisingly efficient. She was deluding herself when she thought she was necessary to him, and the association must end. She was firm on that point. Chick was a comparatively rich man now, and it was absurd that he should share humble quarters with the two women who loved him.

Gwenda's brow puckered.

Mrs. Phibbs had been housekeeper, friend and chaperon, and she adored Chick.

Gwenda loved him, too, but not as Mrs. Phibbs loved him. That lady's attitude was maternal; her interest in the young marquis was centred about his socks and underwear and the state of his digestion. But Gwenda loved him in another way. She deceived herself and yet saw through the deception. She accepted Chick's fait accompli meekly. It was a further excuse for postponing her decision.

She was enchanted with the glories of the Riviera, although she saw it when the spring sweetness of the coast had matured into the exotic glories with which the early summer endows the gardens and terraces of Monte Carlo.

To walk in the garden that faces the Casino, or to sit beneath the wide-spreading fronds of palms, watching the play of the water as the gardener drenched the thirsty ground with his huge hose, to stroll along the terraces facing the blue Mediterranean, or to sit in the cool of the hotel lounge with its luxurious inviting chairs—these experiences were sheer delight. And Chick had hired a motor-car, and they had climbed the mountain road to La Turbie, and explored the ruins of the great tower which Augustus in his pride had caused to rise on the mountain crest.

Gwenda's health showed a remarkable improvement from the moment she arrived. Before a week had passed she felt better than she had ever felt in her life. And with her return to strength she took a more cheerful view of life, and there seemed no urgent necessity for having that talk with Chick.

"I'm going into the gambling place," said Chick one afternoon.

"You mean the Rooms, Chick," said Gwenda. "You mustn't say 'gambling' at Monte Carlo."

Chick scratched his head.

"There are so many things you mustn't do here, Gwenda," he said. "You mustn't wish a man good luck because it brings him bad luck, and you mustn't enter the gam—the Rooms, I mean, with the left foot, and if you spill wine at the table you must dab a little behind your ears. It sounds like superstition to me."

"It probably is," laughed Gwenda, "And, talking of superstition, I am going to put my money on No. 24, because it is my birthday!"

Chick was incoherent in his apologies.

"How could you know that it was my birthday?" she smiled, putting her cool palm over his mouth. "Don't be silly?"

She had an exciting afternoon, for No. 24 turned up exactly twenty-four times in two hours.

"And I've won twenty-four thousand francs," she said triumphantly. "I'm a rich woman, Chick, and I'm going to pay you back all I have cost you on this trip."

Chick's refusal was almost painful in its frenzied vehemence.

For him it was a happy day. The chef at the "Paris," who was surprised at nothing, received and executed an urgent order to manufacture a birthday cake, and the dinner was served in their private sitting-room.

The cake, surrounded by twenty-four bedroom candles—there were no others procurable at short notice—was a success beyond anticipation, and Chick's heart had been full of happiness and pride, when there had entered to the feast a most undesirable skeleton.

He was a plump, cherubic skeleton, and Chick, after his first feeling of resentment, felt heartily ashamed of himself, for he owed a great deal to the Earl of Mansar.

He was, at any rate, as much of a skeleton to Gwenda, but this Chick did not know. He had only arrived that afternoon, he explained.

"I heard you were dining en famille, and as I regard myself as one of you, I knew you wouldn't mind my coming in."

It pained Chick to say he was glad to see his visitor, but he said it.

"No, thank you," said Lord Mansar in answer to Gwenda's invitation. "I have dined already. What is the occasion of this festivity? Not your birthday. Chick?"

"It is not my birthday," said Chick quietly, "but Mrs. Maynard's."

It was strange, he thought, how a nice man like Mansar could cast a gloom over his friends and rob a festivity of its seemingly inextinguishable gaiety. They had planned to spend the evening together, but the arrival of their guest left them no alternative but to repair to the inevitable Rooms.

Chick hated the way Mansar and the girl paired off, leaving him to entertain Mrs. Phibbs, which meant leaving him alone, for she had developed a passion for gambling in five-franc pieces. He left that imposing lady at the roulette table and wandered aimlessly into the cercle privee in the trail of Gwenda and her escort.

The rich interior of the private club has a soothing effect upon disturbed nerves, but it failed signally to inspire Chick. Mansar found a chair for the girl at the trente-et-quarante table, and Chick stood on the outskirts of the crowd, his hands thrust into his pockets, a look of settled gloom upon his face, watching the swift passage of money and counters, and admiring, so far as it was possible for him to admire anything, the amazing dexterity of the black-coated croupier who turned the cards.

He loafed into the refreshment-room, ordered a large orangeade (nobody knows the exquisite value of orangeade until he has drunk it at Monte Carlo), and, sitting in an arm-chair, he allowed himself to brood. Of course he had no right whatever to object to Gwenda's friendship, he told himself, and least of all to her friendship with a man who had not spared himself in securing Chick's advancement.

What distressed him more than anything else was the fact that Gwenda was married, and it was not like Gwenda to encourage the attention of a third party. Chick had a very keen sense of propriety. He was fundamentally good, not in the cant sense in which the word is so often employed, but in the greater essentials. His standard of behaviour was a high one, and the blue of Right and the scarlet of Wrong never merged to produce an admirable violet in his mind. The longer he sat, the deeper grew his gloom, and presently, rising with a jerk, he went to the bar.

"Give me a cocktail, please," he said firmly. He had never done more than put his lips to wine in his life, and he had the illusion that the barman knew this.

But his request created no sensation. There was a great shaking of metal bottles, a dribbling of amber fluid into a long-stemmed glass, the plunge of a cherry, and—

"Five francs," said the bar-keeper.

Chick swallowed something and paid. He held the liquor up to the light, and it seemed good. He smelt it and appreciated its bouquet. He swallowed it down with one gulp and held on to the brass-fender before the bar, incapable of speech. For a second he stopped breathing, and then the fire of the unaccustomed potion began to radiate.

"Another," said Chick when he had got his breath. This time he sipped the alluring preparation and found it excellent. The sting had gone from the fiery liquor. It had a queerly soothing effect which it was difficult to analyse. His ears felt hot. His face seemed to be burning. He could see his reflection in the mirror behind the bar, and outwardly there was no apparent change. He was surprised. "That is a nice cocktail, sir," said the barman.

Chick nodded.

"Personally, I prefer Clover Club," said the friendly man, wiping down the counter mechanically.

"Is there any other kind of cocktail?" asked Chick in astonishment.

"Good gracious, yes, sir—there are twenty!"

"What was the name of that one you said?"

"Clover Club, sir."

"Gimme one," said Chick breathlessly.

The new cocktail was of a delicate shade of clouded pink, and frothed whitely on the top. Chick decided that he would drink nothing but Clover Club cocktails in the future.

He leant against the bar, because it seemed easier than standing. It was remarkable how genial he felt toward Mansar, how large and generous was his view of his forthcoming marriage to Gwenda. He had decided that they would be married at a very early date, and chuckled at the thought. He knew that Gwenda had to get rid of her husband somehow or other, but he could not be bothered to dispose of that encumbrance in detail. He would just vanish. Pouf! Like that. Chick laughed at the smiling bartender.

"Something I thought about," he said.

"I don't think I should have any more cocktails, if I were you, sir," said the bar-tender. "The room is rather hot, and our cocktails are pretty strong."

"That's all right," said Chick.

He planked down a five-franc piece with unnecessary violence and walked steadily back to the Rooms, and the bar-keeper, looking after him, shook his head.

"He can carry it like a gentleman," he said admiringly.

Chick could walk so well that when he came up with Gwenda, who had left the table, she saw nothing wrong in his appearance. She was more than a little agitated, but Chick did not notice this. He noticed nothing except the eccentric movements of the tables, which, for some unknown reason, were swaying gently up and down as though they were floating upon a tempestuous ocean.

"Chick, I want to speak to you very importantly," said the girl.

She took his arm, and they walked out of the Casino together. Even when they were back in their sitting-room she noticed nothing.

"If Lord Mansar doesn't leave Monte Carlo tomorrow, can we go away, Chick?" she asked.

"Certainly, Gwenda," said Chick, looking at her solemnly.

"You see. Chick "—she was not looking at him—"Lord Mansar rather likes me and I like him; but I can't marry—you know that. And I wouldn't marry if I could. You know that, don't you, Chick?"

She raised her eyes to Chick, and he nodded.

"What is the matter. Chick?" she asked.

"Nothing," said Chick loudly.

"Chick," she said, aghast, "you've been drinking!"

"Cocktails!" said Chick impressively. "Clover Club. Not really drunk!"

"Why ever did you do it, Chick?" she wailed, tears in her eyes.

"Miserable" said Chick dolefully. "Very miserable, Gwenda. When you and Mansar get married—bless you!"

He rose, and the sure foundation of his legs held him erect.

"A very good fellow, Mansar," he said, and walked carefully to the door.

Before he could open it, Gwenda had reached him. She dropped her hands upon his shoulders.

"Look at me. Chick," she said. "Do you think I should marry Lord Mansar?"

"Very nice fellow," murmured Chick.

"Look at me. Chick. Hold up your head. Is that why you drank?"

"Cocktails are not drink," corrected Chick gravely.

She drew a long breath.

"Go to bed, Chick," she said gently. "I never thought I should be glad to see you like this, but I am."

The Marquis of Pelborough did not wake in the morning. He emerged from a condition of painful half-consciousness to a state of even more painful half-deadliness, and the half of him which was dead was the happier.

To say that his head ached would be to misdescribe his sensations. There was a tremendous ache where his head had been, and his eyelids seemed to creak when he opened them. Slowly and cautiously he rose to a sitting position. As he moved, his brain seemed to be a flag that was flapping in the breeze. He sat up and looked around. By the side of his bed was a large bottle of mineral water and a glass. There were also two large lemons which had been cut in half. Moreover, he discovered, when he had quenched his raging thirst and the acid bite of the lemon had restored his sense of taste, that his bath was filled with ice-cold water.

Chick dropped into the bath with a splash and a shiver, turned on the shower, and emerged a few minutes later feeling as near to normal as a thumping, thundering heart would allow him to be. He dressed slowly, facing a very unpleasant situation. He had been drunk. There was no euphemism for his experience. He faced the ghastly fact in the cold light of morning without any illusion whatever.

His first sensation was one of surprise that he had accomplished the feat at the cost of twenty francs. He always thought that drunkenness was most expensive. When he had recovered from his surprise, his mind went with a jerk to Gwenda, and he groaned. He remembered having come back to the hotel with her. Had she cut the lemons for him? He shuddered at the thought. It was six o'clock, and, save for the street cleaners, the serene swish of whose brooms came to him, Monte Carlo was a town of the dead. He stepped out on the balcony and filled his lungs with the fresh morning air.

What would Gwenda think of him? He remembered enough to know that he had not made a fool of himself, but it were better that he were the laughing-stock of Monte Carlo and of all the world than that he should have disappointed Gwenda.

"Terrible," murmured Chick, "terrible!"

He shook his head, whence the pain had gone, leaving only a queer sawdust sensation.

A brisk walk toward Cap Martin and back almost completed his cure. Gwenda was at breakfast with Mrs. Phibbs when he went into the sitting-room, and she greeted him with her old smile.

"I'm dreadfully sorry, Gwenda—" he began, but she stopped him.

"It was the heat of the room," said Mrs. Phibbs.

Gwenda turned the conversation in the direction of sea-bathing, and Chick knew that her comments on his behaviour were merely deferred. They proved to be less severe than he had expected.

"I'll never drink again, Gwenda," he said ruefully, and she squeezed the arm that was in hers.

"Chick, this is a very favourable moment for a talk I want with you," she said, as she led the way down the sloping road toward the beach and the bathing huts. "When we get back to London you must set up an establishment of your own. No, no, it has nothing to do with what happened last night," she said, answering his unspoken question. "But Chick, you can't go on living like this, with Mrs. Phibbs and me. You realize that yourself, don't you?"

"No," said Chick doggedly. "Of course, if..."—he hesitated—"if you are changing—I mean if you are—" He stopped, at a loss for the right words. "I mean, Gwenda," he said bluntly, "if you are setting up an establishment of your own—why, of course, I understand."

She shook her head.

"I'm not, Chick," she said quietly.

"Then I'm going to stay with you," said Chick, "until—"

"Until when?" she asked, when he paused.

"I don't know," said Chick, shaking his head. "I wish I could ask you lots of questions." He bit his lip, looking thoughtfully at the white road at his feet. "Gwenda, you never talk about your husband."

"No, Chick, I never shall," she answered, avoiding his eye.

"Is he nice, Gwenda?"

She made no reply.

"Do you like him?"

She put her arm in his and urged him forward.

"Wait a moment." Chick disengaged himself gently. "Does Lord Mansar know anything about him?"

"He asked the same questions as you, Chick." she said, "and I gave him the same reply. That is why he has gone home."

"Gosh!" said Chick, awe-stricken. "Did Lord Mansar—has he—?"

"Did he want me to marry him, Chick? Yes, he did. And I told him I couldn't and wouldn't."

He gazed at her with his solemn eyes, and then: "Have you any children, Gwenda?"

This was too much for the girl. Her sense of humour was not proof against a question which had been asked of her twice within twenty-four hours, and she burst into a fit of uncontrollable laughter.

Presently she dried her eyes.

"Have you?" he asked again.

"Six," she said solemnly.

"I don't believe you," said Chick.

He wanted to say something, and for once his will failed him. Twice in the course of their stroll he began with a husky "Gwenda!", only to be tongue-tied.

They sat on the sands and watched a big white yacht with all its main-sheet and spinnaker billowing whitely, a dazzling object in the sunlight, and there was a silence between them which was unusual.

Presently Chick asked:

"Gwenda, will you let me see your wedding ring?"

She hesitated.

"Why do you want to see it, Chick?"

"I just want to see it" said Chick, with an assumption of carelessness. She slipped the golden circlet from her finger and put it in the palm of his hand.

There was some writing engraved on the inside.

"May I?" he asked, and again she hesitated.

"Yes, Chick," she said.

The inscription was: "From T. L. M. to J. M."

The letters showed faintly, for the ring had been well worn, and Chick gave it back to her.

"What is your full name, Gwenda?" he asked, and thinking she had not heard him he repeated the question.

"Gwenda Dorothy Maynard," she said.

"But, Gwenda, your brother's name was Maynard, too."

She did not reply. Chick was breathing painfully. He found it almost impossible to keep the quiver from his voice when he spoke, and the nervous hands that played with the sand were trembling.

"Gwenda—" he began for the third time, but he could not say it.

He knew her secret. That was the thought that filled him with joy, Gwenda was not married! The ring was her mother's. And then he remembered that once she had said that a girl on the stage was in a stronger position if people thought she was married and had a man at her call.

He trod on air for the rest of the day, and his heart was singing gaily. And yet, when he tried to speak, his vocal chords seemed to become paralysed. The high confidence which brought him to the edge of confession deserted him basely and left him an abject, stammering fool.

The girl saw and understood. If she had not she might have made it easier for Chick to loose the flow of his inhibited speech.

They were in the Rooms that night, Gwenda mildly punting in louis, Mrs. Phibbs, a determined female, flanked by two large columns of five-franc counters.

And then Chick had an inspiration. The course he had elected was a desperate one, but the situation was as desperate.

He drew the girl aside.

"Gwenda, will you go up to the sitting-room in half an hour. There is something I want you to know—it may shock you, Gwenda."

She nodded gravely and went back to the table. Chick waited to see whether she was watching him, and then stole stealthily into the refreshment-room.

"Good evening, sir," said the barman

"A Clover Club," hissed Chick, cutting short the pleasantries of the tender—"in fact, two Clover Clubs, please."

He swallowed them hastily, and they seemed to have no effect. He was dumbfounded. Had he so soon acquired the constitution of the seasoned drinker? He was on the point of ordering the third, when he experienced the beginnings of that genial glow and sat down to wait for its full effect. He walked past Gwenda, apparently not noticing her, strode over to the hotel and went up in the lift to his room. He was feeling good and as brave as a lion.

Chick's courage had never been called into question. He was a notorious glutton for punishment, but then Chick had never had the terrifying experience which now awaited him.

"Gwenda," he said, addressing a great dish of violets which occupied the centre of the table, "there is something I wish to ask you."

He felt so confident that he wished she would come in at that moment; but there were still ten minutes before the half-hour expired, and he must content himself with the violets.

"Gwenda," he said, "there is something I have been trying to tell you. I know you are not married, and I know that I am not the kind of fellow that you ought to marry."

This didn't seem quite right, and he started again.

"Gwenda, I've been trying to say something to you all day, and I'm sorry to say I've been compelled to drink two cocktails in order to work up my courage, so please don't let me kiss you!"

She was a long time coming, and he felt unaccountably tired. He strayed into his dark bedroom and lay on the bed.

"Gwenda," he murmured, "I know I'm a rascal to break my word—but, Gwenda—"

He woke up when the chambermaid brought the tea. She was so accustomed to meeting, in the course of her professional duties, gentlemen who were such sticklers for style that they went to bed in evening-dress, that she made no comment.

When Chick had changed and dressed, he went in to breakfast, and Gwenda's attitude was just a little distrait.

Chick drew out his chair and sat down.

"I broke my word to you last night, Gwenda," he said huskily. "I told you—"

"You told me that there was something you wanted me to know, and that it would shock me. Chick," she said, as she poured out his coffee. "Well, I know, and I'm shocked."

"What do you know, Gwenda?" he asked, startled.

"That you snore frightfully," said Gwenda coldly.

The silence that followed was chilling.

"I'm going home to-morrow," said the girl.

Chick wriggled in his chair.

"You broke your word to me about—about the bar," she said with a catch in her voice.

"Did you see me?" he asked, conscience-stricken.

And she nodded.

"But—but why didn't you stop me?" he stammered.

She shot a glance at him that made Chick wither.

"I didn't dream it would make you sleep, you booby," she said scornfully.

XI

THE MAN FROM TOULOUSE

When Jagg Flower was finishing his sentence in the prison at Toulouse, the authorities allowed him certain books wherewith to improve his mind and direct him to the higher life. One such book he remembers well. It opened thus:

"Il y avait une fois vingt-cinq soldats de plomb, tous frères, tous nés d'une vieille cuillère de plomb. L'arme au bras, la tête droite, leur uniforme rouge et bleu n'était pas mal du tout."

"This," said Jagg Flower, as he flung the improving book from one end of the cell to the other, "is what makes prison life in France so immensely unpopular with the educated classes." Which was duly reported to the governor.

Because Jagg was on the point of release, that official, who had a kindly feeling for the long-faced bank robber, sent him one evening a bundle of English and American newspapers.

"But this," said Jagg, as he opened the Paris edition of The New York Herald, "is both human and luxurious. Regard you, François! Present to Mister the Governor my felicitations and the renewal of my profound respect."

François, the jailer, grinned admiringly.

On the second day of his reading John Jalgar Flower reached a paragraph in a London newspaper which made him sit up.

"Kenberry House, which at one time ranked with the stately homes of England, has been acquired by the Marquis of Pelborough, with whose romantic career our readers are familiar. A year ago the Marquis was an insurance clerk in a City office. His uncle, Dr. Josephus Beane, of Pelborough, laid claim to the peerage, which had been extinct since 1714, his claim being admitted and the title revived in his favour. It was a melancholy coincidence that the doctor died on the very day he received a notification that the peerage had been revived in his favour. The present Marquis, being the only relative in the tail male—"

"Great snakes!" breathed Mr. Flower. He occupied the remainder of his sentence developing an idea.

Whatever pretensions Kenberry House had to stateliness had long since vanished. It was one of those residences for which fire had a fatal attraction. Its history was a history of successive conflagrations, and every time it had been rebuilt a little smaller, a little less stately, so that the battlemented towers and the grim big gate with its portcullis, which had impressed the peasantry of the Tudor era, had been replaced by chimney-pots and a very ordinary front door. Kenberry House was now too big to describe as a villa and too small to justify the description of mansion.

But the grounds, those glorious sloping meadowlands that ran down to the bubbling Ken, the old gardens and the ancient elms, remained very much as they had been when Queen Elizabeth, with her passion for sleeping at other people's houses, had rested a night on her way to Fotheringay.

Gwenda had read the description of the place in a newspaper advertisement, and had gone down one Sunday, on her return from the South of France, to inspect the property. She was enchanted. The house was just big enough for Chick. The price which was asked was absurdly small: the property, on the whole, was in a state of good repair.

This was especially the case with the house itself, and it was due to the excellent condition of the paintwork and the interior decorations generally that the Marquis of Pelborough found himself hustled out of London and into his newly-furnished country seat before he quite realized what was happening.

That he was profoundly miserable goes without saying. Not even the arrangement which gave him Mrs. Phibbs to organize his household compensated for the violent disruption of his pleasant life in Doughty Street. He would lose Gwenda, who had been mother and manager to him, for she was to take a room in the flat below. Such of the furniture as was worthy of transference to the stately home was sent down by rail; the remainder was sold.

Chick had a feeling that he was being abandoned, and dare not let himself think of what life would be without daily association with Gwenda Maynard. He could not deny the beauty of his new situation, the quiet and restfulness of his demesne, nor was he wholly unimpressed by the discovery that he was the employer of four gardeners, a groom and a cowman. He was also over-landlord of two farms, and learnt with interest that, by the terms of an ancient charter granted by the fourth Henry, he might, if he were so disposed, hang, on a gallows which he must erect at his own expense, any "cut-throat, cut-purse, or stealer of deer" from Morton Highgate to Down Wood, these marking the limitations of his sovereignty. The only bright spot in the situation was that, the run of her play having ended, Gwenda was free to spend a fortnight as his guest.

"But only a fortnight, Chick. I can't and won't live on your charity."

"It will be dreadful when you are gone, Gwenda," he said plaintively. "Every day something new is turning up. I had a letter from uncle's lawyers this morning, asking me for some leases he signed. He owned a tiny piece of land outside Pelborough, and there's a law case pending about the present rights of the tenant."

"But you haven't any of your uncle's documents, have you?" she asked in surprise.

Chick nodded.

"There's a huge boxful," he said, a ray of hope shining amidst the darkness of his desolation. "Suppose, Gwenda, you stay down here and help me tabulate the papers? I've never touched them, and this is the second time the lawyers have written."

He explained that when his uncle had died, and he had disposed of his property, he had found a trunkful of letters and memoranda mostly dealing with old Dr. Beane's claim to the peerage of Pelborough, and these had been supplemented by another mass which he had found in the doctor's desk and in his old safe.

"I've always meant to sort them out and classify them," he said penitently, "but I was depending upon your assistance, Gwenda."

"I'll help you," said the girl, with a twinkle in her eye, "but it will not take more than a fortnight, Chick, and then—"

"Let's be cheerful," said Chick, brightening up. "We'll start on those papers next Monday."

"We'll start this morning," said the girl, but here Chick struck.

He had not fully explored his property, and he insisted that that day should be devoted to the purpose. She accompanied him on a tour, and it was a day of sheer delight.

They sat under the overhanging alders by the side of the little river which formed one of the boundaries of his property, and then Chick had to go back to the house for a new fishing-rod he had bought, and another two hours went whilst they fixed the tackle and taught one another to cast a fly. It was a case of the blind leading the blind, but they landed one speckled beauty late in the afternoon, and Kenberry House assumed a new importance to Chick in consequence.

"Don't go, Gwenda," he said as she got up.

"It is late. Chick," she warned him, "and we've had no tea."

"I know," said Chick. "Just sit down a minute, Gwenda. There was something I wanted to say to you at Monte Carlo."

"Don't say it, Chick," she said quietly.

She was standing over him, and her hand strayed to his untidy hair.

"But, Gwenda—"

"I know what you were going to tell me, Chick, and I did my best to encourage you to say it," she said. "I was shameless then, but I have been ashamed since. I was just fishing for you. Chick, as you fished for the trout. Oh, I must have been mad!"

He was on his feet now and had dropped his rod, but before he could speak she stopped him.

"We've had a lovely time, you and I, Chick," she said quietly, "a beautiful, ideal time, and we are not going to spoil it. You are little more than a boy—I know you're older than I am, but girls are ever so much older than men of their age—and you have a big future. You must marry in your own class, Chick."

He made a protesting noise.

"I know it sounds hard and horrid and noveletty, but really behind these class marriages there is unanswerable logic. If I married you, what would the world say of me? That I had taken you in hand from the moment you inherited your title and had kept you so close to me that you never had a chance of meeting a nice girl. I don't care very much what they think of me; it's what they think of you that matters. You would be regarded as a helpless fool who had succumbed to the artfulness of a designing actress."

She shook her head, but avoided meeting his eyes.

"No, that little dream is ended, Chick. If I loved you even more than I do, and I don't think that is possible "—her voice shook for a second—"I could never agree."

"But you've made me what I am," he said huskily.

"I stage-managed you, Chick," she said with a faint smile. "I produced you in the theatrical sense, and you must think of me as your impresario."

Chick stooped and picked up the rod, unscrewed it leisurely, and wound the tackle with exasperating calmness.

"All right, Gwenda," he said, and she felt a twinge of pain that he had taken his rejection so coolly.

Neither of them spoke as they trudged back to the house, to find the resigned Mrs. Phibbs sitting beside the tea-table in Chick's new drawing- room. It was a cheerless evening for the girl. She went up to her room soon after dinner, and he did not see her again that night.

Once, as he was pacing the lawn, he thought he caught a glimpse of her figure by the window of her darkened room, but when he called up, there was no answer.

For Gwenda, that night was the most tragic in her life. Deliberately she had thrust away something which was more than life itself to her. She tried to think of him as a boy, but Chick was a man, a sweet and simple man, and her senior by a year, and the realization that she was putting him out of her life was an agony almost unendurable.

Chick saw the dark shadows under her eyes at breakfast the next morning, and the knowledge that she was suffering added to his own wretchedness.

"We will start on those papers this morning, Gwenda," he said gruffly, and she nodded.

"I don't think I shall be able to help you more than today, Chick," she said. "I shall have to go back to London to-morrow."

"To-morrow?" said Chick in consternation, and then dropped his eyes. "Very well," he said.

He was only beginning to understand what the ordeal meant to her. He was being selfish, considering only his own loss. When they were alone in the pretty library which Gwenda had furnished with such care, he came straight to the point.

"My dear," he said, "if you would like to go today, I won't press you to stay."

It required an effort on his part to say this, a greater effort to restrain himself when she dropped her head and he saw that she was crying softly.

"Thank you, Chick," she said.

"There is only one question I'd like to ask, Gwenda. If it weren't for this beastly title, if we were back again at Brockley and I was working for my living, would you have said the same?"

She did not speak, and the shake of her head was so gentle that he would not have noticed it had he not been watching her so closely.

"Now let us see these wretched papers," he said. "Poor old Uncle Josephus! What a lot of trouble he has given us!"

For the most part the contents of the boxes were copies of letters and petitions addressed to Parliament. There were, too, records of the Pelboroughs, written in the doctor's minute handwriting, which traced the history of the family back to Philip Beane of Tours.

"Will you see Mr. Flower?" asked Mrs. Phibbs, coming in with a card in her hand.

"Flower?" repeated Chick, frowning. "Is he a reporter?"

A month before, when it had been announced that he had purchased Kenberry House, he had been dogged by newspaper men.

"No. I asked him that," said Mrs. Phibbs.

Chick took the card, but was no wiser, for Mr. John Jalgar Flower had modestly omitted both his profession and his address.

"All right. Show him in here. Do you mind, Gwenda?"

She shook her head.

Into the library came a smartly dressed man with a keen, intellectual face and a pair of good-humoured eyes. He bowed to the girl, then, his golden teeth showing in an expansive smile, he advanced upon Chick with an open hand.

"Lord Pelborough?"

"That is my name," said Chick. "Won't you sit down, sir?"

"A delightful place," said Mr. Flower ecstatically. "The most beautiful country I have been in. The air is invigorating, the attitude of the natives deferential and even feudalistic. And those wonderful elms along the drive, Lord Pelborough, they must be at least five hundred years old!"

"I shouldn't be surprised, sir," said Chick.

He was wondering whether the new-comer was selling mechanical pianos or electric-lighting plants. The last genial soul who had called "travelled" in the latter. There had also been three voluble visitors who had specialized in books, and would have stocked his library if he had given them the chance.

Mr, Flower looked meaningly at the lady, who he thought was Chick's secretary.

"I have a very confidential communication to make to you, my lord," he said.

Gwenda would have risen, but Chick shook his head.

"Unless it is something that a lady should not hear, you need not hesitate to tell me, sir," he said.

"It deals with a matter which is vital to you, my lord," said Mr. Flower, with proper impressiveness.

"I think I'd better go," said the girl in a low voice.

Again Chick shook his head. "Let us hear all about it, Mr. Flower," he said, leaning back in his chair patiently.

But Jagg Flower was not inclined to say what he had to say before a third person. He said as much. He did not confess that he objected to a witness, but he intimated that the subject was of so painful a character that a lady might feel embarrassed.

"Go on," said Chick shortly.

All the girl's faculties had become suddenly alert. Her instinct told her that the communication was more than ordinarily important to Chick's welfare.

"I don't think I shall be shocked, Mr. Flower," she said quietly, "but if I am I can easily go."

Jagg Flower was puzzled. He could not define the relationship between the two, knowing that the Marquis of Pelborough was not married. "Very well, then," he said after a moment's deliberation, "I will tell you."

He laid his hat on the floor and took off his gloves. "I am an adventurer of the world," he began. "In other words, I am a person whose actions have never been strictly conformable to the written law."

"Good gracious!" said Chick in alarm.

"I tell you this, Lord Pelborough," Mr. Flower went on easily, "because it is perfectly certain that, after I have made my communication, you will institute inquiries as to my character and my identity. Let me tell you that a week ago I came out of prison at Toulouse, where for three years I have been incarcerated. I was in this particular case a victim of a brutal and perjurous system, for at the hour I was supposed to be making an unauthorized entrance into the Credit Foncier, at Marseilles, I was, in point of fact, robbing an insurance company in Bordeaux. But let that pass.

"Twelve years ago. Lord Pelborough "—he leant forward and his voice was very earnest—"I was working the Middle Eastern States of America with a man who at this moment is in a United States prison "—his utterance was slow and deliberate—"and that man's name was Joseph or, as I happen to know, Josephus Beane, and he was the son of Dr. Josephus Beane of Pelborough."

Chick stared at him. "My uncle was a bachelor."

The other shook his head. "Read these," he said, and took from his pocket an envelope and tossed it on to the table.

Chick extracted two long slips. The first was a certificate of marriage between Josephus Beane, student of medicine, and Agnes Cartwright. The marriage had taken place in Liverpool, and Chick remembered dimly that his uncle had studied medicine at the Liverpool University. The second slip, which was also a copy, was a certificate of birth of "Joseph Pelborough Beane."

"My uncle never told me about his marriage," said Chick steadily.

The other smiled. "He was hardly likely to," he said dryly. "The lady he married died in an inebriates' home seven years after. The boy, as Joe has often told me, was brought up by some friends of his mother. It was one of those marriages which a young man makes in his folly. Joe grew up to hate his father, and I have reason to believe that his father returned the hatred with interest. Joe was an adventurer, but, unlike myself..."—he smiled—"a petty adventurer. He was in prison three times in England, and would have been in prison for the rest of his life, if he had not got away to America, where I met him."

"Where is he now?" asked the girl. Her heart was thumping madly, and she found difficulty in breathing.

"In Sing Sing," was the reply.

Chick did not speak for a long time, and when he did the reason for his smile was wholly misunderstood by Mr. Flower.

"So really he is the Marquis," he said.

"And you are Mr. Beane," said Flower courteously.

So far his startling news had not produced the agitation which he had expected.

"And now," he said, "I really must talk to you alone."

Chick nodded, and when the girl rose and left the room, Mr. Flower followed her, closing the door behind her.

"I am a business man. Lord Pelborough," he said, "for I will call you by that title, and you are a business man. There's nobody else in the world, except my poor friend Josephus Beane, who knows your secret."

"My secret?" said Chick, looking up.

"Well, let us say my secret," said Flower good-humouredly. "Let us get down to business. What is this worth to you?"

"I don't quite understand you," said Chick.

"I am going abroad—to Australia, let us say, I am tired of my roving life, and I wish to settle in some pleasant spot. Would ten thousand pounds be an exorbitant sum to ask?"

"I'm afraid I really don't understand you," said Chick. "Do you mean that I should give you ten thousand pounds?"

"Exactly," smiled Mr. Flower.

"For what?" asked Chick.

The man was staggered. "I thought I had made it clear to your lordship," he said gently, "that I am in a position to produce a new Marquis of Pelborough."

"Produce him," said Chick with a broad smile.

He walked slowly round the desk and came up to the man.

"Produce your Marquis of Pelborough, Mr. Flower," he said, "and I'll give you the ten thousand pounds."

Mr. Flower collapsed on to the chair, "You mean that you want to give up the title?"

"That is what I mean," said Chick.

"To give up this house, these beautiful lands?"

Chick smiled. "They are the property of Chick Beane, my friend," he said almost jovially. "No, I just want to give up the title, and I'm very grateful to you for having called. Sing Sing, I think you said?"

But the man was speechless.

"When you came I was rather annoyed," said Chick. "I thought you were selling pianos. I hope you weren't offended."

Mr. Flower shook his head helplessly.

"I can't ask you to stay to lunch," said Chick, "because "—he hesitated—"if you don't mind my saying so, it wouldn't be nice for a lady to lunch with a gentleman who has just come out of jail, would it? But there's an awfully good inn in the village, and there is a telegraph office."

He frowned thoughtfully at the dazed Mr. Flower.

"I suppose prisoners couldn't receive telegrams in Sing Sing?" he asked. "I don't know the ways of American prisons, but you will know. Could I send him a wire telling him he may come along whenever he likes and claim the title?"

At last Mr. Flower found his voice. "He doesn't know," he said hollowly. "You're not going to put that into his hands—an ancient title like the—er—Pelborough marquisate? Remember, Lord Pelborough, that you are responsible to your ancestors."

"Blow my ancestors!" said Chick. "And if I'm responsible, so is he. Will you wire for me and let me know in the morning?"

Mr. Jagg Flower had been in many peculiar and unnerving situations, but he had never paralleled this experience. He walked down the drive, beneath the shade of those ancient elms which he had so admired, like a man in a dream.

Chick dashed into the drawing room where the girl was watching the departure of the visitor. Before she knew what was happening he had taken her in his arms.

"It is a miracle, Gwenda, a miracle! Isn't it wonderful!"

"But, Chick," she said in horror, "you're not going to accept this man's bare word? You mustn't do it, Chick!"

She pushed him away.

"Of course I'm going to accept it," chortled Chick. "There is no doubt about it. Those were copies of certificates. I know all about birth and marriage certificates. I used to deal with them when I was working for Leither."

"You're going to allow a jail-bird to take this title?"

"I'll allow any kind of bird to take it," said Chick, catching her hands. "Don't you see, Gwenda, that the big thing that hurt you has gone? I'm just Chick Beane. Don't you realize what you said to me yesterday?"

Her hands were trembling in his, and he lifted them to his lips.

Presently she drew them back. "Chick, you have to fight for this title," she said. "I am certain there is something wrong. Did he ask you for money?" she asked quickly.

He nodded. "He said he would shut up about it if I paid him ten thousand pounds. Of course the poor fellow didn't know any better."

"Perhaps he did, Chick," she said breathlessly. "Perhaps he knew that I wanted to be the Marchioness of Pelborough!"

Chick was momentarily staggered. "But you don't, Gwenda," he said in amazement.

She nodded. "Yes, I do. You've got to fight for that title. Chick, just as hard as you've ever fought in the ring, because if you don't want it, I do."

He looked at her steadily. "You are not telling the truth, Gwenda," he said quietly. "You're saying that to spur me on, and I'm not going to be spurred. I think too much of you to believe that a title has any attraction for you. I love you too much to believe that."

Her face was white. The eyes that avoided his were bright with tears. Suddenly she turned and walked quickly from the room. He thought she had gone up to her room, but he was mistaken. She made straight for the library. He came in, and found her sitting at the table in the place where she had been when Mr. Flower had interrupted their search.

"If there are any documents relating to the doctor's marriage, they will be here," she said.

"Do you think that fellow lied?" asked Chick.

She shook her head. "He expected investigations, he told us that," she said, "and he wouldn't have forged these copies. I don't think there is any doubt at all that he spoke the truth. The doctor was married and he did have a son."

Naturally, when they were searching for something else, the first things they discovered were the lost leases. It was not until just on midnight that Gwenda discovered a small locked ledger marked "Accounts of my practice, 1884." She tried to open the lock and failed.

"There won't be anything there, Gwenda," said Chick.

"You never know," said the girl.

She tried to put her thumb-nail between the leaves, and found they were glued together. That determined her. A hasty search of their small stock of tools resulted in the find of a pair of pincers, and the lock was wrenched off.

Gwenda uttered an exclamation of astonishment. The ledger had at one time served the purpose for which it was designed, but the doctor had industriously cut out the centre of the pages, gumming the edges together to give it the appearance of a book, leaving in the middle a deep cavity in which lay a blue envelope, innocent of inscription.

It contained two slips of vellum, and one glance at them made her drop her hands on her lap.

"Oh, Chick!" she said.

"What is it?" asked Chick quickly.

"He did tell the truth! These are the original certificates," she wailed.

"Good egg!" said Chick.

"Don't say that," she said impatiently. "Chick, I could cry!"

There were three other papers in the envelope. The first of these was a letter in the doctor's handwriting, evidently a copy of one he had sent to his son.

It was not pleasant reading, for the old man had not minced his words. The second was a long list of payments, made also in the doctor's hand, "Payments made in re J. Beane," and the size of the total explained why Josephus Beane had died a poor man. To this last a newspaper cutting was pinned, Gwenda did not see it until she had laid the paper down on the table. She took out the pin, rusty with age, and read the cutting, and as she read, Chick saw her face change.

"What is it, Gwenda?"

She did not reply, but, folding the cutting, took an envelope from the stationery rack and enclosed it.

"When is Mr. Flower calling again?" she said softly.

"He promised to come in the morning," said Chick. "What was that cutting, Gwenda?"

"I'll tell you to-morrow," said the girl.

Mr. Jagg Flower had completely recovered from the shock by the next morning. He was a shrewd student of men and women, and he realized that any hope he had of making easy money was centred in the girl. His inquiries as to the nature of her relationship with Chick had not produced very illuminating results, but he felt sure that the appeal must be made to her, if it was to succeed at all, and when he came to Kenberry House the next morning and found the girl and Chick in the library, he made no suggestion that his communication was for Chick's private ear.

"I've been thinking over your proposition, Mr. Flower," said Chick.

"I'm glad to hear that, my lord," replied Mr. Flower, relieved. "You understand that I court the fullest investigations. I have come here prepared to give you the name of the minister who married the parties, the address at which the child was born."

"They are all on the certificate, aren't they?" said Chick.

"Well, yes, they are," admitted the other, a little disconcerted. "His lordship explained to you, Miss Maynard, my suggestion?"

Gwenda nodded. "He has also explained to me his alternative plan," she said, "namely, that you should produce Josephus Beane, and I quite agree that ten thousand pounds would be a small price to pay for that miracle."

"I don't get you," said the man.

"You see, Mr. Flower," said the girl sweetly, "when poor Mr. Josephus Beane was executed at Vermont, Virginia, for the murder of a bank manager, he rather upset your plans. I've got the paragraph here. I think it is from The Vermont Observer, and it gives a very full description of the trial. The bank manager was shot at his home when he was disturbing two burglars who had broken into the house. One was Mr. Beane, who was captured. The other was a man who escaped, and for whom there is still a warrant."

"Good morning," said Mr. Flower, accepting the situation. "I seem to be wasting my time here. Good day to your lordship," He nodded smilingly to the dumbfounded Chick. "A beautiful house this, and a lovely country. I'd give anything to own those old elms of yours."

He paused at the door. "I suppose it is no use asking you to defray my out-of-pocket expenses?" Chick could only stare at him.

Two hours after Mr. Flower had taken his unobtrusive departure from the village of Kenberry there arrived, whilst Chick was at lunch, a thick-set American who claimed an instant audience.

"Sorry to bother you," said the new-comer, wiping his perspiring brow, "but I understand there's a man in this house, or he was seen coming into this house this morning, named—well, never mind his name— he's an American."

"That's true," said Chick. "Mr. Flower."

"Oh, he's given his own name, has he?" said the other with a smile. "Can I see him?"

"He's been gone some time," said Chick.

"Do you know where he's gone?"

"I haven't the slightest idea. He was staying at 'The Red Lion,' I believe."

"He's not there now," said the detective. "He told the people, when he took his grip away, that he was staying with your lordship. That is twice I've missed him, but the third time pays for all."

"Is he a friend of yours?" asked Chick.

The girl had come from the dining-room, and was an interested listener.

"Friend?" smiled the other. "No, sir. My name's Sullivan. I'm from police head-quarters, Vermont, and I've an extradition warrant for him. I arrived at Toulouse Jail an hour after he'd left. He's wanted for a murder committed twelve years ago—at least, he was one of the two guys that shot Mr. Stizelhouser. We got one, but the other dodged us. We've been after him for twelve years, and I guess we'll get him sooner or later. He's not a friend of yours, I suppose, my lord?"

Chick shook his head. "No," he said. "He was a friend of my cousin's."

XII

THE BEATING OF THE MIDDLE-WEIGHT

There is a sixth sense which all criminals acquire, and which, whilst it is of the greatest value to them in the active pursuits of their profession, must invariably bring their careers to a disastrous finish. It is the sense of immunity. The ostrich is popularly supposed to share this characteristic, but even if it were true that the ostrich, when hotly pursued, dives his head into the sand, he at least does not adopt this suicidal policy except as a last desperate resort.

Mr. Jagg Flower, who had described himself as a gentleman at large, had been in the habit, throughout his chequered life, of hiding one crime by committing another, and when, as it occasionally did, the strong hand of the law came upon his collar and he was retired to a place where, in the argot of his class, "the dogs did not bite," he regarded his punishment as both a penance and an atonement, which wiped out all his earlier indiscretions and produced him to the world, at the conclusion of his sentence, more or less spotless.

A certain burglary, which had been accompanied by murder, had disfigured his earlier career; but thanks to the assistance of friends, a swift voyage to the other side of the Atlantic, and his subsequent arrest and punishment for a breach of the European laws, he had forgotten that Vermont, Virginia, was on the map until, in the solitude of his Toulouse cell, he had read that the Marquis of Pelborough had acquired a country seat, that his name was originally Beane, and he was the nephew of Dr. Josephus Beane.

Whereupon Mr. Flower had remembered that an erstwhile companion of his, one who, indeed, had been a fellow-adventurer in the Vermont enterprise, was the son of Dr. Josephus Beane, and therefore, had he lived, would be the holder of the title. Unfortunately, Joe Beane had not lived. The outraged laws of Virginia had been vindicated, and that dissolute young man had been electrocuted, regretted by none.

To resurrect him was an easy matter to a man of Mr. Flower's plausibility, and, having failed in his object to extract money from Chick Pelborough by a promise of silence, he had accepted his defeat, and there the matter might have ended.

"That girl was surely a queen," he thought on his way to town.

He harboured none of the malice against her which had brought him in stealth to Anita Pireau, in Marseilles, to impress upon her the enormity of the offence she committed when she stood up in the courts and testified against him. He was so philosophical a man that he could admire the force which had beaten him. His sense of immunity, however, had received a jar. He had been uncomfortably reminded that there was at least one offence which had not been erased by various imprisonments, and he decided that, on the whole, Holland, in the role of an American tourist, might offer him a successful livelihood.

For a week he lay low, enjoying the hospitality of a private hotel in Bloomsbury, and then one of his fraternity, a London "confidence man," gave him the first hint that the police were searching for him. He had only hidden in case Lord Pelborough had communicated with the police, and when he received the first warning, he attached only that importance to the search.

Nevertheless, he decided to leave England. He had taken his place in a first-class carriage on the Harwich boat train, when there appeared at the open door a thick-set man, whom Mr. Flower recognized before he spoke.

"Say, Jagg, come a little walk with me, will you?"

Behind the American detective were two obvious London policemen.

"Sure," said Jagg, rising slowly and taking down his bag from the rack. "I guess you've been having a talk with dear little Gwenda."

The detective had his foot on the carriage floor to enter, when the bag struck him in the face and sent him floundering back upon the platform. The next second Jagg Flower pulled open the door on the other side of the carriage, crossed the rails, mounted a farther platform, and was racing through the goods yard at Liverpool Street Station before the alarm was raised.

He slackened his pace to a walk as he came to an open gateway, at which, in his windowed lodge, a station policeman was sitting. He came out into High Street, Shoreditch, and mounted a tram which was on the move. At Islington he changed cars and reached King's Cross. Here a train was on the point of leaving for the North, and he had time to take a first-class ticket before it moved out.

So that queen of a girl had set them on to him! Jagg Flower smiled. Women had betrayed him before, and had been sorry. Given the leisure and the opportunity, Gwenda—that was her name; he had heard the Marquis address her—would be sorry, too.

The train's first stop was at Grantham, and there were an unusually large number of policemen on the platform.

"Gwenda!" said Mr. Jagg Flower softly, as he dropped on to the line on the side opposite to the platform. He was in one of the last carriages, and the ground was clear for him. Again he made use of the goods yard and succeeded in getting clear of the town.

"These English police are surely maligned," said Mr. Flower, as he took to the open road.

The quietude of Kenberry House was not disturbed by news of Mr. Flower's peril.

After his unsuccessful attempt at blackmail, he passed out of Chick's life and his thoughts, representing no more than an exciting interlude. At one time it seemed that the news he had brought would reshape the life of the youthful Lord of Pelborough. Chick almost wished it had.

"Chick is a curious man," said Mrs. Phibbs, his housekeeper.

Gwenda's thoughts were running on the same lines, but she was not ready to agree even with the criticisms offered by such a good friend of theirs as Mrs. Phibbs.

"Why?" she asked.

"He has so many unexpected moods," said Mrs. Phibbs, putting down her book and polishing her pince-nez. "He came here in the depth of gloom. Really he was most depressing, Gwenda. And then the day that very nice American called I found him capering round the library like a demented child. And now—"

"Now?" said Gwenda inquiringly.

"Now he's neither one thing nor the other. He's just quiet. I don't suppose he has spoken a dozen words in the last three meals."

Gwenda had noticed that too. The time was coming for her departure, but the situation had changed so often that to be consistent now would mean perpetuating her inconsistency.

Chick's avoidance of any discussion of her future she could understand. He was trying to help her, but somehow she did not want help in the way he intended.

"Where is he?" she asked.

"He's fishing."

Gwenda took her mackintosh over her arm and walked across the sloping meadows toward the river. Chick, she knew, would be in his favourite spot, a hollow in the river-bank secluded by a screen of trees from wind and rain and observation.

He turned his head as she came stumbling down the bank, and reached up his hand to help her.

"Fishing, Chick?" she asked unnecessarily.

"Fishing," agreed Chick, his eyes on the stream.

They sat for a long time without speaking.

"What is the matter with you, Chick?" she demanded.

"Nothing," he said, not turning his head.

"Don't be silly, Chick. Of course there's something the matter. Are you angry with me?"

He looked at her and smiled. "No, dear, I'm not angry with you," he said. "Why should I be?"

There was a glint of a silver-grey body, a snap of voracious jaws, and the fly went under. She watched him curiously as he played the trout.

Chick seemed to have aged in the past two or three months, she thought. The boy had become a man. He had thickened a little, and the face which in other days carried a hint of indecision, had grown stronger.

"You have become quite a fisherman," she smiled, as he landed the struggling trout.

"Haven't I?" he said.

His reply piqued her.

"Don't you want to talk to me, Chick?"

He put down his rod and turned to her, clasping his knee in his hands.

"Gwenda, the last time we were here I talked to you about marriage," he said quietly, "and you refused because I was a marquis, and people might think that you were after my title. And then, when I thought I was losing that title, I talked to you, and you said you would marry me if I kept it. I dare not talk to you now, Gwenda, because "—he hesitated—"I know you only said that to make me go after that American fellow and prove he was wrong."

She was silent.

"There is only one thing I can talk to you about, Gwenda, and that is you and I," said Chick, and took her hand from her lap and patted it. "You used to be so much older than I, Gwenda, and now you're so much younger I feel quite grown-up beside you, but not grown-up enough to do what I want."

"What is that, Chick?" she said in a voice a little above a whisper.

His arm slipped round her and her head dropped upon his shoulder.

"Just to hug you like this," he said huskily, "and hold you until—until you behave!"

"This isn't behaving, Chick," she murmured.

His fishing-rod slipped into the water, and he watched it float in the swift stream,

"You'll lose it," whispered Gwenda, her face against his,

"I can buy another," said Chick, "but I can't buy the minute I'd lose."

Mrs, Phibbs saw them strolling back hand in hand, and did not see anything extraordinary in the circumstance. And when she detected them holding hands under the tablecloth at dinner, she thought no more than that some little quarrel which had occurred, unknown to her, had been patched up. But when she walked into the library to find a book, and a sepulchral voice said from the window recess. "Don't turn on the light; it hurts my eyes, Mrs, Phibbs," she very wisely withdrew, realizing that something had happened—something for which she had prayed.

At the moment the interruption came, Chick was talking about boxing, although Mrs, Phibbs would never have guessed this, had the light been turned on, for amateur champions, when they lecture upon the noble art, do not find it necessary to sit so close to their audience.

"I'll build a gym. when I can afford it," he said.

"One day I'd like to see you box. Chick," she whispered. There was no need to speak louder; her ordinary speaking voice would have deafened him—in the circumstances.

"I don't think you'd like it," he said. He did not shake his head, because it would have meant shaking two heads—in the circumstances.

"But I should really. Lord Mansar said—please don't shudder, Chick; it shakes me—Lord Mansar said that you had a 'miraculous left'; your left arm doesn't feel any different from the other. It is terribly hard, but so is the right arm. Do you mind me pinching you, or don't you feel it?"

"I'm supposed to hit harder with the left," said Chick. "but I hope you'll never see me hit with either. Boxing is wonderful for boys. That is why people shouldn't sneer at these big champions who fight for money. It seems degrading, but it isn't. It stimulates the little people, the school-boys and chaps like that, to do a little better."

"What is the use of boxing, Chick? I know it is splendid to be able to defend yourself, but there's nothing—spiritual in it."

Chick laughed softly.

"Gwenda, the man who loses his temper in the ring is beaten before he starts; the man who doesn't fight fair is beaten by the people who see him. Discipline and respect for the laws are spiritual—what's the word?"

"Qualities?" suggested the girl.

"Yes, spiritual qualities. But, darling, let's talk of Monte Carlo. I never want you to see me fighting; I'd be scared to death."

So they talked about something else until the hall clock struck midnight.

In the midst of the third day of his sublime happiness came a stocky man whom Chick had seen before. He was not exactly in the same state of repair as he had been when he had left Kenberry House, for his eye was a dark purple and the bridge of his nose was heavily plastered.

"Just as I thought I'd got him," he explained to Chick bitterly, "he threw a forty-pound bag in my face and bolted."

"What makes you think he will come here?" asked Chick.

The interview took place behind the closed doors of his library.

"That's Jagg's way. He's got an idea that you or the lady squealed to the police," said Detective Sullivan, "and he's a pretty dangerous man. You've heard of Jagg Flower, my lord? I understand you take an interest in boxing."

"Jagg Flower!" Chick frowned. "I don't remember his name."

"He'd have made a fortune in the ring if he'd only gone straight—the finest light—middle we ever had in America, and a dead shot, too," he added significantly. "He carries a gun. We know that, because when the English police searched his lodgings in Bloomsbury we found the remains of a box of cartridges. Now, I'll tell you, my lord, why I've come to you." He drew his chair nearer to the desk and lowered his voice. "I'm as sure as anything that he'll return here. The country is closed to him, and he can't get out, and, naturally enough, he'll come after the people who have squealed—I mean who have betrayed him.

He did the same thing in France, and he did it once in America. There isn't a meaner fellow in the world than Jagg."

"He seemed quite nice," said Chick dubiously.

The detective laughed, and related briefly what had happened to Anita Pireau, a companion of his who had given information to the police.

Chick listened and shivered.

"So you see, sir," said Sullivan, "it is not safe for you to be living in this house, the only man here."

"How did you know that?" smiled Chick.

"I've a tongue in my head," said the detective good-humouredly. "What I want to know. Lord Pelborough, is, will you let me sleep in this house for the next week?"

Chick hesitated.

"I'll have to consult my—my fiancee," he blurted, cherry-red.

Gwenda was inclined to treat the matter lightly, but she had no serious objections to offer. Mrs. Phibbs, on the other hand, who saw in this a sinister plot on the part of the detective to have a week's lodging in a pleasant country village free of all charge, was sceptical.

In the end, Mr. Sullivan's one bag was taken to a room adjoining Chick's. To relieve them of the embarrassment of his presence, he asked that his meals might be set in the servants' hall, but Chick insisted upon his dining with the "family," and he proved to be an entertaining guest.

He had a fund of fascinating stories of crime and criminals, and Chick learnt of a world of which he had never dreamt, a world of human tigers that preyed alike upon the weaklings of their own species and upon the society which had offended them by its prosperity.

"Jagg had a friend named Beane," said Sullivan, on the third night of his visit, "a weak fool of a fellow. He was an Englishman, too. His father was a doctor in this country, and he could have occupied any position, but Joe Beane just naturally hated work. He was pulled in once or twice in New York for mean little crimes, and then he drifted down to Virginia and met this fellow Flower."

He went on to describe the erring Beane's career, and Chick listened to the story of his cousin's life and death without a muscle of his face moving. It was a curious thought that far away in Virginia, in a neglected corner of a prison yard, lay one who, if Fate had been kinder, might have taken his seat in the House of Lords.

After the meal was over, Chick took the girl's arm and led her into the study.

"I was so sorry for you, dear," she said. "I tried to stop Mr. Sullivan."

Chick shook his head.

"It didn't matter a bit," he said. "Poor old Uncle Josephus! No wonder he was impatient with me. It must have broken his heart. You're marrying into a queer family, Gwenda," he said, his arm about her, his hand gently stroking her face. Then he remembered a half-brother of hers, a slinking thief of a brother, and when he saw her smile he knew that she had remembered, too.

He went to bed a little later than usual. He had a number of letters to write, for Chick, since his adventures in the oil market, had acquired two directorships—he traced the hand of Lord Mansar in each appointment.

He did not go straight to bed, but wearing a dressing-gown over his pyjamas he sat on a seat in one of the windows looking out over the grounds. It was a moonlight night, and he could see almost to the stone wall that bounded the tiny park. He had not been disturbed by Mr. Sullivan's ominous prophecy, partly because he did not believe that the man held him responsible for the attentions of the police, and partly because he did not know Jagg Flower.

Chick said his prayers, and went to bed and was asleep in a minute. When he woke, the first grey of dawn was in the sky, and he wondered what had aroused him to instant wakefulness.

He listened. There was no sound but the distant faint tick of a clock in the hall below. And yet something must have awakened him. There was no sound coming from Sullivan's room, so he had evidently slept through the noise, whatever it was.

He slipped out of bed, pulled on his slippers, and opened the door softly. The corridor was in darkness, and there was a profound silence. Tightening the string of his pyjamas, he stepped noiselessly along the carpeted floor and stopped at Gwenda's room, listening. He was on the point of returning to his own room, when he heard the faintest of whispers.

He tried the handle of the door gently, for fear of disturbing her if she were asleep, but it was locked, and he went along to the door of the bathroom, from which a second door communicated with Gwenda's room. This was open, and the door of her room was ajar. He pushed it open with the same caution.

The room was in darkness, save for the faint light supplied by the dawn, and he saw standing by Gwenda's bed the figure of a man. His back was toward Chick, and he was bending over the bed, one hand over the mouth of the girl, who was lying motionless. There was an electric switch near the door, and Chick pressed it down.

Instantly the room was flooded with light. The man turned quickly, and Chick looked into the smiling face of Jagg Flower.

"You did hear, then," said Mr. Flower pleasantly. Chick walked slowly toward him, heedless of the automatic pistol Flower held in his hand.

"Stop right where you are," said the intruder. Chick looked at the girl. Her nightdress was torn at the neck, and there was a big ugly scratch on her white shoulder. His eyes went slowly from her to the man, and then down to the levelled pistol, and he spoke no word.

Then suddenly he leapt. One hand closed round the wrist of the hand that held the Browning, the other struck straight at the man's throat a blow which would have paralysed a less hardy mortal than Jagg Flower. As he staggered back, there was a crash of glass as Chick sent the pistol through the window. He never underrated an opponent, and a voice within him whispered a warning. The man was a middle-weight.

The lightning stab that the smiling Flower aimed at him missed his face. A second blow he lowered his head to meet, a third quick uppercut met the air.

Then the slim figure was on him, and in the heart of Chick Pelborough was cold murder.

The girl, leaning on her hand, watched in horror as Chick's arm swung left and right so quickly that she could not follow the blows.

"Hands up, Flower!" It was Sullivan in the open door of the dark bathroom, pistol in hand.

"Leave him alone!" snarled Chick. His lip was cut, and a great red bruise showed where Jagg Flower's fist had reached him.

"On the whole, I think I will put up my hands," drawled Flower. One eye was closed, and he bore the marks of his punishment conspicuously. "If I had known what I know now, I would have tackled you first, young man—with a hammer."

Chick walked to the table by the side of the girl's bed, and his hand closed over a blue bottle before she had realized it was there. Then he faced the man, about whose wrists Sullivan had snapped a pair of American handcuffs.

"The reason I haven't killed you. Flower," Chick said, his face as white as death, "is because you're going back to Virginia to be electrocuted. Mr. Sullivan says that the State will make it a point of honour to get you to the chair."

He showed the bottle in the palm of his hand, and Mr. Flower was no longer smiling.

Two people in their dressing-gowns watched through the library window the departure of Mr. Sullivan and his prisoner. It was six o'clock, and the house had not been aroused.

"What will happen to him?" asked Gwenda.

"He'll be executed," said Chick. He bit his lip thoughtfully. "I should like to see it," he said.

"Chick," said the girl reproachfully, "how can you say such a thing?"

She had been awakened in the night by the pressure of Flower's hand on her face, and had screamed. It was the scream which had awakened Chick, and which had even aroused the detective.

"I struggled a little. That's when he scratched me." She nursed her shoulder with a smile. "Oh, really, dear, it is nothing. And I did see you fight?—you were terrifying!"

Chick smiled uncomfortably,

"Chick, what was that little blue bottle you took from the table by my bed?" she asked.

"That was nothing, either," smiled Chick.

"But really, what was it? Did Flower bring it?"

"I brought it in myself," said Chick, "Didn't you see me put it down?"

"What was it?" she asked again.

"It was liniment. I thought Mr. Flower might want it."

Later he emptied the contents of the bottle in a secluded part of the grounds, and watched it smoke and steam, and the grass wither, and he shivered as he had when the detective had told him of the horrible vengeance which Jagg Flower had wreaked upon the French girl who had betrayed him.

Chick really took the most unexpected views, thought Gwenda, when they were discussing plans in the library that night. She had thought that he, whose painful shyness had first awakened her interest in him, would prefer the quietest of weddings, but Chick, to her astonishment, had vetoed that suggestion.

It was to be at St. Margaret's, Westminster, and was to be a wedding of the most ostentatious character.

"I'm going to be married so that everybody knows that you're the Marchioness of Pelborough," he said firmly.

And so they were married one dull October day, and the church was filled with people in all stations of life, varying from the Lord Chancellor to the boxing instructor at the Polytechnic.

There was a crowd to see them go in and come out, and on the edge of the crowd was a very pretty girl who had figured alarmingly in Chick's life. Miss Farland, the lady in question, wept silently as the newly-married couple drove away.

"He was engaged to me once," she sobbed to her friends, "but you know what these lords are. When an actress gets after them—"

She attracted the attention of a press photographer who was just folding his camera.

"Excuse me," she said, "I was the young lady who was engaged to Lord Pelborough."

"Fine," said the photographer. "I hope it was a good job. How did you lose it?"

Richard Horatio Edgar Wallace was born on the 1st April 1875 at 7 Ashburnham Grove, Greenwich. His mother, Mary Jane "Polly" Richards was born into an Irish Catholic family in Liverpool in 1843 and had worked in theatres, both as an actress in bit-parts and as a stagehand and usherette, until she married a Merchant Navy Captain, Joseph Richards, in 1867. He too had been born into an Irish Catholic family in Liverpool. His father had also been a Captain in the Merchant Navy, and his mother's family had a marine background. Mary was eight months pregnant with Joseph's child when he died at sea, and it was once the child had been born that she first turned to the stage, taking the stage name Polly Richards.

She joined the Marriott family theatre troupe in 1872. It was managed by Mrs. Alice Edgar, Richard Edgar, Grace Edgar, Adeline Edgar and Richard Horatio Edgar, Wallace's father. In late 1874 Mary and Richard Horatio Edgar had a brief sexual encounter at the party following a successful show, and she fell pregnant. Worried about the scandal which would ensue and fearing that she might forever lose her job at the troupe, she fabricated an obligation in Greenwich would detain her there for at least six months. She lived in a room in the boarding house on Ashburnham Grove until her son, Edgar, was born. She had already made preparations through her midwife for a couple to foster the child, and when Edgar was born the midwife presented her with Mrs Freeman. Her husband was a fishmonger at Billingsgate market and she already had ten children. She was happy to foster the child and for Polly to make frequent visits to see him in exchange for a small sum of money which Polly made from her work in the theatre troupe.

Wallace was now known as Richard Horatio Edgar Freeman, taking his father's forenames and his foster family's surname. Broadly speaking his childhood was a happy one. The Freemans looked after him lovingly and he had good friendships with his foster siblings, particularly Clara Freeman, twenty years his senior, who often looked after him as a child. After a few years Polly's finances tightened and she was no longer in a position to afford the fee she had been paying the Freemans. However, they had grown to love the young Wallace and opted to adopt him in order to keep him out of the workhouse. Polly could no longer visit him. George Freeman was keen to ensure that he had equal opportunities and did all he could to secure him an education at St. Alfege with St. Peter's, a Peckham boarding school. Despite his adoptive father's efforts, though, Wallace left the school aged twelve for truancy.

Instead he went to work and by the time he was fourteen or fifteen he had experience selling newspapers at Ludgate Circus, near Fleet Street, as a worker in a rubber factory, as a shoe shop assistant, as a milk delivery boy and as a ship's cook. He stole from the milk company which resulted in his dismissal, and in 1894 was engaged to a local girl from Deptford named Edith Anstree, though he broke this off and instead joined the Infantry. He adopted the name Edgar Wallace which he took from Lew Wallace, the author of *Ben-Hur*, and his medical record records a diminutive 33" chest and a stunted growth. his first posting was with the West Kent Regiment in South Africa in 1896, though he did not enjoy military life, arranging to be transferred to the Royal Army Medical Corps. Though this was a less strenuous job, it was also significantly less pleasant and so he again transferred to the Press Corps, which he found suited him far better.

He was in Cape Town in 1898 where he met Rudyard Kipling and was inspired to begin writing and publishing poetry and songs. His first collection of ballads, *The Mission that Failed!* and was enough of a success that in 1899 he paid his way out of the armed forces in order to turn to writing full time. His first work was as a war correspondent for Reuters who kept him in Africa to cover the Boer War, and then for the Daily Mail in 1900 and various other periodicals after that. It was while he was in South Africa that he met and married Ivy Maude Caldecott, who was 21 when they married in 1901, despite her

Wesleyan missionary father's strong opposition to the union, for several reasons, one of which was that Wallace's writing was not turning quite the profit he had expected it would. *War and Other Poems* and *Writ in Barracks,* both published in 1900, had not proved as popular as his first collection. Eleanor Clare Hellier Wallace, their first child, died of meningitis in 1903 and, in rather deep debt, they returned to London. Wallace used his contacts with the Daily Mail to get work with them in London, electing to write detective novels as a means of making quick money.

Wallace met Polly, his birth mother, in 1903. He didn't remember her from his childhood as he had been too young when she became unable to visit, so it was as though they were meeting for the first time. She was sixty years old and terminally ill, living in abject poverty. She had come to Wallace seeking financial support, but he turned her away. She died in the Bradford Infirmary later that year. In 1904 he and Ivy had a son, Bryan. He was still writing and had completed his first thriller, *The Four Just Men.* Since nobody would publish it he resorted to setting up his own publishing company which he called Tallis Press and he published a serialised version of *The Four Just Men* in 1905. He received promotional assistance from the Daily Mail in which he ran a competition for entrants to guess the method of murder in the final chapter, with a prize of £1,000 for a correct guess. Although the paper's proprietor, Lord Alfred Harmsworth, refused Wallace the £1,000 prize money, Wallace persisted and went ahead with the competition, recklessly advertising on billboards and buses all over the country, hoping to expand his advertisements across the Empire. His worried colleagues at the Daily Mail managed to convince him to lower the prize money to £500, split into a first prize of £250, a second prize of £200 and a third of £50, but with the total cost of his advertisements nearing £2,000 he would need to sell £2,500 worth of copies before he could see any profit. He was confident that this could be achieved in just three months.

Though he had remarkable enthusiasm, it became clear that his managerial skills left a lot to be desired. It soon emerged that nowhere in the competition terms and conditions had he included a clause limiting the competition to one single winner; instead, any entrant with a winning answer was entitled to their corresponding prize money. Thus, if ten entrants guessed the first prize answer, the competition was obliged to pay each entrant £250. This error was only noticed after the competition had been closed and the solution had been printed in the final installment of the novel, meaning that not only was there no opportunity to write his way out of enormous financial obligation, but the entrants who had guessed correctly would by now have read the final chapter and know they had done so. £250 was an enormous amount of money to the average Edwardian family and those entitled to it were likely to make a lot of noise if they didn't receive their money. Despite this, Wallace's fist instinct was to attempt to ignore the issue entirely, even as he discovered that he initial calculations had been dramatically over-enthusiastic and it would take nearer to two years of continuous sales to break even at the initial cost of £2,500, let alone the new figure which included every correct guesser. Compounding the problem even further was the awful realisation that as sales continued throughout the initial three month period and Wallace approached the £2,500 break-even figure, new readers were still eligible to enter and guess correctly. Though it is unknown how much he eventually owed his readers, Lord Harmsworth found himself having to loan over £5,000 in order to protect the reputation of the newspaper, since 1906 had come around and there still hadn't been a list printed of all prize-winners. It was less a charitable act than one of a man anxious that the failure would reflect ill on his own paper. Wallace filed for bankruptcy shortly thereafter and as a token gesture to his creditors sold the rights to the novel to Sir George Newnes, a publisher and editor, for £75. In the midst of this chaos though, Wallace managed to write and published *Smithy*, which would become the first of a series of *Smithy* novels.

Following this fiascos Wallace was dismissed from the Daily Mail in 1907 when inaccuracies which were found in his reporting, resulting in libel cases being brought against the paper. That year he became the first reporter to be fired from the Daily Mail and was his awful reputation prevented him from finding work at any other papers. Despite all this, though, he travelled to the Congo Free State later that year and reported on the criminal treatment of the Congolese people by King Leopold II of Belgium and the Belgian rubber companies. Up to fifteen million Congolese were killed in various atrocities, and Wallace was asked to serialise stories based on his experiences for her penny magazine *Weekly Tale-Teller*. He and Ivy had another daughter, named Patricia, in 1908. Though his new work for *Weekly Tale-Teller* was bringing in some money, their financial situation was still dire and Ivy was occasionally forced to sell off her jewellery and possessions in order to pay for food. In 1911 his Congolese stories were published in a collection called *Sanders of the River*, which quickly became a bestseller. He would publish eleven more such collections featuring a total of 102 stories of adventure and tribal life set on the river Congo.

From 1908 he started to enjoy a revival of both his success and his reputation. The majority of his initial writing he sold outright in order to make money as quickly as possible and placate his creditors in the United Kingdom and South Africa, but as his success saw the reestablishment of his reputation he began to find work once again as a journalist, beginning in horse racing for the *Week-End*, the *Evening News* and then as an editor for the *Week-End Racing Supplement*. Following this success he started his own racing papers, *Bibury's* and *R. E. Walton's Weekly*, eventually buying his own racehorses and losing thousands gambling. His success was insufficient to support his newly extravagant lifestyle and his marriage began to fail in the light of his financial irresponsibility. He and Ivy had their last child together, Michael Blair Wallace, in 1916, and she filed for divorce in 1918 moving to Tunbridge Wells with her children.

Wallace began to fall for his secretary Ethel Violet King and they married in 1921, having a child, Penelope Wallace, in 1923, who would herself go on to become a successful crime writer. Wallace now began to take his career as a fiction writer more seriously, signing with Hodder and Stoughton in 1921. He now began to organize his contracts more carefully, arranging for royalties and properly organized promotions, run by people more business-minded than himself. He was marketed as the 'King of Thrillers' and they gave him the trademark image of a trilby, a cigarette holder and a yellow Rolls Royce. He was truly prolific, capable not only of producing a 70,000 word novel in three days but of doing three novels in a row in such a manner. His publishers signed off on almost everything he wrote as soon as he turned it in, estimating that by 1928 one in four books being read at any time was written by Wallace, for alongside his famous thrillers he wrote variously in other genres, including but not limited to science fiction, non-fiction accounts of WWI which amounted to ten volumes and screen plays. Eventually he would reach the remarkable total of 170 novels, 18 stage plays and 957 short stories.

Wallace became chairman of the Press Club which to this day holds an annual Edgar Wallace Award, rewarding 'excellence in writing'. In 1923 he broadcasted a report on the Epsom Derby horse race for the British Broadcasting Company, making him the first ever radio sports correspondent. His ex-wife Ivy had suffered from breast cancer between 1923-1924, and it eventually killed her in 1926 despite a successful operation to remove a tumour the year before. He wrote the essay "The Canker in our Midst" in 1926 which dealt, aggressively and controversially, with the problem of paedophilia in show business, describing how children were unwittingly left open to sexual abuse, and linking paedophilia with homosexuality. Its tone has been described as "intolerant, blustering, kick-the-blighters-down-the-stairs". He was appointed chairman of the British Lion Film Corporation on the back of the success of *The Ringer* and on the agreement that he give British Lion first choice on all his future work. This contract gave him an annual salary and a large amount of stock with the company, along with a stipend on all British Lion production of his work and 10% of their annual profits. This extraordinary contract gave him annual earnings by 1929 of almost £50,000, or almost £2 million in 2014.

He now became an active figure in politics, entering the 1931 general election as a Liberal contestant in Blackpool, rejecting the current government in favour of free trade. He lost the election by over 33,000 votes and went to America in late 1931, once again deeply in debt after buying the *Sunday News* which closed six months later. In America he quickly found work as a script doctor for RKO Pictures, enjoying early success with the 1932 adaptation of *The Hound of the Baskervilles*. This success, along with that of the play *The Green Pack*, established his reputation in America and he was able to see his own work adapted for film, beginning with *The Four Just Men*. His most successful theatrical work, *On The Spot*, which explores the life of Al Capone, has been described as "arguably, in construction, dialogue, action, plot and resolution, still one of the finest and purest of 20th-century melodramas". These successes led to his assignation on RKO's "gorilla picture" which would become famous as King Kong in 1933.

He worked on the first draft though he was beginning to experience severe headaches which brought about a diagnosis of diabetes. Despite taking medication to address his condition, it deteriorated in a matter of days. His wife booked him passage home but soon heard that he had entered a coma and died of his condition and double pneumonia on the 7th of February 1932 in North Maple Drive, Beverly Hills. In his honour the bell at St. Bride's church on Fleet Street tolled for the duration of the morning while the flags flew at half-mast. He was buried near his home in England at Chalklands, Bourne End, in Buckinghamshire. Once again, at the time of his death he was in severe debt, mostly to racing bookkeepers, though these debts were settled within two years thanks to the enormous royalties his estate continued to receive from his contracts. His writing has been translated into 29 languages, and is considered one of the most important bodies of Colonial writing.

Edgar Wallace – A Concise Bibliography

African Novels
Sanders of the River (1911)
The People of the River (1911)
The River of Stars (1913)
Bosambo of the River (1914)
Bones (1915)
The Keepers of the King's Peace (1917)
Lieutenant Bones (1918)
Bones in London (1921)
Sandi the Kingmaker (1922)
Bones of the River (1923)
Sanders (1926)
Again Sanders (1928)

Four Just Men (Series)
The Four Just Men (1905)
The Council of Justice (1908)
The Just Men of Cordova (1917)
The Law of the Four Just Men (US title: Again the Three Just Men) (1921)
The Three Just Men (1926)
Again the Three Just Men (US title: The Law of the Three Just Men) (1929) a.k.a. Again the Three

Mr. J. G. Reeder (Series)
Room 13 (1924)
The Mind of Mr. J. G. Reeder (US title: The Murder Book of Mr. J. G. Reeder) (1925)
Terror Keep (1927)
Red Aces (1929)[27]
The Guv'nor and Other Short Stories (US title: Mr. Reeder Returns) (1932)

Detective Sgt. (Inspector) Elk series
The Nine Bears or The Other Man or The Cheaters (1910)
revised as Silinski - Master Criminal (1930)
The Fellowship of the Frog (1925)
The Joker or The Colossus (1926)
The Twister (1928)
The India-Rubber Men (1929)
White Face (1930)

Educated Evans (Series)
Educated Evans (1924)
More Educated Evans (1926)
Good Evans (1927)

Smithy (Series)
Smithy (1905)
Smithy Abroad (1909)
Smithy and The Hun (1915)
Nobby or Smithy's Friend Nobby (1916)

Crime Novels
Angel Esquire (1908)
The Fourth Plague or Red Hand (1913)
Grey Timothy or Pallard the Punter (1913)
The Man Who Bought London (1915)
The Melody of Death (1915)
A Debt Discharged (1916)
The Tomb of T'Sin (1916)
The Secret House (1917)
The Clue of the Twisted Candle (1918)
Down under Donovan (1918)
The Man Who Knew (1918)
The Strange Lapses of Larry Loman (1918)
The Green Rust (1919)
Kate Plus Ten (1919)
The Daffodil Mystery or The Daffodil Murder (1920)
Jack O'Judgment (1920)
The Angel of Terror or The Destroying Angel (1922)
The Crimson Circle (1922)
Mr. Justice Maxwell or Take-A-Chance Anderson(1922)
The Valley of Ghosts (1922)

Captains of Souls (1923)
The Clue of the New Pin (1923)
The Green Archer (1923)
The Missing Million (1923)
The Dark Eyes of London or The Croakers (1924)
Double Dan or Diana of Kara-Kara (US Title) (1924)
The Face in the Night or The Diamond Men or The Ragged Princess (1924)
The Sinister Man (1924)
The Three Oak Mystery (1924)
The Blue Hand or Beyond Recall (1925)
The Daughters of the Night (1925)
The Gaunt Stranger or Police Work (1925) revised as The Ringer (1926)
A King by Night (1925)
The Strange Countess (1925)
The Avenger or The Hairy Arm (1926)
'The Black Abbot (1926)
The Day of Uniting (1926)
The Door with Seven Locks (1926)
The Man from Morocco or Souls In Shadows or The Black (US Title) (1926)
The Million Dollar Story (1926)
The Northing Tramp or The Tramp (1926)
Penelope of the Polyantha (1926)
The Square Emerald or The Woman (1926)
The Terrible People or The Gallows' Hand (1926)
We Shall See! or The Gaol-Breakers (US Title) (1926)
The Yellow Snake or The Black Tenth (1926)
Big Foot (1927)
The Feathered Serpent or Inspector Wade or Inspector Wade and the Feathered Serpent (1927)
Flat 2 (1927)
The Forger or The Counterfeiter (1927)
Terror Keep (1927)
The Hand of Power or The Proud Sons of Ragusa (1927)
The Man Who Was Nobody (1927)
Number Six (1927)
The Squeaker or The Sign of the Leopard or The Squealer (US Title) (1927)
The Traitor's Gate (1927)
The Double (1928)
The Flying Squad (1928)
The Gunner or Gunman's Bluff (US Title) (1928)
Four Square Jane or The Fourth Square (1929)
The Golden Hades or Stamped In Gold or The Sinister Yellow Sign (1929)
The Green Ribbon (1929)
The Calendar (1930)
The Clue of the Silver Key or The Silver Key (1930)
The Lady of Ascot (1930)
The Devil Man or Sinister Street or Silver Steel
or The Life and Death of Charles Peace (1931)
The Man at the Carlton or The Mystery of Mary Grier (1931)

The Coat of Arms or The Arranways Mystery (1931)
On the Spot: Violence and Murder in Chicago (1931)
When the Gangs Came to London or Scotland Yard's Yankee Dick
or The Gangsters Come To London (1932)
The Frightened Lady or The Case of the Frightened Lady or Criminal At Large (1933)
The Green Pack (1933)
The Man Who Changed His Name (1935)
The Mouthpiece (1935)
Smoky Cell (1935)
The Table (1936)
Sanctuary Island (1936)

Other Novels
Captain Tatham of Tatham Island or Eve's Island or The Island of Galloping Gold (1909)
The Duke in the Suburbs (1909)
Private Selby (1912)
"1925" - The Story of a Fatal Peace (1915)
Those Folk of Bulboro (1918)
The Book of all Power (1921)
Flying Fifty-five (1922)
The Books of Bart (1923)
Barbara on Her Own (1926)

Poetry Collections
The Mission That Failed (1898)
War and Other Poems (1900)
Writ In Barracks (1900)

Non-Fiction
Unofficial Despatches of the Anglo-Boer War (1901)
Famous Scottish Regiments (1914)
Field Marshal Sir John French (1914)
Heroes All: Gallant Deeds of the War (1914)
The Standard History of the War – Volumes 1 – 4 (1914)
Kitchener's Army and the Territorial Forces:
The Full Story of a Great Achievement (1915)
Vol. 2-4. War of the Nations (1915)
Vol. 5-7. War of the Nations (1916)
Vol. 8-9. War of the Nations (1917)
Famous Men and Battles of the British Empire (1917)
Tam of the Scouts (1918)
The Real Shell-Man: The Story of Chetwynd of Chilwell (1919)
People or Edgar Wallace by Himself(1926)
The Trial of Patrick Herbert Mahon (1928)
My Hollywood Diary (1932)

Screenplays

King Kong (1932, first draft of original screenplay, 110 pages) While the script was not used in its entirety, much of it was retained for the final screenplay.
The Hound of the Baskervilles (1932, British film)
The Squeaker (1930, British film)
Prince Gabby (1929, British film)
Mark of the Frog (1928, American film)
The Valley of Ghosts (192

Short Story Collections
The Admirable Carfew (1914)
The Adventure of Heine (1917)
Tam O' the Scouts (1918)
The Fighting Scouts (1919)
Chick (1923)
The Black Avons (1925)
The Brigand (1927)
The Mixer (1927)
This England (1927)
The Orator (1928)
The Thief in the Night (1928)
Elegant Edward (1928)
The Lone House Mystery and Other Stories (1929)
The Governor of Chi-Foo (1929)
Again the Ringer The Ringer Returns (US Title) (1929)
The Big Four or Crooks of Society (1929)
The Black or Blackmailers I Have Foiled (1929)
The Cat-Burglar (1929)
Circumstantial Evidence (1929)
Fighting Snub Reilly (1929)
For Information Received (1929)
Forty-Eight Short Stories (1929)
Planetoid 127 and The Sweizer Pump (1929)
The Ghost of Down Hill & The Queen of Sheba's Belt (1929)
The Iron Grip (1929)
The Lady of Little Hell (1929)
The Little Green Man (1929)
The Prison-Breakers (1929)
The Reporter (1929)
Killer Kay (1930)
Mrs William Jones and Bill (1930)
Forty Eight Short-Stories (1930)
The Stretelli Case and Other Mystery Stories (1930)
The Terror (1930)
The Lady Called Nita (1930)
Sergeant Sir Peter or Sergeant Dunn, C.I.D. (1932)
The Scotland Yard Book of Edgar Wallace (1932)
The Steward (1932)
Nig-Nog and other humorous stories (1934)

The Last Adventure (1934)
The Woman From the East (1934) Co-written By Robert George Curtis
The Edgar Wallace Reader of Mystery and Adventure (1943)
The Undisclosed Client (1963)

Other
King Kong, with Draycott M. Dell, (1933), 28 October 1933 Cinema Weekly

Plays
An African Millionaire (1904)
The Forest of Happy Dreams (1910)
Dolly Cutting Herself (1911)
The Manager's Dream (1914)
M'Lady (1921)
Double Dan (1926)
The Mystery of room 45 (1926)
A Perfect Gentleman (1927)
The Terror (1927)
Traitors Gate (1927)
The Lad (1928)
The Man Who Changed His Name (1928)
The Squeaker (1928)
The Calendar (1929)
Persons Unknown (1929)
The Ringer (1929)
The Mouthpiece (1930)
On the Spot (1930)
Smoky Cell (1930)
The Squeaker (1930)
To Oblige A Lady (1930)
The Case of the Frightened Lady (1931)
The Old Man (1931)
The Green Pack (1932)
The Table (1932)